THIEVES LIKE US

STEPHEN COLE

BLOOMSBURY

First published in Great Britain in 2006 by Bloomsbury Publishing Plc
36 Soho Square, London, W1D 3QY

This paperback edition published in 2007

A CIP catalogue record of this book is available from the British Library

ISBN 978 0 7475 8951 8

All papers used by Bloomsbury Publishing are natural, recyclable products made
from wood grown in well-managed forests. The manufacturing processes
conform to the environmental regulations of the country of origin.

Typeset by Dorchester Typesetting Group Ltd
Printed in Great Britain by Clays Ltd, St Ives Plc

1 3 5 7 9 10 8 6 4 2

www.bloomsbury.com/stephencole

For the inestimable P –
Philippa Milnes-Smith

CHAPTER ONE

To open a door, and not know what lay on the other side. That was what Jonah dreamed about, day and night. That was what freedom meant.

He kicked back the covers on his thin mattress, unable to sleep, listening out for the same old noises of night here. The lazy scuff of heels in the corridor outside, low voices and laughter as the warders trudged the night beat. Banging about somewhere down the passage, a foul-mouthed yell for silence, taken up by other prisoners too bored or too wired to sleep.

Jonah guessed that Young Offenders' Institutions weren't exactly designed with sweet dreams in mind.

Two months so far. Two months into a year-long stretch and already it seemed like for ever. They called it 'doing time', but to Jonah it felt more like time was doing *him*, and roughly. Every day hung loose about him like a sweater on a stick-man, no matter how he tried to bulk out the hours.

There were peer literacy workshops, where he helped other inmates with their reading for an hour – well, until they threw their next strop and threatened to ram the books down his throat, anyway. Then there were the personal health classes, focusing chiefly on drugs and sex – but since they never told you how to get your hands on either, few people bothered to go. You could try a bit of music and drama if you didn't mind being beaten up by the hard cases afterwards . . . Just as long as you made time for the biggest joy of all – Resettlement Class. This was where they made you practise filling out work applications for jobs you didn't want and wouldn't stand a chance of getting anyway.

'*I want to work somewhere with computers,*' Jonah had insisted.

'*After what* you *did to get put in here?*' His personal officer had laughed, about as impersonal as you could get. '*Dream on, son.*'

Jonah couldn't remember how to sleep, let alone dream. Here he was, seventeen years old, with a future as dismal as his past. He checked his crappy watch with the luminous hands for the tenth time that minute.

Nearly five to three in the morning.

In the distance, an echoing crash sounded. Jonah didn't react, didn't question it. Outside was another world, one that had little meaning here. Nothing could reach him through the gates and the guards and the high walls. Even the sunlight was scrag-end stuff, thin and grey over the gardens and the exercise yard, like the days had a job just to drag themselves past dawn.

Jonah closed his eyes and pictured himself flying beyond the dreary confines of the detention centre, running barefoot outside through wide-open fields, splashing in the sea – all the crap he'd never contemplated for a second when he'd actually had the chance. While others basked in the warmth of the sun on their skins, Jonah had only ever felt it faintly through closed curtains, fighting to keep the glare off his monitor screen. That was his window on to an easier world, one where he could break the rules and it was OK, it was *clever* . . .

Jonah Wish – the great code-breaker. Or the great freak, in the eyes of just about everyone else. Cracking ciphers. Inventing his own. Encrypting stuff, translating stuff – all just a big game to him until –

Sudden footfalls in the corridor distracted him. He pictured the warders in their grey uniforms, black boots slapping down on ivory tiles, grumbling as they were goaded into action. Someone caught using again? Another suicide?

Jonah sighed. Who cared? It would be all over the block by breakfast, and he would know then. For what it was worth.

His watch read a minute closer to three.

Restless, he shifted on to his side. Stared resentfully at his cell door – a black rectangle, edges bound with a miserable light stealing in from the corridor. The room was dark as pitch – not that there was much to see even when the lights snapped back on at seven-thirty.

It was kind of weird. He'd known so many rooms – in care homes, hostels, or with foster families all around the country – that in his head, they all blurred into one nothingy, threadbare little place. All he could bring to mind with clarity were the makes and models of the computers he'd used and abused over the years, feeding his growing talent. He'd clogged their memories with pattern matches and character substitution, crushed their processors under the weight of calculations they weren't built to handle, crashed –

That crashing sound. There it came again, just a little louder, a little harsher. And raised voices too, somewhere close by.

The feeble light skulking about the edges of the cell door brightened for a few moments with neon intensity. Men shouted in surprise and alarm before a sudden silence fell, thick as the darkness in Jonah's room.

It was broken only by the sound of nimble footsteps on the tiles. Getting louder. Closer.

Unnerved now, Jonah got up from his bunk.

The footsteps had stopped.

He strained to hear anything out in the corridor. After that commotion, why wasn't everyone banging on the doors, yelling and shouting, seizing on a break in the boredom?

It was quiet as the grave out there.

'It's all right,' he told himself, wiping the cold sweat from his forehead. 'It's all right. You're locked in. Nothing can get through that door.'

There came a snatch of tuneless whistling from outside, and some sinister scrapes and ratchets.

Then, with a roll of heavy tumblers, the door opened a crack.

Jonah felt frozen like a rabbit in a truck's headlights. There was nowhere to hide. In desperation he dropped down and slid under his bunk.

The door was kicked wide open and yellow light

spilled in from the corridor. From his hiding place Jonah saw a kid a few years younger than him, fourteen or fifteen maybe, standing in the doorway. He had a cheeky face, scattered with freckles. The black joggers and clinging polo neck he wore emphasised his scrawny physique. He sported a black patch like a pirate's over his left eye.

'Hey,' the skinny kid said. 'Jonah Wish?'

Jonah held his breath, closed his eyes.

'Oi! You under the bed, I'm talking to you.' The intruder spoke with a rough London accent. 'Jonah?'

Swearing under his breath, Jonah wriggled out from under the bunk. 'Who the hell are you? How'd you get in here?'

'Wasn't much of a lock. Any majorly talented individual could have sorted it.'

'But you're just a kid!'

'Oh, is *that* what I am?'

'I mean, how did you get past the screws, the security –'

' "Gain entry to target's cell, identify target and observe." That was my job. That's what I've done.'

Jonah got slowly to his feet. 'What do you mean, "target"?'

'Uh-uh.' The boy peeled back his patch to reveal what looked to be a perfectly good eye underneath. 'I don't answer the tough questions – that's Con's job.'

'Con? What are you –?'

'Sorry, mate, got to get on with observing you now.' With a wicked smile, he pushed apart his eyelids with two fingers and popped out his eyeball. It glistened as he held it between finger and thumb. 'The name's

Patch. I'm keeping an eye on you, Jonah Wish.'

Jonah just stared, speechless and revolted, with no idea how to respond. There was a scuffling noise from outside in the corridor.

'Did Patch get his eye out already?' It was a girl's voice calling, high and prim; she sounded foreign, French maybe. 'He is trying to intimidate you, yes? But don't let him freak you out. It's only glass.'

'Aw, Con,' Patch complained, placing his bogus eyeball back in place beneath the black fabric. 'Why d'you have to spoil all my fun?'

A graceful silhouette appeared behind Patch in the doorway. So this was Con – for Constance? Connie? Confidence, from the sound of things.

'Look,' said Jonah, finding his voice at last. 'You want to tell me what the hell is going on here?'

The girl ignored him, turned to Patch. 'I thought Motti was fixing the lights.'

They snapped on in the cell, blinding and brilliant.

'Right on cue,' said Patch.

Jonah blinked furiously, willing his sight to return. When it did, his gaze lingered on Con. She was tall, almost his height. Eighteen or nineteen, he reckoned, and striking rather than beautiful: her neat nose just a little crooked, her eyes just a fraction too far apart. Her hair was blonder than Jonah's, almost white, held back off her forehead by a thick band as black as the rest of the clothes she wore.

She looked aloof and sophisticated, while Jonah stood there cowering like a prat in his prison pyjamas.

'Now just hang on,' he said. 'I don't know what kind of stunt you're trying to pull here, but –'

12

Con cut him short. 'You are Jonah Wish, the cipherpunk, yes?'

Jonah grimaced. 'Cipherpunk?'

'It's him all right, Con,' Patch said, checking the corridor was still clear. 'He's changed a bit since the pictures were taken, but this is the right cell. And there's no roomie to worry about, just like the man said.'

Con walked casually into the cell. 'You do not look like a computer geek, Jonah.' She talked slowly and carefully, like she was tasting each word in her mouth. 'You quite cute. Even with bed head.'

'I could just about handle the "cipherpunk" thing,' said Jonah, smoothing a hand through his tangled sandy hair, 'but now I know you're taking the piss.'

'Uh-uh.' Con smiled, the kind of smile you saw pinned up in dentists' waiting rooms. 'We are taking *you*.'

'Taking me?' He bunched his fists. 'This is crazy. What *is* this?'

'Get dressed. Hurry.'

'Why?'

Con threw him a look hard enough to bruise. 'We'd hate for you to catch cold out there.'

'Out there?' He looked at her, bemused. 'What, you're here to spring me?'

'Duh!' said Patch. 'Kind of early for visiting hours, innit?'

'And we will be late for our exit if we don't get moving.' Con picked up his blue prison jeans from where they lay crumpled on the floor and threw them at him. 'So move.'

'Late. Right.' Jonah's mind was grappling numbly

with events and coming off worst.

Then, as he slowly pulled on the threadbare jeans, he noticed the warder in the corridor start to stir. Was that good news or bad? Did he *want* to be rescued – shoved back in his cell and locked up again? Hadn't he just been fantasising about getting out of here?

Funnily enough, a tall blonde and a kid with a removable eyeball hadn't figured prominently in those fantasies.

The warder's eyes flickered fully open. He was a new screw – Wilson, his name was. He stared first in confusion, then in alarm at these unlikely night visitors.

As Jonah continued dressing, he could see from the corner of his eye that slowly, quietly, Wilson was getting to his feet. Should he say something, alert Con and Patch? Or should he be glad there was someone ready to put a stop to this madness? He struggled into a white T-shirt, trying not to shake, feeling the light cotton snag on his sweaty back.

'Come on!' Con urged him.

Wilson pulled out his baton and raised it, ready to bring it down on the back of Patch's head. If Jonah was going to say something, he would have to do it right now before –

He never got the chance.

As Wilson brought down his club, Patch ducked and dodged neatly out of the way. At the same time, Con slipped behind the warder. Jonah blinked, and so almost missed the bit where she knocked the baton from Wilson's hand and struck him in the stomach. Next thing he knew, Patch was wielding the club while Wilson lay sprawled on the concrete floor, gasping for breath.

'Now come on, you kids,' Wilson said weakly, like he thought he was still somehow in control. 'I don't know what your game is, but give it up. You can't hope to walk out of here.'

'Kids?' Con hauled him up by one arm. 'Look at me, you patronising little man.' Her green eyes were unblinking, as green and cold as Arctic waters. 'What is his name, Jonah?'

The warder looked at him warningly.

'She asked you a question, Jonah,' said Patch quietly. 'What, you're on *his* side, now?'

At least I understand his side, thought Jonah, his mouth dry.

'Wilson,' he croaked at last. 'His name's Wilson.'

'Well, well, Mr Wilson. I am glad you woke up. We have need of you.'

'If you think you can use me as a hostage –' He broke off, wincing as she placed a hand on the back of his neck.

'Mr Wilson, you are going to do something for us. You are going to walk to the main gate and tell them to open up.'

'You must be out of your –'

'Shhh.' Con leaned in to the warder's face like she was going to kiss him, her eyes boring into his own, her voice soft and soothing as her fingers stroked his neck. 'You *will* walk to the main gate,' she assured him. 'You will tell the guards there to open up so that a white van may gain entrance.'

Wilson just stared at her, kind of glassily.

'The driver will not be carrying identification, but you can vouch for her. Ask that they bend the rules and let her through. She is . . . some entertainment you have arranged for Doug Hurst, no? It's his birthday today.'

'Entertainment,' said Wilson, nodding as if this was a perfectly plausible idea.

'For Doug's birthday,' Con reminded him gently. It was weird; the way she spoke, her words . . . She sounded so much older than she looked.

Patch didn't. 'Say you'll show them some juicy photos of the gig later,' he smirked. '*Well* juicy photos.'

Con ignored him, all her attention on Wilson. 'Once you have told them this, you will go back inside, sit at the front desk and fall asleep.' Her voice grew softer, huskier. 'You will fall into a deep, deep sleep, and when you wake up you will remember nothing of this evening's events whatsoever. Do you understand me, Wilson?'

The warder nodded meekly.

'Then off you go.'

She let go of him and he shambled off out of the corridor.

'I'm the one in the deep, deep sleep,' Jonah muttered, pulling on his trainers. 'I've got to be dreaming, right?' He sank back against the cell wall and checked his watch. It was three o'clock exactly. 'Got to be.' Five minutes ago, the world stank but at least it was sane. Now . . .

'Two minutes till Motti's due at the main entrance,' hissed Patch. 'Come on, Con, fix up the geek and let's get going!'

'Who's Motti?' Jonah demanded. 'And what do you mean, fix up the –?'

'How long have you been in this pit, Jonah?' Con started walking slowly, steadily towards him.

'Too long,' he said stiffly.

'I'll bet you have dreamed of all the things you would like to do.' She unzipped her black jacket, which fell open to reveal a high-necked blouse. 'You have dreamed of *this* moment, yes? The moment of release.'

'Release?'

'Life is about opportunities.' She moved in close, her slim fingers slipping around the topmost of her blouse's tiny black buttons. 'And this is the biggest opportunity you'll ever have, Jonah. This is the chance of a lifetime.'

He stared transfixed as the little buttons popped open, one by one. 'What are you . . . I mean, you can't . . . We only just –'

But Con had already tugged open the neck of her blouse. Jonah's voice died in his throat as he saw the two glass ampoules glowing a sickly yellow, affixed just beneath her collarbone.

'But like any other chance – before you take it, you have to make it.' She plucked both ampoules deftly from the pale skin without even glancing down. 'One for you and one for me.'

'What are they?' Jonah said as she pressed one into his hand.

'We may need them if Wilson does not convince. And if we run into any more trouble on the way out.'

Jonah felt reality falling away. This was all a joke, it had to be – some big elaborate wind-up. 'You're really going to do it? You'll get me out of here?'

17

'Do not let go of this till I say.' Con closed Jonah's fingers around the ampoule. 'Phosphor caps are quite stable at body temperature, but away from the skin they cool quickly and . . .' She puffed up her cheeks then blew out the air as if by way of demonstration.

Jonah stared at his fist. 'You used these to get in here.'

'Amongst other things.'

'Why's it gone so quiet out there? What did you do to everyone?'

'Your questions can wait. *We* can't.'

Patch nodded. 'So are you coming, or what?'

Jonah stared at them helplessly. 'Who *are* you people?'

'Maybe your best friends. Maybe your worst nightmare.' Con's eyes seemed to glitter as she gestured to the cell door, which still stood wide open. The shadowy corridor was waiting outside. 'Want to find out which?'

CHAPTER TWO

Jonah's heart started to race as he was pushed out of his cell. How many times had he trudged along this corridor, eyes down, trying to keep out of trouble? But suddenly the unit seemed like another world, strange and unreal to him. The lights were down low. Wisps of white smoke coiled about his ankles. He started to walk. Con had one hand on his shoulder, steering him onwards. It was unnaturally quiet, no one about, save for a few officers slumped against the walls or sprawled on the floor.

He didn't want to know if they were dead or just sleeping. His mind had locked on a single thought, bright like the glass pellet trapped in his sweaty fist: *You're getting out.* Jonah was picking up speed now, his feet slapping down on the corridor, breaking into a stumbling run. *It's really going to happen.*

They were headed for the next wing. It seemed a roundabout route to the main exit. Jonah glanced back at Con, puzzled.

'Not safe to go out the same way we came in,' she told him. 'The caps only stun. The screws we zapped will be waking up.'

A turn in the corridor revealed a heavy iron door

blocking their way.

'What the hell is this?' Con looked at Jonah accusingly as if he'd put it there himself. 'This wasn't on the plans.'

'Looks new.' Patch sniffed. 'Yeah, smell that oil. The lock's still lubed.' He plunged two delicate metal rods into the keyhole and shook his head. 'They use five-pin tumblers and call a place secure. It's a bleedin' insult.'

'Could you stop being offended and just pick the damn thing?'

'What, Con?' The door swung open and Patch smiled cheekily. 'Couldn't hear what you said. Too busy picking the damn thing.'

'That's faster than the screws manage with a key,' said Jonah.

Con shoved him through the doorway. 'You can praise him later.'

'Don't let her boss you, Jonah,' said Patch. 'You can praise me right now. I can take it.'

Con was pushing them both along the corridor now, forcing them into a run. Noise was starting up, hoarse shouts and swearing from the cells, jeering and laughter. When no screws slapped them down, they grew bolder, louder, started banging on their doors. Jonah could feel the fear and excitement building around him.

'Animals,' said Con darkly. 'We should have drugged the whole lot of them, not just your block.'

'You drugged my whole *block*?' Jonah skidded to a halt. 'How the hell did you –?'

'Keep moving,' Con told him.

'We spiked the chicken and the tuna in the canteen,' Patch told him, ignoring a glare from Con. 'You're a veggie, aren't you?'

'How'd you know that?'

'Only four lettuce-lovers in your whole block.' Again, Patch grinned. 'Guess the other three sleep heavy.'

'We knew noise like this would only make you more scared,' said Con. 'Harder work.'

Jonah folded his arms. 'Right. Nothing to do with the fact that you can't do that creepy hypnotism unless it's quiet?'

'Mesmerism,' she corrected him with a tight smile. 'It is called *mesmerism*, yes? Now, *move*.'

She shoved Jonah forward, urging him to run through the harsh contours of the block. But his mind was racing way ahead. Drugged food? Stun bombs? Just what the hell was he getting himself into? These people had the cash and the know-how to pull off a spectacular jailbreak, and yet they were pretty much kids like he was. Con had mastered some freaky hypnosis thing, Patch could open a door faster than Jonah could open an envelope. But was Motti their boss or just another specialist – good with electrics, perhaps?

Whatever, they were going to big trouble to break Jonah out. It didn't take a genius to know they must need him for *his* little speciality – Jonah Wish, the cipherpunk.

But what if he didn't want to play ball? What would happen to him then?

'We made it!' Patch kicked open the door that led

out to the reception area. Jonah ran through, saw two officers slumped on the desk, snoring softly. One of them was Wilson. Clearly he'd done just as he was told.

The main doors stood unbolted.

'Worked like a charm. No one lifted a finger to stop us!' Con smiled. 'Lock that door behind us, Patch.' While her accomplice got busy, she held out a hand to Jonah. 'OK, let me have that cap I gave you.'

Jonah looked between her and the main doors. Then he smiled, reached out his hand . . .

Shut his eyes and threw the cap down at her feet.

The glass burst with a blinding light and a thick fog of smoke. He heard Patch swear. Con shouted as she jumped back and crashed into the reception desk. But Jonah was already running for the doors.

'Sorry,' he called over his shoulder, 'but you did say life was about opportunities.'

Heart in his mouth, Jonah slung open one of the doors. He felt the night air cold on his face, and a moment's euphoria. They'd wanted him to go with them, and he had – as far as the exit. Now it was time to make and take his *own* chances.

The yard outside was dark and silent. A white van was parked close by – had to be Con and Patch's friend, OK'd by Wilson and let through at the main gate. Jonah swiftly changed direction, backing off round the side of the reception building. He'd never make it past the guards on foot, but there had to be some other way of getting out of this –

He gasped as something fell on him from above, knocking him to the ground – or rather, some*body*.

Before he could catch his breath, he was dragged to his feet and shoved up against the wall by a tall, rangy guy with black hair pulled back in a ponytail and a razor-cut goatee.

The guy's hand closed threateningly on his throat. 'Going somewhere, Jonah?'

'S'pose not,' gasped Jonah, and the pressure on his throat relaxed a little. The guy was maybe twenty, sounded American. His fierce scowl would have been more intimidating if his round-rimmed glasses hadn't come loose in the tumble – the left lens was now perched on his nose. 'You must be Motti. The boss man.'

'Boss man? *Him?*' Jonah turned to find Patch and Con slipping through the shadows towards them, Patch laughing like a drain. 'Wait till Coldhardt hears!'

Jonah frowned. 'Coldhardt?'

'Shut your dumb mouth, Patch,' Motti hissed, quickly straightening his glasses. 'What gives with the geek getaway, Con? Losing your touch?'

'He's got more nerve than we thought.' Con shrugged. 'I didn't want to put him under. I thought it best he could watch out for himself if we found trouble.'

'Looks to me like he *is* trouble,' said Motti. 'Maybe we should just off him now. Say *sayonara.*'

Con arched an eyebrow. 'You want to explain that to Coldhardt?'

He shrugged. 'Shit happens.'

'Smells to me like it already did.' Jonah forced him-self to face Motti's stare; he'd learned a thing or two about standing up to creeps these last two months inside. 'What happened, get scared up on the dark spooky roof all by yourself?'

Patch sniggered, but Motti only tightened his grip on Jonah's throat once more. 'Careful, geek. Working the lights from up there was a cinch – and I can punch out yours just as easily. You got a big mouth.'

'And a fair-sized brain,' Jonah gasped, acting about twenty degrees cooler than he felt. 'Which is why Coldhardt sent you here to spring me, right? So how about you stop wasting time and get on with it.'

'He's right,' said Con. 'We're pushing our luck already. Come on, Tye is waiting.' She grabbed Jonah by the hand and pulled him free of Motti's grip.

Now, as well as fear, Jonah felt embarrassed as he was dragged towards the white van. He knew Con must be able to feel him trembling. But to his surprise, as Motti and Patch caught up with them she simply gave his hand a little squeeze of reassurance.

Motti slid open the rear door. 'Get in, Patch. C'mon, Con, you too. Guards on the gate need to think Tye's come back out alone.'

Con shook her head. 'I'm taking the front. I'll crouch down out of sight.'

'No way. What if the guards on the gate look in and see you?'

'They won't. It'll be cool.'

'Jeez, Con, you knew the plan. As soon as we're clear of this dump you can get out and –'

'I'm *taking the front*!' Con opened the passenger door and climbed nimbly inside, slamming it shut behind her.

'What was all that about?' hissed Jonah.

'Don't go there,' muttered Motti. He roughly bundled Jonah inside after Patch, then scrambled in himself.

The moment he'd shut the door, the van engine roared into life. It was pitch black – the windows were blanked out and a divider had been put up between the front and the rear. Jonah felt sick with nerves.

'Don't make a sound,' said Motti. 'Do anything to get the guards' attention and I swear I'll kill you.'

'Go easy, Mot,' muttered Patch.

The van pulled away. Thirty seconds later, when it came to a sudden halt, Jonah's heart almost stopped with it.

A quiet hum: electric window winding down. Footsteps outside.

'Dougie's show over already, is it, love?' A man's voice, smug and knowing; you could almost hear the leer in it. 'Didn't take long.'

'Do you imagine it *ever* takes long with Dougie?' a girl's voice replied, to guffaws of laughter. This had to be Tye. She had a nice voice – a touch rougher than Con's, warmer, with just an edge of Caribbean accent.

'Come on, sweetheart,' said a second guard suddenly. 'Who're you trying to kid?'

A pause. Tye acted innocent. 'What d'you mean?'

Someone banged hard on the side of the van. Jonah held himself dead still, not even daring to breathe.

'Got the poor sod tied up in the back, ain'tcha? Taking him off for a private performance, right?'

More laughter. Jonah blew out his breath, cradled his head in his hands.

'He wishes,' said Tye. 'Well, so long, guys. Oh – here's my agency's card. If you want to see what you missed, give them a call. Ask me nice, I might come back . . .'

Amid wolf whistles and filthy laughter, the van pulled away. Jonah heard a whirring, grinding noise as the gate lifted up to let it pass. Then Tye stepped on the accelerator, turned hard on to the road.

'We did it,' breathed Motti. He whooped loudly. 'We *did* it!' He and Patch shifted forward and pulled down the partition. Suddenly Jonah was staring out at streetlights and shops and office blocks. At windows with blinds, not bars. At the wide, black night and the stars that shone over the sleeping city.

'I'm out,' he murmured. 'Free.'

Con clambered up from the footwell of the passenger seat, grinning broadly, no trace of her earlier mood remaining. 'Look what I was hiding under!' She lifted up a big brown paper bag, spotted with grease. 'The smell was driving me crazy!'

'Mac attack!' cheered Patch. 'Gimme.'

'I almost dug in there and then, and screw the guards!' Con started flinging burgers and fries into the back. The van soon began to stink of fast food.

'It's all cold by now,' said Tye. She didn't turn around, her eyes fixed firmly on the road. All Jonah could see was the smooth, dark skin of the nape of her neck, the way her straightened black hair bounced with every bump.

'Big Macs taste better cold,' Patch informed her.

'It's official. How God intended.'

'Nah, God's a quarter-cheese man.' Motti bit off a chunk. ''S why it tastes like heaven.'

'Got you a beanburger, Jonah,' said Tye. 'Is that cool?'

Jonah was speechless. A few minutes ago these people had stormed a prison, calm as you like. And they'd actually got him out. It had been like something out of the movies. Now suddenly all that was forgotten, and they were just kids hanging out in a van, stuffing themselves with junk food.

Con passed him the burger. 'Eat.'

'Why not?' he said, peeling off the shiny paper and taking a bite of cold stodge in breadcrumbs. 'It's three-fifteen in the morning, I've just been broken out of prison, I've no idea who you are or what you really want or what happens now –'

'Did you get me a strawberry shake, Tye?' wondered Patch. 'You know I love a strawberry shake.'

'They only had vanilla.' She passed the drink over her shoulder.

'Shouldn't you be dumping this van?' asked Jonah. 'I mean, those phosphor caps just stun, you said.'

'Pretty much. A bright flash and some smoke.' Con had already all but devoured her chicken sandwich, and looked a lot less sophisticated with mayo round her mouth, giggling as she tried to snag a piece of lettuce from her lips with her little finger. 'Still nasty at close range. Lucky for you, I don't bear grudges.'

'Unlucky for you, she don't bare nothing else,' sighed Patch. 'Not even for money.'

'So they'll be up and after us any time,' said Jonah through another mouthful of burger. 'They'll be looking for a white van, circulating my description. And Tye's, and Con's and –'

'Gee, d'you think?' said Motti.

'They won't find us.' Con sounded utterly sure of herself. 'Not a hope in hell.'

Jonah saw they were heading out of the city now, for the thin strips of countryside beyond. He pinched the bridge of his nose, suddenly tired. 'Does Coldhardt live nearby, then?'

Knowing looks passed between them, some smiles. But they said nothing.

'Fine. Have fun with your little in-joke,' said Jonah. 'S'pose I'll find out soon enough.'

'Sorry, mate.' Patch dug an elbow in Jonah's ribs. 'But cheer up. You'll soon be in on the joke too. Coldhardt thinks you should join up.'

'Lucky us,' drawled Motti. Con threw her last fry at him.

'Why would he go to all this trouble for me? What does he want?' Jonah dropped the half-eaten bean-burger in his lap. He felt sick now, as well as tired. 'Who the hell *is* this Coldhardt, anyway?'

Con grinned at him. 'The man who is going to change your life.'

Motti nodded. 'Or maybe end it.'

'You got a real chip on your shoulder today, man,' Patch observed.

'Con threw it there,' he joked, and the two of them cracked up.

Jonah shook his head. 'What did I do to get

mixed up in this?'

'You got noticed,' said Tye, quietly rejoining the conversation as she swung the van on to a minor road. 'You stood out.'

'I spent my whole life trying to avoid standing out.' Jonah said. 'Good to know that's one more thing I can't do.' He knew he was sounding like a whining kid, but he didn't care. He was angry, tired and feeling sicker than ever. 'Listen . . . What if I don't *want* to join up with you and your precious Coldhardt? Will . . . will you let me go?'

No one spoke.

'Only . . . if I see where he lives and stuff, and I want out . . . I'm a threat to him, aren't I? I could – I could lead the cops to him . . .'

'Only if you sleepwalk,' said Con, almost fondly. 'You seem very tired, no? Too sleepy to move. No threat to anyone.'

'Wanna bet? I can snore loud enough to make your ears bleed.' Jonah shook his head, tried to clear it. 'It's late. I didn't get any sleep . . .'

He jumped as Patch slipped an arm round him, leaned in with a confidential air. 'It could also be to do with the way we spiked the chicken and tuna in your block last night.'

'I never ate that stuff.'

'True.' He crumpled up a greasy plastic wrapper. 'But y'know, it's even easier to spike a single bean-burger.'

'You . . .' Jonah willed his eyes to focus, but it was no good. He felt he was falling into a dark, dark tunnel. 'You load of –'

'Oi, watch the language, mate,' Patch's echoing voice carried distantly through the blackness. 'I'm just a kid. Remember?'

CHAPTER THREE

Jonah woke up in his boxers, with a headache, a back-ache and no idea where the hell he was. His bunk in prison had been more like a slab in the morgue, but now he was lying in the middle of a soft, springy double bed. Dark blue curtains stirred at the open window, letting golden sunlight spill over the spotless white walls.

He pushed off the enormous, squashy duvet and sat up, taking in the antiqued floorboards and the marble bathroom through the doorway. A chunky dark wooden chest of drawers was loaded with salon grooming products, while the open wardrobe was crammed with clothes for just about every occasion – suits and jeans and hoodies. He recognised some of the labels: as pricey as everything else seemed to be around here.

But then Jonah's eyes fixed and lingered on a serious-looking media-centre PC, with a widescreen flat panel display and surround sound, dominating a desk in the corner. He recognised the make with a quake of surprise – a flash new breed, not meant to be hitting the high street for ages.

Jonah flexed his fingers, started to scramble out of

bed. He'd dreamed of owning a machine like this. And it was so long since he'd heard the comforting click of the keys as he –

He froze, remembering some old, old advice about sweets and strangers. This must be Coldhardt's place.

Whose room was this?

A chair had been placed beside the bed. A glass of water sat on the arm with a note beside it in an extravagant scrawl: '*Drink me – I will refresh. PS I am not spiked.*'

'Ha, ha,' said Jonah darkly. But he drained the lot. Almost straight away his head seemed to clear a little.

He pulled aside one curtain, shielded his eyes from the bright blue sky. The view was as five-star as the rest of the room – a vineyard sloping away down a hillside, lawns that looked trimmed by nail scissors, and in the distance, a narrow, winding country road snaking between cornfields.

No clues as to where he was, or how long he'd been out. He couldn't see a single person, a solitary car. It could be miles and miles to civilisation, so even if he could get out undetected, running away was hardly an option.

Jonah lay back in the bed, perspiring slightly. His abductors had planned things perfectly. But what now?

There was a noise outside the bedroom door. Someone coming. At once, he closed his eyes, curled up on his side, shammed sleep.

The door opened smoothly, silently. Opening his eyes a fraction, Jonah saw that Motti had come to call. Black was clearly the guy's colour – like last night, he wore black jeans and a T-shirt with an all-but-destroyed white logo on the front.

Motti just stood there, all Gothic and grungy in the doorway for a few moments. Then he advanced stealthily towards the bed.

Jonah tensed, kept up the pretence he was dead to the world. But as Motti reached out for his throat, Jonah lashed out with his foot, landing an evil blow to the guy's family jewels. Motti bellowed in pain, doubled up. But Jonah wasn't finished yet. He sprang out of bed, wrestled Motti to the floor.

'OK, go easy, geek,' Motti gasped, trying to twist free.

'The name is Jonah.' He straddled Motti's chest, pinning him to the floor. 'What d'you want from me? Why'd you sneak in here?'

'To wake you up, asswipe.' Motti grimaced, stopped struggling and went limp. 'We were gonna show you around. Answer your questions and stuff.'

Jonah looked at him warily. 'How can I trust you?'

Motti smiled. 'You can't.'

Suddenly he bucked his whole body. Jonah wasn't prepared, overbalanced. In a second, Motti was on top of him, pinning him to the floor.

'You two are getting to know each other better, huh?' Jonah looked across to see Con smirking in the doorway, in jeans and a tight red top. 'I should shut the door, hang a Do Not Disturb sign, no? Give you boys some privacy?'

'Funny,' Motti muttered. He looked down at Jonah. 'Are we through here?'

'Whatever,' said Jonah.

Con nodded approvingly. 'See you downstairs.'

Motti got up, pushed his glasses back on his nose. 'Nice move there,' he said grudgingly, rubbing his balls ruefully. Then, to Jonah's surprise, he offered his hand.

Jonah grimaced. 'I'll take the clean one, thanks.'

Motti half-smiled, swapped hands and helped him up. 'Learned to take care of yourself in the slammer, huh?'

'Used to get visits from guys whose idea of fun was to load a sock full of batteries and cosh the crap out of you. If you don't get in first . . .' He shrugged. 'Sorry. I s'pose.'

''S OK. I know how it is.'

'You've been inside?'

'Few times.' Motti paused. 'But you know, man, you gotta learn a whole new way of fighting now. Coldhardt's taught us some real moves.'

'Didn't notice you using them.'

'Not allowed to kill you on the first day.' Motti smiled wryly and gestured at the wardrobe. 'Look, there's clothes in there – Con chose 'em for you, so bitch at her if they don't fit. You want to shower first, that's cool.' He headed for the door. 'Meet us downstairs in twenty, 'K?'

Jonah stared after him. 'Con chose this stuff for *me*?'

'And the curtains and shit. All of it. You wanna redecorate, it's down to you. It's your room, geek.'

'My room?' Jonah stared round bewildered. 'So, is this place where you live?'

'Live. Plan. Play. One of the perks of the job.' Motti

was looking impatient, still rubbing at his tender parts. 'Come downstairs, shut your mouth and open your ears – in twenty. You'll find out all you wanna know.'

The shower was hot and powerful, the scented gels and foams light years away from the stuff he'd had inside. Engulfed in a thick white towel, Jonah chose a pair of dark boot-cut jeans and a black V-neck T-shirt. They were a perfect fit. His old trainers had been dumped in the bin and he could understand why. They hardly measured up to the Nikes and New Balances crowding the polished floor of the wardrobe.

He looked in the mirror on his chest of drawers, grimaced at how pale and pasty he looked. Then he noticed a tub of hair gel sitting open beneath it. A note had been placed inside the lid, in the same flamboyant pen – *For bed head*.

'Looks like Con thinks of everything,' he murmured, and felt once again that familiar sense of unease. He looked at the PC. A bribe? Or just a tool for him to do whatever it was he was here for?

Cautiously, Jonah opened his door, and felt a cooling breeze. Two enormous fans turned silently in the high ceiling, which was studded with spotlights. He saw now that his room gave on to a wide swathe of polished mahogany, a kind of gallery area extending from the landing. Incongruously, a retro tabletop Scramble arcade game stood beside the intricately carved balustrade.

To his left was a wide wooden spiral staircase. A strip of deep white carpet snaked down its length, bolted into the well-crafted angles with chrome stair rods. 'Where do you lead, I wonder?' murmured Jonah, as he crossed to the gallery and looked down on to a huge space that was more like a common room or a club than the expected grand entrance hall. The floor, painted black, was littered with fat brown cracked-leather sofas, arranged around a full-sized snooker table that dominated the room. Drinks and snacks dispensers flanked fruit machines, a wall of flickering neon to the right of the room.

'Perks of the job,' he breathed, smiling despite himself.

But it was the wall facing the gallery that really grabbed Jonah's attention; a giant mural stretched across it, hazy shapes of colour against an unfocused landscape. Darker, spindly figures that might be trees or people lent uncertain detail to the scene, reaching upwards or outwards, or crouched over. It was cool, but kind of creepy, and did little to soothe the uneasy feeling in his guts.

He knew what it was. Nerves. Time and again he'd had to psyche himself up for his 'please like me' act – first day at a new school, or a new foster home. New faces checking him out. He'd spent his whole life trying to read the crowd, to fit in.

Except this time he didn't long to belong.

All he wanted were some answers.

Jonah checked his watch – his twenty minutes were up. He started quickly down the spiral staircase.

But as he reached the final turn, he stopped. They were waiting for him, lined up at the bottom of the stairs: Motti, Patch, Con – and Tye.

It was Jonah's first proper view of her, and he wasn't disappointed. She was a black girl, cute, maybe sixteen, dressed in combats. Her hair was no longer straight but scrunched up into little braids and adorned with a couple of gauzy red ribbons. She had an oval face with well-proportioned features – no make-up, and her brows weren't plucked like Con's. But her eyes were striking, wide and dark as she looked up at him through thick lashes. There was something hard in her stare, something old beyond her years, and wary. She did not smile to see him.

'Hey, cipher boy,' said Con, effortlessly taking his attention. 'This is the hangout. Welcome to the wrong side of the tracks.'

'Where is this place?' he asked, his eyes flicking from one to the other in turn.

'Want some coffee?' Patch, dressed in slobby blue track pants and an Anime T-shirt, headed for the rear of the room, the part Jonah couldn't see from the balcony. It looked like it had been airlifted out of a Starbucks – a chrome counter top with industrial-sized coffee makers, juicers, even a slush-ice drink machine assembled behind it. 'Latte? Espresso?'

'No, thanks.'

'You sure, mate? We got hazelnut syrup, vanilla . . .'

'You've got a lot of stuff here,' Jonah agreed, his attention wandering to a large alcove on his right. It had been turned into a full-on amusement arcade, with car simulators, shoot-em-ups and pinball machines.

'Wait till you see the gym,' Con told him. 'The

pool, too. Heated, with a wave machine . . .'

'And the garage is awesome,' Motti added. 'We got a race circuit where we test drive stuff. You like cars, geek?'

'I can't drive.'

''S not like you need a licence here.' Motti grinned. 'Just take out a car and floor it. Best way to learn.'

'Best way to kill yourself,' said Tye, crossing to the nearest sofa and flopping down.

'Tye's the designated driver round here,' Con explained with a slightly disparaging look. 'She takes it all very seriously.'

'She's a pilot, too,' Patch called over admiringly from the counter. 'She flew us here.'

They'd taken a plane? No wonder they weren't worried about the van being hot. And if they'd flown here, Jonah supposed he could be just about any-where.

'How long did you make me sleep? What's the date?'

'See for yourself.' Con tossed him something. He was glad he managed to catch it. It was a Rolex watch, beautiful, a Datejust with a steel strap. Had to cost a fortune. The date on the cool blue face read 26 – the same day they'd taken him. So he couldn't be anywhere too far-flung . . .

Then again, they'd fixed everything else. Why not the date?

He let the Rolex fall from his fingers to the stair. 'I have a watch, thanks,' he said coldly.

Con turned her back on him, and Motti smiled. 'Aw, you've hurt her feelings, geek. She stole that specially, just for you.'

'Poor bastard only wanted to buy her a drink,' said Tye, a sandpaper edge to her voice. 'She told him to just give her the money.'

'That's one thing you don't seem short of round here,' Jonah observed, glancing around the impressive space. 'I'm guessing you didn't get all this stuff doing paper rounds.'

Patch rejoined the group with a steaming mug of coffee and a look of amusement. 'Jonah, you never reckon we *stole* all this stuff?'

'We earned everything you see here,' Motti declared, 'fair and square.'

'What, pulling stunts like you pulled on me?'

'Guys, I think we have got us a choirboy here, yes?' There was no smile on Con's face now. 'I thought we got you out of prison, Jonah. Not a convent. What makes you think you can stand there and judge us?'

Motti joined Tye on the leather couch. 'See, we heard you helped your last foster dad launch a new business – what was it, Patch?'

Patch didn't hesitate. 'Designing secure encryptions for company computer payroll systems.'

''S right. Only once he was up and running, you cracked your own ciphers and siphoned off the cash for yourself.'

Jonah started forward angrily. 'It wasn't like that.'

Motti smirked. 'C'mon, who you kidding?'

'I had reasons.'

'The *best* reasons,' grinned Patch. 'You wanted cash and you knew how to get it easily.'

'You just didn't know how *not* to get caught,' Con added.

Jonah glared at Tye, waiting for her to chip in. But she stayed silent, looking down at her hands. 'I don't care what any of you think,' he said. 'But if you've dragged me out here to crack some encrypted bank account or something, so I can make you and this Coldhardt guy any richer –'

Motti laughed. 'As if! Credit us with *some* imagination.'

'Well, what *do* you want, then?' He gestured angrily down at himself. 'The designer gear, the computer up there . . . You're trying to buy me.'

'No. We're just trying to help you fit in.' The ghost of a smile returned to Con's face. 'This is what life's like when you're one of Coldhardt's children.'

'His *children*?' Jonah stared. 'OK, this is getting kind of creepy now. I suppose we're not talking adoption here?'

'Coldhardt saved us,' said Con. 'From ourselves.'

Motti yawned. 'From total boredom, you mean.'

'From a lifetime of nothing,' said Patch, going one better. 'No breaks, no future. Just marking time, doing what the law says . . . Trying to fit in with every other no-hoper.'

'And he brought you all here. I get it.' Jonah stared round at each of them in turn. 'You're all special in some way. You have talents.'

Motti looked at Patch. 'Think he's hitting on us?'

'Talents that Coldhardt can use,' said Jonah, undeterred. 'Patch, you're the lockpick. Tye's good with transport. Con does her hypnotism –'

'Mesmerism!' she protested.

'You don't even know what mesmerism really is,' sneered Motti.

'I know it sounds cooler than hypnotism, OK?'

'Motti . . . I dunno,' Jonah went on slowly. 'You handled the electrics. You're good with security systems, maybe. You get the others in and out, let them do their job.'

'Oh, is *that* what I do?' he said levelly.

'He gets an A for effort,' Tye observed.

Con shook her head. 'He's barely scratching the surface.'

'Whatever else you can do, the point is, you're all exceptional. Exceptionally talented misfits. What was it you said, Con – welcome to the wrong side of the tracks?' Jonah nodded. 'That's where Coldhardt found you, isn't it? In jail. Or in trouble. Alone – and easy pickings.'

'Gee, it's like my whole misspent youth passed before my eyes,' said Motti sarcastically. 'Well, listen, man – the pickings didn't come any easier than you.'

'I'm not for sale,' said Jonah firmly.

'You're happier on your own, Jonah?' Tye was holding him fixed with those big dark eyes of hers.

'I get along fine.'

Con gave him an uncomprehending look. 'Why settle for fine when you can have *fabulous*?'

'Aw, it's probably best he's acting way above it all for now,' said Motti. 'He ain't had the valuation yet. He could be leaving here faster than a cat with a firecracker up its butt.'

'Valuation?' Jonah looked at them uneasily.

'You say you're not for sale. We say we don't know what you're really worth,' said Con, green eyes sparkling. 'So it's time you met Coldhardt, cipher boy. In person.'

CHAPTER FOUR

Jonah had to admit he was intrigued as the others led him outside. Especially when he found out that the place where they'd been hanging was just an oversized outbuilding in the grounds of a huge chateau, all crumbling stonework and sash windows. It seemed Coldhardt owned the whole estate – you'd think it was home to some crusty earl and a butler or something, not four sociopathic dropouts and their rich benefactor.

If benefactor was the word. What if his 'children' got caught – would Coldhardt himself show up to break them out? Or would they sit rotting in a cell till he trained up another miniature teen army?

Maybe Motti hadn't just been mouthing off for once. If they pulled off stunts like last night's on a regular basis, they damn well *had* earned all that they'd got. And none of them seemed to feel short-changed . . . Except Tye maybe. The quiet one.

'So, I'm guessing the locals don't have you down for a bunch of criminals who hit the big time,' he ventured.

He'd aimed the question at Tye, but it was Con who answered. 'They think this is a kind of special school.'

'An academy,' Patch corrected her. 'Like the X-Men, yeah?'

'Except Patch is the only mutant we got here,' said Motti. 'Right, Cyclops?'

'Why d'you wear a patch when you've got a glass eye in?' Jonah asked bluntly.

''Cause Motti's got a thing about eyes.'

'Stow it,' said Motti.

'He has, and specially when I have to pop it out.' Patch beamed. 'Which is often. See, there's more to my glass eye than meets – er, the eye.'

'Lame,' grumbled Motti under his breath.

'In any case, the villagers are right, in a way,' Con went on. 'This *is* an academy, and Coldhardt's a good tutor. He has taught us so much.'

'I can imagine,' said Jonah. 'Quite a youth training scheme.'

They were approaching the main door to the chateau, a massive slab of dark oak framed by a thick sprawl of ivy. Jonah swallowed down his nerves. He wasn't so much angry now as apprehensive. So far, his abductors were treating him well enough. But if he couldn't deliver whatever it was they wanted, or if he refused even to try . . . what then?

There was no more time to worry. Tye pushed aside some of the ivy to reveal a small keypad. Her slim fingers beat a brief tattoo on the numbers and the door clicked open.

'Doorbell not working?' Jonah ventured.

Patch smiled. 'You could say the chief is security conscious.'

'And I designed the defences for this whole place,' said Motti.

'It's what he used to do in the real world,' said Con. 'He worked for a firm of security specialists.'

'Man, I *was* the firm.'

'Till he started turning over the places he was making so secure,' chimed Patch.

Motti straightened his glasses. 'Had to test my systems worked right, didn't I?'

Tye must have noticed Jonah's expression. 'No, the judge didn't believe him either.'

'All ancient history.' Motti led the way through to a large, immaculate hallway. 'But it got me noticed – by Coldhardt. Anyway, like I say, I designed the defences. Like that door? It ain't just wood, geek. It's lined with steel, two inches thick.'

Jonah nodded vaguely. His attention had been taken by a large, unsettling statue of a man locked in combat with some weird demonic figure. The marble tableau dominated the centre of the hall, bathed in golden sunlight from two enormous windows.

'Er . . . is the glass bulletproof?'

'It's everything-proof,' said Motti mysteriously.

'You're expecting trouble, then?'

'Always a possibility.'

Patch yawned again, flipped up his eye-patch and scratched the skin. 'Motti's completely paranoid.'

'Am not.'

'Yeah?' Patch pulled a spooky face. 'How do you *know* you're not?'

'Can we just get on, guys?' Con pushed through, past the eerie statue and through one of two vaulted archways set into the back of the room.

Jonah followed with the others and turned hard right into a long, wide passage. Or was it just a long, narrow room? Huge arched windows lined the outer wall, affording a view out on to a well-manicured courtyard.

'Cloisters,' said Tye softly, as if listening in on his thoughts. 'Built in 1801. It's so peaceful here.'

'S'pose it is,' Jonah conceded. Some of the glass in the windows was stained – coats of arms, some churchy-looking stuff in Latin . . . and a creepy little recurring figure that looked like the thing the man-statue was fighting. He almost asked Tye what the thing was supposed to be . . . but thought better of it, for now.

Motti had pulled some little gadget from his jeans pocket. When he pressed it, the wooden double doors at the end of the cloister hummed open automatically. They gave on to a short walkway, beyond which was a slate-floored room lined with portraits and colonnades.

The group paused to linger in the walkway. But just when Jonah was beginning to fear a complete guided tour was on the cards, Motti hit his gadget again and the floor lurched beneath them. Suddenly they were disappearing down into the ground. The walkway was a hidden lift.

Jonah looked round in alarm. 'Super-techno eleva-tor *not* built in 1801, I take it.'

'This takes us down to the hub,' said Con rever-ently. 'The heart of Coldhardt's operations.'

'Installed underground in case of trouble, right?'

Jonah rubbed his hand through his hair, as the lift reached a halt.

Down here, old world elegance made way for high-tech minimalism. The spacious chamber seemed to be a bunker, boardroom and workplace all in one. Eight brushed steel chairs were arranged round a table, a huge oval of heavy oak. Black, unmarked filing cabinets stood like sentries down the length of one wall, while twelve plasma screens clustered on the other like an enormous compound eye. They showed CNN, BBC World Service and news services in languages Jonah couldn't even guess at, as well as fish-eyed views of the house and grounds courtesy of a few well-placed spy cams. There was a wide desk, on which sat a computer – looked to be a wireless set-up – and a slim glass vase, in which sat a single black rose.

Then his ears pricked up at the steady rush of a serious air-con system behind a set of frosted glass doors. Data centre, he reckoned. In which case that computer would have some serious power behind it.

'So where's Coldhardt?' said Jonah to the others, trying to act casual. 'Stepped out for a pee? Gone to pick another black rose? Both at once, if the neighbours aren't watching?'

'There's always *someone* watching, Jonah Wish.'

The voice was velvet and rich, with a slight Irish lilt to it. Jonah turned automatically to see, but the lights cut out the same second. The TV feeds seemed to go the same way, and the room was plunged into blackness. Then the plasma screens flickered on again.

Jonah felt a cold feeling in the pit of his stomach. All twelve monitors showed the same picture of *him*.

There he was on his doorstep, waving goodbye to Marion, his foster mum. Jonah could tell from her clothes – from the look she was trying to hide in her eyes – it was the day the police came calling.

The image changed. A close-up of him in the street, livid with rage, face all snot and tears, screaming. The photographer pulled back a little to show the police gripping his arms. Out further to reveal his foster dad pushing Marion back inside the house. A little more to show the waiting police car with its doors wide open for him, and the gawping crowd gathered on the pavement.

'What is this?' he croaked. The next picture showed him inside a shabby grey room, sitting behind a desk, head bowed. 'That's the bloody police interview room for God's sake.' He looked at Con and the others, who were studying the picture dispassionately. 'How'd you ever get to take pictures inside – ?'

'Like I say,' the heavy voice steamrollered over his own, 'there's always someone watching.'

The lights came back up. And now a dark, gaunt figure sat at the head of the huge oak table.

His head was crowned with white hair, brushed up stiffly from his lined forehead. He looked to be in his early sixties, but there was a lean and hungry look about the pale, craggy features that put Jonah in mind of someone far younger. His eyes were a piercing blue, one eyebrow raised in either challenge or amusement. The thin lips curled into a half-smile as he rose now to his full imposing height, which had to be way over six feet. He was dressed like a big businessman: a dark suit, a silk shirt open at the neck to reveal a glint of gold – an amulet of some kind, clearly nothing so mundane as a St Christopher.

Jonah took a deep breath. 'You're Coldhardt?'

The pale man looked disappointed. 'You need to ask?'

'Nice entrance. Hope we didn't leave you crouched behind the filing cabinets for too long.' Jonah swallowed hard. He wasn't going to give this joker the satisfaction of knowing how rattled he was. 'How did you get these pictures?'

'I've had you on file for some time, Jonah. Along with several other interested parties.' Coldhardt smiled again, a cold smile that never came close to his eyes. 'In fact, this photographic material comes from one of them. I can't claim credit. I only stole it.'

'So, what, now I'm supposed to be intimidated and impressed at the same time?'

'Just be thankful I got to you first.'

'Yeah, well, cheers for making me a fugitive.' Jonah pulled up a chair and slouched into it. He pointed to the screens. 'Got any of me looking to the left? Only that's my best side.'

The image switched to the outside of the detention centre, ugly and stark. A shudder ran through him at the sight of it.

The strange smile still flickered round Coldhardt's lips. 'The Bible talks of a Hebrew prophet named Jonah, who lived around 800 BC. He was consumed by a giant fish, and vomited out three days later, unharmed. I'm afraid you had to wait two months to escape the place that swallowed *you* up.' Coldhardt crossed to one of his dark cabinets. 'But then, you have to allow for inflation.'

'Bible? Don't tell me you're all mad religious cultists?'

'Our faith is in *you*, Jonah. I do hope it's not been misplaced.' Coldhardt nodded to the others, acknowledging them for the first time, and they all took a seat at the table. Then he slid some papers to Jonah along the table. They were colour copies of parts of what looked to be old parchment, covered in exotic symbols. Many of the signs were barely visible, blotted out by stains or age. But Jonah recognised a few, and guessed what it was he was looking at.

'It's a scytale cipher. Simple matrix transposition.'

Patch frowned. 'Simple what?'

Jonah shrugged. 'Just a way of scrambling letters, making a code.'

'And what's a scytale?' asked Con.

'Kind of a special-sized stick,' he told her. 'The Ancient Greeks, Egyptians – they all used them to send coded messages. See, you take a strip of parchment and wrap it around the scytale in a spiral till all the wood is covered. Then you write your message, one letter on each pass of the parchment along the length of the stick.'

'What if you run out of room?'

'You just start a new row underneath. When you've finished, unwrap the strip of parchment, and hey presto: the message becomes just a jumble of letters. Until the person you send it to wraps it round a scytale that's the same size, and the message reads normally again.' He smiled over at Coldhardt. 'You know, you could have saved yourself a lot of trouble by looking that up in a book.'

This time, Coldhardt didn't smile back. 'The fragments are believed to be part of a Spartan military cipher, hailing from the fourth century BC. I want you to tell me what this message says.'

'You have a scytale handy, and the rest of the parchment? Oh, and a crash course in Ancient Greek would help.'

'I don't believe you're taking me altogether seriously. And you really should, you know.'

'Amen to that,' breathed Motti.

Coldhardt gestured to his computer. 'Use this, Jonah. Tell me what the message says.'

So here it was: the inevitable test. 'What's in it for me?'

'A new start.' Coldhardt's eyes seemed to stare into his soul. 'A life that most people your age could only dream of.'

Jonah stared down at the fragments of paper. He'd wasted so much time inside, bored and listless – no computers, no challenge. And now suddenly he was in a different world, being asked – no, *told* to do what he loved.

What was written here that was so important, worth so much?

He realised he was dying to find out.

Without a word he got up and walked over to the desk: Coldhardt stepped smartly aside to let him pass, and Jonah caught the tang of some subtle, expensive cologne. He studied the computer, located an internet icon on the plain black desktop and double-clicked. At once, a request for a password came up.

Jonah was about to ask Coldhardt what it was, when he bit his lip. Might as well show initiative.

It was the work of seconds to hack into User Account Properties. From here, Jonah reset the Administrator and cleared all user passwords. He rebooted the computer in safe mode, then created a new Windows account for himself, one that allowed him full access to everything on the system. He checked the internet connection – as he'd expected, it was secure, all file traffic encrypted.

The parchment copies gave him only fragments to work with, but that was cool. That made it more of a challenge. A scytale was only a basic cipher; a systematic guess-and-check approach would crack it in the end, and without much personal effort. A year or so back he'd created a shadow directory on a local server – an invisible folder, its location known only to him. It was filled with all the cipher-cracking software and algorithms he'd acquired or written over the years, waiting to be downloaded as and when he needed them. Now was the time, so he clicked on some old favourites to get the party started.

There were obstacles, of course. While he didn't need an actual scytale – you got the same effect just by fitting the characters into the rows and columns of a blank grid – he had no way of knowing the length of the original message, and so didn't know how long and wide the grid should be. But if it was a military cipher, then the message was most likely a command. Brisk and to the point – say, no more than a hundred characters . . .

Jonah had written some code way back that would

calculate the various permutations. But he'd also need to patch in a language program that would recognise and retrieve genuine Ancient Greek words from the random gibberish. That, together with some skill and a little intuition . . .

Slowly, Jonah allowed himself to become entirely engrossed in his work. All through his life, no matter where he was, whatever the circumstances, the world he looked in on through the screen was always home turf. And with a rush of excitement, he realised that Coldhardt's computer was faster than anything he'd ever worked on. The software was working at an incredible rate, cross-checking thousands of possible matrix sizes against millions of possible character substitutions, trying to crack the cipher.

But as the minutes passed, Jonah sensed something was wrong. Something he was missing. Sure enough, the program told him that no matches were found. Either the translation software was dodgy or there was something else going on with this mystery message . . .

He became aware of Coldhardt's shadow beside him, black and heavy across the desk.

Jonah drove all doubts from his mind. He *would* crack this. Column substitution? Seemed unlikely. The Spartan sending the message would have to copy out the characters on his scytale into a grid first, then arrange the columns in a different order before copying it out on to a new strip of parchment. The person receiving the message would have to go through the same process in reverse at the other end. That was a lot of faffing about . . .

But perhaps the message was important enough to warrant it.

He upped the size of the possible grids, patched in a new program to test his theory. Come on, come on . . .

Jackpot!

His heart beating faster, Jonah watched as a handful of words tumbled out of the translator. Then he frowned.

The answer to life, the universe and everything it wasn't.

'OK, I think this is it,' he announced.

Con raised an eyebrow, prepared to be impressed. 'After just twenty minutes?'

'It's better encrypted than anything I've seen from that time. But there's only fragments – not much sense.'

'Go on,' said Coldhardt softly.

' "Catacombs . . . north . . . stars buried in patterns." That's the main bit. Then there's just gibberish . . . Doesn't sound like real words. "Imhotep"? And um, how do I say this? "Oph . . ." '

'Ophiuchus.' Coldhardt looked at the others. 'That's *oh-FEE-yoo-kus*. It's a mouthful, but get used to it. It's a name you'll be hearing a lot of.'

'So I did it, then,' said Jonah. 'Do I win a coconut?'

'Your interpretation matches that given to me by the original parchment's owner – a man who wishes to avail himself of our services.' Coldhardt seemed pleased. 'Although I believe he took a little longer to come by the solution.'

'Well, now you know what it says,' said Jonah, erasing the account he had just created. 'But what does it mean? What *is* Ophiuchus?'

'You mean, *who* is Ophiuchus. You'll find out in due course.'

'Great, we're back to the man of mystery thing.' Jonah shut down the computer and stood back up. 'Look, if you already knew what the fragments said, why did you need me at all?'

'I wanted to be sure I was being told the truth,' said Coldhardt. 'And while I know of many celebrated geniuses who could have confirmed the information for me, those same geniuses are known to my opponents.' He gave a wintry smile. 'Secrets are hard to keep. And true new talent is hard to find.'

'So you break me out of jail –'

'– to be sure of exclusive access to your very capable mind.'

Jonah felt a shiver run through him. 'And I'm *your* prisoner now, is that it?'

'I prefer to use the word *employee*.' Coldhardt took the parchment copies and walked purposefully back to the black cabinets. 'I want you to work for me, Jonah. Like I say, you're fresh talent. There are harder tasks and greater challenges ahead.' He carefully filed the papers away. 'I can help you reach your full potential, boy.'

'Yeah? What if I turn you down?'

Coldhardt turned and stared intently at Jonah. 'Then you must leave us, of course. We shall have to release you somewhere remote, and since you have no passport and no money – nothing save for the clothes you stand in – getting back to England might prove difficult. But you can always hand yourself over to the local police. They'll gladly deal with you, I'm sure . . .'

Jonah couldn't meet the intensity of the gaunt man's gaze any longer. He looked away, down at his Diesel jeans, at the brand new NBs on his feet. Thought back to the sumptuous cool of the room he'd woken up in, and the hangout down the spiral stairs.

What was the alternative? Back to prison, with time added on for breaking out. And after a few years, out again with a record. No home, no family or friends to speak of.

No future.

'Well, Jonah?' Coldhardt prompted him. 'Will you join my fold?'

Jonah imagined that once the decision was taken, there was no going back. He looked at the others. Con was watching him expectantly. Patch nodded in encouragement, polishing his glass eyeball on his sleeve. Motti's attention was on the detention centre that loomed large and pin sharp on the dozen screens.

Tye was looking right at Jonah, her expression unreadable.

'I s'pose I'm in,' Jonah said.

CHAPTER FIVE

The luxury Range Rover was as big and black as the night. Tye was playing chauffeur, enjoying the smoothness of the ride, taking the tight mountain bends with ease. Con sat beside her in the passenger seat, peering into the sunshade mirror as she applied yet another coat of lip gloss. Coldhardt sat brooding in the back, gazing out over the dark jagged landscape of foothill, forest and crag, sipping champagne from a pewter goblet.

No junk food allowed in *this* car.

Con pouted her glistening lips and sighed. 'Why can't you tell us what all this is about, Coldhardt? At least fill us in on some background.'

'I want Tye to come to this fresh,' he said. 'I want her to hear the story for the first time as Demnos tells it. She'll be able to tell if he's on the level.'

'Right. We can always depend on our human lie detector to deliver.'

Tye shot her a sideways glance. Con excelled at the straight-faced sarcastic remark.

'So then why do you need *me* here?' she continued.

'I don't. But I know how you enjoy a party.'

The sat-nav prompted her to take a right turn, a

narrow road that spiralled steeply round a leafy hill-side. Coldhardt's base was in Geneva, not far from the French border, and Tye loved the feeling of freedom of driving through Alpine country. The sweeping views, the moonlit calm all soothed her nerves, reminded her of happier times in the Léogane mountains where she grew up. She was always tense at the start of a new job.

And now there was the new boy to think about – or rather, to try *not* to think about. He seemed so . . . well, unspoiled, despite all the crap he'd been through.

Don't join us, she'd been willing him. *Stick with the world you know.*

Do as I say, not as I do.

'Wonder how Jonah's settling in,' she remarked.

Con pulled a face. 'Still sulking, I expect.'

'It's been a shock for him. Not everyone adjusts as fast as you.' She bit her lip, didn't want to make out she was bothered one way or the other – give Con a few scraps and she'd make a real meal of it.

'I want you all to watch him closely,' said Coldhardt. Tye eyed him in the rear-view, distractedly swilling round his champagne. 'I believe he could be of great importance to us in our next enterprise. Keep him happy. Try to keep conflict to a minimum.'

'Well, Patch is such a softy, he will give no trouble,' said Con. 'And Motti likes him better now they've had a fight. Respects him more, yes?' She laughed to her-self, started applying another layer of mascara. 'Such silly things, boys. So easy to make them happy.'

Well, you'd know, Tye thought, but kept her thoughts to herself as usual.

'So Jonah can look after himself? That's good,' said

Coldhardt. 'But he needs proper training in self-defence. See to it, Tye.'

She nodded. A chequered flag had appeared on the sat-nav, warning them their destination was close by. Tye caught a blur of warm and welcoming light through the dark trees, some way off. 'This is the place?'

'Yes. The Gallery Rimbaud.'

'What's going on tonight?'

'A charity soirée for the great and good of the art world, in celebration of the gallery's guest of honour – the beneficent Raul Demnos.'

Con looked at Tye. 'That means he does things for charity.'

'I know.' Tye gripped the wheel harder, quietly seething inside. Growing up in Haiti she'd never had much of a formal education, apart from English and elocution lessons, her father's obsession – so she could talk like the woman who'd left them both. Con, on the other hand, had been educated in the smartest schools all over Europe, shunted from one remote relative to another after her parents –

'Demnos has recently donated some splendid Futurist paintings,' Coldhardt went on. 'He's reputed to have one of the finest collections of unusual art treasures in the world.'

'How'd you get to crash his party?' Tye wondered.

'I've made some . . . significant purchases here in the past. When I received the invitation it made sense that we all attend.'

'Are we going to rip them off?' Con asked eagerly.

'We're going to hear what Demnos has to say in a

neutral and elegant setting,' said Coldhardt. 'Now, you're clear on your cover stories for the other guests?'

'I'm your niece, trailing the art critic for *Les Temps* – who tragically can't be here.'

'And I catalogue exhibits for galleries, and private collections,' said Tye, turning the Range Rover into an impressive driveway. 'I'm hoping to catalogue Demnos's.'

'Giving us the perfect excuse to withdraw from polite society to a quiet room with dear Raul while we discuss the matter.' In the rear-view, Tye caught him smiling to himself. 'Many matters.'

The deceptions started the second they arrived. Having parked the car outside the impressive stately home, Tye shimmied into the back seat. In her sheer black silk halterneck she made an unlikely chauffeur. The footmen who swooped down to open the doors for the elegant trio were all far too well-trained to peer inside the car, and that – plus the mirrored windows – successfully concealed the fact that there was now no one in the driving seat.

Soon they were ensconced in a cream and crimson drawing room that rang with the dull drone of worthy conversation. Tye felt awkward and uncomfortable in her feminine frills and three-inch heels, sipping water and avoiding eye contact wherever possible. Con of course was loving it all in her lacy gold Lagerfeld with the cowl neck that bared pretty much her whole back – she could easily pass for someone in her twenties. Off duty for now, she was seizing whatever time she had: mingling, flirting, acting like she knew everyone in the room – or like she was someone who everyone there *ought* to know. She made mesmerising company, in every possible way.

Tye turned to Coldhardt, who looked debonair as always in his tux, a white rosebud pinned to the lapel. 'Have you seen Demnos yet?'

'Be patient.' He was staring across the room at an Indian woman in pale, shimmering green. And he wasn't the only one. The small group around her were clinging to her every word like drowning men to driftwood, laughing when she joked, intent when she was serious. She was maybe forty, tall and willowy, her thick black hair swept up on her head, her ears pricked at least a dozen times with fierce yellow diamonds. She wore a snake bracelet on her upper arm, the gold curling sensuously around her dusky skin, twin diamonds for eyes. Her chin was thrust out at her audience, her shoulders pushed back. She was fully in control.

'Who is she?' Tye asked. Coldhardt didn't answer, and she didn't push it. She was well aware that his silence signalled he didn't want to have to lie – he knew she'd pick up on the deceit at once. That particular skill was, after all, one of the reasons he'd bothered with her in the first place.

'This is a wonderful party!' Con reappeared beside them, her green eyes sparkling. 'Come with me and mingle, Tye. It'll be fun.'

Tye considered. The woman in green was leaving the room, tugging along a crowd of admirers in her wake. Perhaps she could steer Con over in that direction, find out for herself who –

'You'll stay right here, both of you,' said

Coldhardt, looking past them. 'Our man has arrived.'

Tye turned to see a huge bull of a man moving purposefully through the crowd, besieged by beaming faces, his smile as strained as the crimson cummerbund holding in his girth. His dark hair was slicked back, slathered to his head with Brylcreem. His features seemed bunched up in the middle of his fat face: beady brown eyes too close together, a strong nose and thin lips peeping through his jet-black moustache and beard. Two young men in tuxes, solid and clean-shaven, walked watchfully behind him, obviously bodyguards. Just behind them came a third bruiser, with a small, delicate young woman clinging to his burly arm. She was in her early twenties maybe and dragged one foot as she walked, ignoring the circus about her, a look of furious determination on her sharp, aquiline features.

Coldhardt moved effortlessly through the crowd to intercept the guest of honour, Tye and Con at his heels. 'Raul Demnos,' he announced smoothly, 'how the devil are you?'

'Nathaniel Coldhardt!' Demnos shook him by the hand delightedly, ignoring his minders' wary looks. He spoke English with barely a trace of accent. 'I have been anticipating our meeting for so long!' He lowered his voice. 'Save me from these vain fools and hangers-on, *please*!'

Coldhardt nodded to Tye. She stepped forward, held out her hand. 'My name is Tye Chery, of the European Art Archive Project. Mr Coldhardt informs me that your collection has never been fully catalogued. I'd love to talk to you about how we work.'

Demnos nodded knowingly, cast some fleeting smiles round at his entourage. 'If you'll excuse me? Regrettably, I must let a little business detain me.'

'Will you be long, Father?' The slender girl with the bad leg was acting casual, only her dark, sunken eyes betraying her anxiety.

'Forgive me, Yianna, my dear. You must amuse yourself for a while without me.'

Yianna set her mouth in a defiant pout, shifting her weight awkwardly on her bad leg. 'Nothing changes,' she muttered.

Tye, not used to her heels, had difficulty keeping up with Demnos and the others as they hurried down a corridor to a quietly elegant curator's office. He directed one bodyguard to stand at the door. The other followed him inside.

'We can talk freely here,' said Demnos. He turned to Tye, and looked her up and down coldly. 'You're quite right, my dear. My collection has never been catalogued. Nor will it ever be.'

She shrugged. 'Just a cover.'

'You have great secrets in your collection, yes?' Con enquired, a greedy gleam in her beautiful eyes.

'Many. But it is the greatest secret of all that I seek to add to it. And why I come to you, Coldhardt.' He narrowed his eyes. 'These girls . . . I take it you trust them?'

He didn't hesitate. 'Implicitly.'

Tye glanced at him, surprised but pleased. Con was actually blushing with pleasure; Coldhardt threw her a brief smile, which she caught and devoured.

Then Coldhardt's manner grew serious. 'What you've

intimated to me so far has been most interesting. Now I'd like you tell us the whole story.' He nodded to the bouncer. 'Provided *you* trust *your* . . . assistant?'

'He does not speak English.' Demnos smiled grimly. 'He cannot know what I am saying. That is why I trust him.' He paused. 'My story begins with a man named Imhotep.'

Tye nodded. One of the names that Jonah had pulled out of the Spartan cipher.

'He lived in the 27th century BC. He is known as the world's first doctor. The first to map the human body. The first to accurately diagnose and treat disease, to bring the art of healing to mankind. But he was not only a healer. Imhotep was a great architect. He built the first pyramid in Egypt. He was a priest, a scribe, a sage, a poet, an astrologer.'

'And a big bore at parties, yes?' Con was silenced with a warning look from Coldhardt.

Demnos was not amused. 'To you, in your ignorance, he is a joke. But to the ancient peoples, he became something to be worshipped. A hundred years after his reported death, he was made a medical demigod. Two thousand years later he was declared a full deity – a man who truly *became* a god.'

'Two thousand years . . .' Tye was impressed. 'That's a long time to stay famous.'

'His story does not stop there.' Demnos's dark eyes were burning into her own. 'Greek and Egyptian cultures became intertwined after the death of Alexander the Great in 323 BC, and the Ancient Greeks honoured him too. They made him as one with their great god of healing, Aesculapius – or, as he is better known,

Ophiuchus, the serpent handler.'

That name again, thought Tye.

'He received his title – and his reputation – from the day he witnessed a serpent restore a dead serpent to life. From then on, he somehow used the power of the snake to heal *people* – even to bring them back from the dead.' Demnos lowered his voice. 'But Hades, the god of the underworld, grew tired of this upstart stealing souls from his domain. He asked that Zeus slay the healer, to bring order back to his world. Zeus did so – but placed Ophiuchus in the sky as a constellation of stars, that he might be remembered for all time.' He paused. 'Ophiuchus is the thirteenth sign of the zodiac.'

Con looked puzzled. 'Thirteenth sign? I've never heard of it.'

'Few have,' he sneered. 'His figure towers in the sky between Scorpio and Sagittarius.'

Tye glanced back at Coldhardt and gave him an *Is this going anywhere?* look. But he ignored her, listening in silence.

'It is said that he once held the secret of immortality itself – Amrita, the drink of deathlessness.' Demnos was starting to sweat, and dabbed at his high forehead with a white handkerchief. 'Ambrosia, that brings unending life to the body of one who tastes it.'

'It is easy to say that once he's dead and gone,' said Con. 'It builds his cult, yes?'

'But he is *not* gone, my dear,' hissed Demnos. 'The memory of Imhotep was kept alive because the man himself was kept alive.' Demnos's eyes held a shining passion, his voice had grown hoarse. 'I have evidence to suggest that Ophiuchus was not simply linked to that great architect and healer . . . *he was the same man.*'

Tye stared at him. 'You're saying he drank this Amrita stuff, and lived for over two *thousand* years?'

'Perhaps longer,' breathed Demnos. 'It is even possible that thanks to the Amrita . . . he *cannot* die!'

CHAPTER SIX

'Hey, Jonah,' called Patch. 'You're on TV.'

Jonah looked up sharply, put down his snooker cue. He'd spent most of the evening taking practice shots, and had just failed to pot a red for the sixth time. He'd never played on a full-sized table before; predictably he was just as crap as he was on a smaller one.

He followed the sound of a grave-voiced newscaster to a cosy room leading off from the main hangout. Patch and Motti were slouched on a massive couch in front of an even more massive home cinema system. The TV screen was maybe a little larger than Mars. It showed a reporter outside Jonah's old prison.

'. . . *Wish was described by staff at the Young Offenders' Institution as a quiet and amenable boy. He had received no visitors and corresponded with no one . . .*'

'Geek, they're calling you a loser on TV!' honked Motti.

'They should look at you now, Jonah,' said Patch with an encouraging smile.

'*Security is being tightened in the wake of the extraordinary jail-break,*' the reporter went on, '*but accusations of incompetence have been denied by the governor . . .*'

'How can he deny it?' Motti looked genuinely affronted. 'Geek, I dunno how you stuck it.'

'Motti, would you stop calling me "geek"?'

'Sorry, geek.' He grabbed the remote and zapped to a music channel.

Jonah said nothing, but he was relieved. His legs had gone kind of wobbly. He wished he was tougher. But the truth was, hearing about his own breakout on TV had suddenly made it all more real. It had rammed home the fact that there really was no going back now.

Patch knelt up against the back of the couch. 'Got the most amazing satellite dish out in the grounds,' he said. 'Can pick up just about anything on earth. All the pay channels, even hot girl action and stuff!' He paused. 'Only thing is, Con said she'd brick my balls if I ever tried to watch any.'

'Don't lose no sleep over it,' said Motti. 'She'd have to find them first.'

Patch laughed good-naturedly. 'Anyway, Tye says I'm a big enough jerk-off already.'

Jonah forced a smile, weighed down by his thoughts. 'Where'd Tye learn to fly and stuff?'

'Smuggling in the Caribbean. She's from Haiti,' said Motti.

'What did she smuggle?'

'What *didn't* she?'

'Never met no one smarter than Tye,' Patch said, moving the subject along. 'You can't get nothing past her.'

'What about Con?' Jonah asked. 'How'd she pick up the mesmerism – join the Magic Circle or something?'

'One of her old-timer relatives had this stage hypnotist act back in the 1960s,' said Motti. 'They call it neurolinguistic programming now – like big words can explain it all away.' He snorted. 'Anyway, Con's a real quick learner. And when Grandpa couldn't teach her no more she cleaned him out, quit school and struck out on her own. Conning nice, rich old men who wanted to adopt her. Know what I mean?'

'Looks like Coldhardt succeeded where they didn't,' said Jonah.

'Yeah, well, Con and Coldhardt speak the same language.' Motti idly drummed his fingers on the couch along to the music. 'Green and crisp.'

'Apples?' joked Patch.

'Cash, numbnuts.'

'Will Coldhardt bring the girls back tonight?' Jonah wondered.

Motti looked up at him sharply. 'Miss the eye candy, huh? Well, you better make sure looking's all you do.'

'I didn't mean that!'

'Coldhardt don't allow nothing else, see. We got a working relationship. Anything else, shit gets messy.'

'You've got a lovely way with words, Motti.' Jonah shook his head. 'I just meant, will Coldhardt be bringing them back here tonight?'

'When they've done what he needs them to do.' Motti turned back to the TV. 'They ain't gonna turn into pumpkins if they're out past midnight.'

'So are *you* free to come and go?'

Motti rolled his eyes. 'If we want. But since there's nothing to do for miles around and we got all we need in here –'

'Isn't it kind of like being under house arrest?'

'Yeah, maybe.' Patch gestured around. 'But what a house!'

'You need to cool it some, geek,' said Motti. 'Why not go to the fridge, open the door and stand there for a minute? Then grab a beer from inside and bring it to me.'

Jonah smiled despite himself. 'Good of you to think of my welfare like that.'

Patch followed him out into the main room. 'I'm glad you're in with us, Jonah.'

'Yeah? Why?'

'Well, it's just nice. You know, there being more of us.'

'Right. Sugar-daddy Coldhardt and his five clever children. Just a normal happy family.' As he opened the fridge door, he saw Patch do his best to hide a hurt look. 'Hey,' he sighed. 'I'm sorry, OK?'

'It's kind of messed up, and it ain't always happy, but it *is* family.' Patch smiled, an honest, simple smile. 'I'm glad you've joined us, mate. See, we're all each of us has. To me, this place is home. And I'll do anything not to lose it.'

Jonah nodded. 'And you'd take me into your family, just like that?'

'Another person watching my back?' He grinned. ''Course I would. Life's too short to waste it freaking out over stuff. You gotta go with the flow, right?'

'How long have you been with Coldhardt?'

'Just over a year and a half. Coldhardt and Motti found me on my thirteenth birthday.'

'And threw a surprise party?'

'Could say that.'

Jonah took out a beer. 'Were you inside like me?'

'No. Squatting.' Patch held out his hand for a beer. Jonah passed him a Dr Pepper instead, and he rolled his eyes. 'These blokes, they let me squat with them, all round the country. I got 'em inside really cool places, see? So long as you don't use force to break in, you can squat anywhere.'

'And I'll bet you could break into 10 Downing Street without scratching the lock.'

'Probably,' he agreed brightly. 'See, most people think it's tools that get you in. That all you got to do is shove it inside and fiddle around. Well, they're wrong. That pick's gotta be an extension of *you*. It's just running over the pins, sliding through the keyway, sending you a little picture of what's going on inside.' The tone of his voice grew reverent. 'You have to listen to what it's saying to you, learn its personality. You gotta feel the tiniest turn of the pins and the plug . . .'

Jonah looked at this kid who was fourteen going on forty. 'Spiritual lock-picking?'

'Sound like an arsehole, don't I?' Patch smiled sheepishly. 'Sorry. Just that I've been picking locks since for ever. My mum used to dump me with the guy downstairs while she . . . Well, anyway, he was a lock-smith. I spent a lot of time there. I could torque before I could talk, you know?'

Jonah looked at him blankly.

'Torque – you know, you use a torque wrench with the pick to open . . .' Patch shrugged. 'Never mind. Locksmith joke.'

'Don't call us, we'll call you.' Jonah cracked open Motti's beer on a black marble countertop. 'So that was all you were doing? Getting inside squats?'

Patch paused, his one good eye clouding over as if at a bad memory. 'No.'

'And I'm guessing Coldhardt hasn't taken you under his wing to help people who've locked themselves out of the house. Right?'

'Nah. I'm a thief. Only thing I'm any good at.'

Jonah decided he might as well just come out and say it. 'Well, I don't want to sound like a Boy Scout here, but . . . Don't you ever feel bad? Ripping off people's houses and stuff?'

'We don't go burgling *normal* people!' Patch protested. 'Coldhardt ain't no ordinary crook. And he don't plan ordinary jobs.' He looked suddenly shifty, lowered his voice. 'You saw those photos he got hold of. He moves in some pretty freaky circles.'

Jonah hesitated to ask, 'Freaky how?'

'How come such a little kid got such a big mouth?' Motti had come slouching into the room, huffing on his glasses, polishing them on his sleeve. 'Listen, geek, let's just say that the types Coldhardt rips off, they don't exactly rush to call in the fuzz. These people are rich enough – *powerful* enough – to work outside the law.'

'No one's outside the law,' said Jonah automatically.

'Is that so?' Motti smiled and took his beer. 'Well, anyway, with Coldhardt's interests, it ain't just modern, high-tech places we have to break into. We've gone to work on temples, mausoleums . . .'

Jonah stared. 'Grave-robbing, you mean?'

'No, I *don't* mean.' He smirked. 'But you'd be amazed what stuff gets buried.'

'You superstitious, Jonah?' asked Patch.

''Course not.'

'I never used to be.'

Jonah raised an eyebrow. 'And what? You are now?'

'Sleeps with the lights on, doncha, Cyclops?' sneered Motti.

'So?' There was an uncomfortable pause. Then Patch gave him two fingers, Motti gave him one in return and Patch wandered back off towards the TV room. But Jonah found his eyes lingering uneasily on the eerie mural on the wall, at the shadowy, undefined figures ranged across it.

'Who painted that?' he asked.

'Coldhardt. Kind of freaky, huh?' Motti paused for a deep swig of beer. 'He calls it *Still Life*.'

'I thought that meant when you painted flowers and fruit and stuff.'

'Maybe he means, whatever freaky bad stuff's happened in that picture . . . there's still life.'

'If you can call it that,' said Jonah quietly.

'Hey. It's OK.' There was no sneer in Motti's voice now Patch was out of earshot. 'I told you before, I fixed this place. We're safe. Nothing can get in here.'

Jonah looked at him. 'No *one*, you mean.'

Motti nodded, half-smiled. 'Whatever.'

* * *

Ophiuchus, also known as Imhotep – the man who couldn't die? Tye searched Demnos's face for signs he was trying to deceive them, but his gaze was clear and confident.

Con, however, was looking at Demnos with barely disguised contempt. 'You expect us to believe there's some four-and-a-half-thousand-year-old man running around?'

'There are many who do believe. A great many.' Demnos let his stare linger on Tye. 'The scraps of the Spartan scytale cipher I have in my possession were . . . *recovered* together with fragments of a further document. It is marked with the sign of the snake. I believe it is a copy of Ophiuchus's prescription for Amrita, in his own hand. And that it is genuine.'

Tye's mouth had dried. 'Fragments, you said?'

'Fragments that Mr Demnos does not wish to share with us,' said Coldhardt casually.

Demnos's dark eyes flashed. 'I am not a fool,' he snapped. 'I know the value of the prescription, even incomplete.' He paused, regained control. 'But I have come to believe further parts of the same parchment exist in the hands of another collector, who may or may not appreciate the true importance of what they possess.'

'Who is this collector?' Tye asked.

'Her name is Samraj Vasavi. A cheating harpy, obsessed with her own cleverness.'

'You didn't always think so,' murmured Coldhardt.

Demnos glowered at him. 'That was many years ago.'

'I heard people talking about Samraj out there,'

Con said. 'How she's just funded a private hospital for sick children. She is worth a fortune, yes? Runs a multinational.'

'Serpens Biotech,' said Demnos, like the words tasted bad in his mouth. 'The company trades in genetic research. If Samraj has opened a hospital, it's to secure a steady stream of guinea pigs for the experimental cures she hopes to sell to the world.'

'You think she may be pushing Amrita as one of those "experimental" cures?' asked Tye.

'It is possible. But the only way I can know for sure is to find out how much of Ophiuchus's prescription Samraj has in her possession.'

Coldhardt idly pulled flecks of dust from the white rosebud on his lapel. 'Which is why Raul is in need of our services.'

'I am paying you well to uncover the truth,' Demnos stated. 'And I must know quickly.'

'Why the sudden rush?' Con's gold lacy dress shimmered as she crossed one leg over the other. 'I mean, if these fragments have been lying around for thousands of years . . .'

'Word has reached me that a great mastaba was recently unearthed at the Sakkara necropolis, outside of Cairo.'

'An Egyptian tomb,' Coldhardt translated, 'in the ancient city of the dead.'

Demnos nodded impatiently. 'Many artefacts were discovered inside, many personal effects. Experts believe this could be the tomb of Imhotep.'

Con couldn't contain herself. 'But if Imhotep – or Ophiuchus, or whatever he's calling himself today

– never died –'

'So far, there has been no mention of a body.'

Tye felt a tingle up her spine in the silence that followed.

But Con still wasn't ready to be convinced. 'Maybe they did find one, but they're keeping it quiet,' she argued.

'Why would they? Don't you see, girl? Imhotep left Egypt to become Ophiuchus. He faked his own death and stored away his possessions.' Tye could tell Demnos wasn't just hoping. He was utterly convinced. 'This mastaba must be a kind of strongroom, a place for secrets.'

Tye nodded. 'And you think another copy of the full prescription could be inside?'

'Perhaps. That is what *you* must discover.'

'Because even if only fragments remain, they could still complete the parchment,' Con realised. 'For you – or for Samraj.'

'I *must* know how much of the prescription she possesses. Any ingredient, any clue could be vital. And I imagine that, like me, she will be moving swiftly.' Demnos mopped his forehead again and checked his gold wristwatch. 'Now, you must excuse me. Yianna – my daughter – she needs me. She is very frail.'

'She's beautiful,' said Tye.

'The image of her mother.' Demnos lowered his face and crossed himself. 'Now I must rejoin her, see that she is all right.'

'Of course,' said Coldhardt smoothly. 'We've detained you long enough.'

The big man pulled out a crisp white envelope from

76

inside his jacket and placed it on the curator's desk. 'A downpayment. I have already provided you with the details of the mastaba's location. I wish to hear of your success within three days. Do not disappoint me, Mr Coldhardt.' With that, he nodded at his bodyguard to join him, and both left the room without another word.

The second he left, Con pounced on the envelope and started to purr. Coldhardt held out a hand for it while turning to Tye. 'Well?'

'Good, steady eye contact, no fidgeting . . . Faced us the whole time, his posture was good. Didn't cover his mouth, no real elaboration . . .'

'He was sweating like a pig,' said Con, pouting as she surrendered the envelope.

'But he didn't try to hide it. He's a big man, it's warm in here.' Tye shrugged. 'I think he was telling the truth. At least, he *believes* it's the truth.'

'Then he is seriously deluded,' Con retorted. 'But a madman's money is as good as anyone else's, yes?'

'I don't believe he's mad,' said Coldhardt, tucking the envelope away without bothering to check its contents. 'He's just very well informed.'

'Who by?'

'By *whom*.' Coldhardt smiled wanly. 'You'll travel to Cairo first thing tomorrow morning. In the meantime, shall we enjoy the party a little longer?'

'Yes,' said Con without hesitation, flinging open the door.

'Why not?' Tye muttered, feeling her blisters burn beneath the elegant strap of her shoe.

But she found Coldhardt had paused just outside

the door. At the end of the corridor, the woman in green was deep in conversation with an attentive couple.

Coldhardt held a polite hand over his mouth and cleared his throat noisily.

The woman looked up, saw him and excused herself brusquely.

'Nathaniel,' she said, her tongue lingering over the word as she leaned in to press a kiss on each cheek. The accent of her English was heavy, as exotic as her dark, glittering eyes. 'I thought I spied you earlier.'

'Good evening, Samraj.'

Con and Tye exchanged startled looks. So *this* was Demnos's rival. Their opponent. Their target.

'Allow me to introduce my niece, Constance, and her friend –'

'You've acted unwisely, Nathaniel,' said Samraj, ignoring both Tye and Con completely. 'Been terribly irresponsible.'

'I have?'

A light danced in her eyes. 'Leaving an old friend to mix with bores all night when you could have been entertaining me yourself. I shan't forgive you this neglect, you know.'

'Oh?' Coldhardt took her hand and raised it to his lips. He pressed a kiss against the very tip of her fingers, an oddly intimate gesture, his eyes meeting the yellow diamonds of the snake bracelet coiled round her arm.

Con's pale eyes had turned almost as hard; Tye knew well that she didn't take kindly to being ignored. 'Uncle, dear, we really must be going. There's so much to prepare before my trip tomorrow.'

Now Samraj turned to face her, amusement on her handsome features. 'You are going somewhere, my dear?'

'Back to Paris,' said Con unflinchingly. 'I must write up an account of this *memorable* event for my newspaper.'

'Of course you must,' she said softly.

'Then if you'll excuse us, Samraj?' Coldhardt was dabbing at his mouth with a handkerchief as if wiping his lips after a meal. 'It seems I must neglect you once more.'

'And just as the evening was getting interesting.' Now she glanced at Tye with ill-concealed disdain. 'We'll all meet again soon, I am sure.'

And as Tye nodded and turned to follow the others, she knew one thing with certainty: Samraj was speaking the truth as well.

CHAPTER SEVEN

If you had to be squeezed in five to a car, Jonah reflected, it might as well be a flash convertible on a blazing hot day, somewhere exotic. And cruising along the road from Cairo to Sakkara was better than squashing up inside a crappy white van in a prison car park, at any rate. Maybe things *were* looking up.

They were heading west now in their hire car after a long stretch north. The road was flanked by fields of fig palms. A large, crumbling pyramid was looming ever closer in a fine, smoky haze.

'Step pyramid,' said Motti, beside him. 'Says here it's the first of its kind. Built by our old pal Imhotep.'

'Maybe we should knock on the door, see if he's at home,' said Con sourly. She had bagged the front seat beside Tye as ever, her long, pale legs pushed up against the dash.

'I need a pee,' Patch complained.

'Hey, and the desert needs irrigating,' said Motti. 'Drop the Cyclops here, Tye. They were meant for each other.'

'Don't take your hangover out on Patch,' said Tye, with the air of someone well used to talking to brick walls. She was wearing pale cotton trousers, and a little pink shirt that looked great against her dark skin and the deep blue sky.

The others had taken it for granted, but Jonah couldn't get over how she'd switched from piloting an eight-seater Beech King Air 350 to driving a hired BMW without effort or complaint, and given such a smooth ride in both – especially in the kamikaze insanity of the Cairo traffic. But nagging at the back of his mind was the thought of all she must have done to *get* so good, to come to Coldhardt's attention. He wondered how she'd got into smuggling so young. Whether she'd had a choice. What her choices were now.

'This job better not be like that crypt we had to get into in Lima,' Motti said suddenly, prompting a round of pained and noisy remembrance from the others. 'I mean, sure, it was a pretty crystal, but those ancients knew a bit too much about self-defence if you ask me.'

'Thought my hair was gonna turn white,' said Patch with a shudder.

'I can't believe we got out of that one with all our fingers intact,' said Con. 'And no way am I ever dressing up as a leper again . . .'

Jonah chose not to question them; he wasn't sure if they were trying to wind him up again. And in any case, for now he just wanted to enjoy the view and the sunshine. Staring out of the window, he drifted off into his own thoughts.

The day had kicked off at 6.30am with a wake-up call from Con. She'd told him to get his ass out of bed, pack some light clothes and get downstairs. They were going to Egypt, to track down some old relics linked to Ophiuchus in some newly discovered tomb, stuff that might or might not be linked in to the secret of eternal life.

Jonah's money was on 'might not'. But the job didn't sound too scary. Just nuts.

He'd been given a perfectly forged passport under the name Johann Sypher, 'just in case' he needed to show it to anyone, and Con led him out on to the chateau's private runway. Jonah had a grin on his face a mile wide as he watched the twin-engine turbo-prop plane glide out of its hangar. He'd always wanted to fly. Up till now, he'd never even been abroad.

'Coldhardt not coming with us?' he asked.

The mention of his name brought a glacial frown to Con's face. 'Why would he? The job is simple. A child could do it.'

He smiled innocently. 'So how *was* last night?'

'Just get on board,' she told him.

The five-hour flight from Geneva to Cairo passed quietly. Con and Patch wasted little time crashing out in the luxury seats. But Jonah was too excited to shift his eyes from the circular windows. He could hear Motti crouched over a thin sheaf of plans and papers and a seltzer, puzzling something out and muttering about the injustices of life. It seemed to have been a late night. Jonah had wisely gone to bed around one, when Motti was already on to his sixth beer and fourth tournament of *Fatal Conflict* against Patch. The sound of electronic gunfire had carried faintly to his room like distant thunder, as clouds swallowed the moon through his window like a bad omen.

'We're here,' Tye announced, jerking Jonah from

his memories as a big welcome sign came into view.

Guards in dark uniforms loitered near the entrance with bored faces and big guns. The landscape had been bleached of all colour by the fierce sun. Tourists milled about in roped-off areas, lingered in front of impressive tombs. But there were wide tracts of sandy desolation too, and excavations in progress. Figures in white djellabas and turbans drifted about the mounds and rubble, working or overseeing others.

'If this place is so old, how can there be anything left to uncover?' Jonah asked.

'Egypt's dead were buried here for more than three thousand years,' Tye informed him. 'They've been excavating for maybe a couple of hundred.'

He blushed. 'OK, when you put it that way . . .'

'I'll get us access all areas,' said Con.

'Can you ask if we can use their toilet, too?' Patch called.

Con gave him a withering look as she got out of the car. Patch stared back dreamily as she smoothed out her short denim skirt and black top and walked over to the guards. She started talking confidently and fluently in a language Jonah didn't recognise.

'Is that Arabic or something?'

'Duh!' said Motti. 'What else is she gonna speak in Egypt?'

Jonah was impressed. 'How many languages does she speak?'

'Fluent in eight,' said Tye. 'Good working knowledge of eleven more.'

'Including "goddess",' Patch added.

A few minutes later Con got back in the car,

looking pleased with herself. 'We can drive through to the dig office. The guard's calling through to Professor Allein now – he's the team leader. We're archaeology students with special clearance.'

'Got it,' said Tye.

They drove on along the bumpy, dusty track, Con reeling off directions. The office was a battered old Portakabin, its weatherproofing dried out and cracked by the sun. A thin, balding man in a linen suit, his tanned face scored with deep wrinkles, was frowning down his long nose at them.

'I don't have time to speak to students,' he said in a thick French accent. But when Con started gabbling at him in his own tongue, he smiled broadly and said something back.

'The professor says he's about to make an important phone call,' Con reported. 'He is sorry he was rude. He thought we were all English.'

Tye muttered something that was probably deeply offensive in Creole.

As Con continued her chat, Motti shrugged. 'Whatever. Saves *us* having to speak to old Leather Face.'

'Not quite,' said Patch. 'I gotta ask him one thing.' But the way he staggered out of the car, clutching his crotch with his legs held tight together was eloquence itself, and the old man wearily gestured he go inside the cabin.

'Interesting,' Con reported after a high-speed flurry of *français*. 'The tomb of Ophiuchus was found to be full of anachronistic stuff.'

'What, spiders, you mean?' Tye ventured.

Jonah shook his head. 'Not arachno, *anachro*. They found objects there from the wrong period of history.'

'I was just kidding,' Tye snapped at him. Motti looked away, saying nothing.

The professor was speaking again. 'They've recovered items from many different cultures and centuries,' Con translated, 'placed there long after the tomb was first sealed. The experts are baffled – this would suggest tomb raiders have got inside the tomb, and yet nothing valuable has been removed. This other stuff has been added to what was already there – treasures dating right up to the fifteenth century.' She paused again. 'The smaller objects have been cleared out and placed in a museum lockup until they can be examined thoroughly.'

'Better than some goddamn crypt,' grumbled Motti.

Con paused while the professor went on, her face slowly clouding. 'Oh, but one thing *was* missing. A corpse. They can find no trace there was ever a body here.'

'Then Demnos was right,' Tye realised.

'A tomb with no body, and stuff dumped here regularly for thousands of years?' Jonah nodded thoughtfully. 'Sounds like the storehouse theory is bang on.'

'Con, ask him for a list of the stuff,' said Motti.

Con did so, but the professor went tight-lipped and shook his head. He tapped his watch, nodded cordially at the others, made to duck back inside his office. But Con took him by the arm, smiled, started to stare deep into his eyes . . .

Just then Patch appeared in the doorway, relief all

over his face. He pushed past the professor, who was jolted back into puzzled awareness. Con was about to try again but the professor said a polite but firm good-bye and closed the door on them both a moment later.

'Patch, you idiot.' Con folded her arms crossly, which drew his eye like lightning to the deepening line of her cleavage. 'I was going to get the list of the contents of that tomb!'

'No point,' said Patch. He reached into his baggy orange shorts, tugged out a folded, slightly soggy wad of paper and offered it to her. 'I already got it.'

Con surveyed it dubiously.

'It's just water what's made the ink run,' said Patch, blushing red. 'It is, honest!'

'Yeah, Con,' sniggered Motti, 'don't take the piss.'

'You think it's so funny, *you* look it over,' said Con, turning her back on both of them. 'I am not touching anything that has been down Patch's trousers!'

'And another dream dies,' sighed Patch, passing the papers to Motti.

They all piled back into the car, and Tye roared away. By the time the professor realised his precious list was missing, they were already on the home straits to the city.

Cairo was a maze of streets and lanes and different quarters. Tye steered them through half-finished suburbs, old neighbourhoods where the houses crowded close together as if for comfort, sprawling sweeps of brown, boxy blocks. There was a sense of decay all around, as if the city itself was worn ragged by the endless bustle and bother of its people. Even the slicker downtown offices showed signs of neglect, the proud steel letters of their logos pitted and discoloured by the fine blown sand and polluted air. Jonah's throat was burning after only twenty minutes, and Tye had wisely raised the roof on the convertible.

But that and even the pumping stereo couldn't hope to shut out the incredible noise as they stop-started through the dense five-lane traffic. Jonah found it terrifying – cars swung out without warning, drove directly at you. Horns honked and headlights flashed. Sometimes Tye would swerve aside, sometimes she'd stand her ground, like there was some logic to this mental metal ballet only those behind the wheel could understand. Bikes, pedestrians, donkey carts – they all added to the full-on chaos. A traffic cop stood in the middle of the street with a white hat and whistle, apparently ignorant of the madness all around him, contentedly chewing on a tangerine.

Somehow they made it unscathed to a hotel, a decent enough building but with bags of overripe rubbish piled up against the scuffed walls. Motti asked for two twin rooms for the five of them.

'What gives?' said Jonah. 'Coldhardt's expense account not stretch to separate beds?'

'Protection,' Motti told him, heading for the lift. 'This ain't no holiday, geek. We got to expect trouble at any time. And there's safety in numbers.'

'As well as a queue for the bathroom.' Patch smiled.

The rooms were fine, up on the tenth floor. Con and Tye came through to the guys' place, and they all bundled on the bed to go over the list Patch had pinched.

'It is a pity, yes?' said Con, flicking through. 'No parchment marked "Secret of Immortality" here.'

'Maybe the prof nicked it for himself,' Patch suggested.

She shook her head. 'He's the sort who'd hand it in for the good of mankind. The honest type.'

Tye prodded her arm, smiling. 'You wouldn't know honest if it bit your ass.'

Motti unpacked a laptop with Bluetooth from his rucksack and signalled to Jonah. 'We'll read out everything on the list. Type in the key words. Then we can check online, see if anything stands out.'

Patch snorted. 'Who died and made you king, Motti?'

'I'm oldest,' he argued.

'With the biggest mouth,' said Tye.

Jonah held up his hands. 'I'll do it, it's fine.' At least he could contribute *something* round here.

The list was a long one, but Jonah duly searched each item. Royal robes, wishing cup perfume vases, necklaces, pendants, caskets, figurines, sandals, fruit baskets . . . Nothing that hadn't been found in a dozen other Egyptian tombs. Pinky-grey fingers of cloud were soon dusking the blue sky as the sun slowly set.

Then, finally, something odd was thrown up.

'*Lekythos*, age uncertain . . . Sealed,' Patch read carefully. 'Red figure style. Engraved characters, obscure. What's a lekythos?'

'Sounds Greek,' said Con.

For a minute or so, the only sound in the room was Jonah's fingers clicking on the keys as he checked it out.

'Lekythos,' he read, as he reached a page on Greek

antiquities. 'Special type of oil jar . . . often used at funerals and for making offerings to the dead.'

Tye frowned. 'But if there never was a body in that tomb, what was it doing there?'

'Looking pretty?' Jonah turned round the laptop so they could see the accompanying image. A lekythos looked a little like an earthenware trumpet. Cylindrical in form, it had a single vertical handle attached to its slender neck, with a slightly wider mouth at the top.

'Imhotep's one is sealed,' Con reminded them. 'Why seal up some oil?'

'Could be something stuffed inside,' Patch offered. 'An old scroll, maybe?'

'Take a good look at that thing,' said Motti. 'We've got to steal something looking like that tonight.'

'How do we find this lock-up?' asked Jonah.

'Wait!' said Con, putting both hands to her head and frowning. 'I'm hearing the thoughts of the professor in my mind . . . I see a museum close to Sharia Ramses . . . Not far from this hotel . . .'

Jonah stared in amazement. 'You can really *do* that?' Then he caught the smirks creeping over Patch and Motti's faces. Finally Con could keep up the act no longer and burst into bright peals of laughter.

'Coldhardt already tracked down the address of this lock-up,' said Tye, nudging Con in the ribs. 'That's why we chose this hotel. It's in the area.'

Jonah felt himself reddening. 'Thanks for sharing the news.'

'We talked about it in the car! Guess you were too busy dreaming, looking out the window.'

Patch shrugged. 'Hey, it's Jonah's first time abroad. He just wants to take it all in, don't you, mate?'

Jonah looked away. He appreciated Patch's defending him, but it was weird, having a fourteen-year-old with one eye stand up for him.

Con was still giggling away. But she stopped when Motti pulled out a big hunter's knife from his black denim jacket.

'Insurance,' he explained, slapping it down on the table by the bed. 'OK, Cyclops, you're with me. Coldhardt got us plans of the museum, but I want to check it out myself. Make sure we got no surprises waiting.' He swaggered over to the door, Patch trailing after him. 'You guys, chill out, grab some sleep maybe. We're going in at three.'

CHAPTER EIGHT

To kill time, and to work off some nervous energy, Jonah decided to use the hotel pool. He was pleased to find he had the whole place to himself. The turquoise pool sat in a big, red-bricked room that reeked of chlorine – but clearly not enough to kill the cloud of flies dizzying about overhead. The night was black and noisy outside.

He was finishing his seventh length and wishing he were fitter when he looked up to see Tye had entered the room. She was wearing a deep blue high-necked swimsuit and trailing a fluffy white towel behind her.

'Get out of the pool,' she said. 'Now.'

He frowned, and hauled himself out as she strode towards him. 'What is it? What happened?'

'It's what's *going* to happen you should be worried about,' she said gravely. 'Your ass is going to get whupped!'

With that, she crouched into some martial arts-style pose and then kicked his legs out from under him. With a surprised shout, Jonah fell back into the water.

'What the hell are you playing at?' he spluttered.

'Self-defence,' said Tye. 'Coldhardt trained us. Now we have to train you. Get out of the pool.'

'So you can kick me back into it?'

'You've got to start somewhere, Jonah.' She watched him climb out, her dark eyes intense. 'When we're out on a job we don't fool around. We can't afford to. You need to learn how to handle yourself.'

He frowned. 'What, in just a few hours?'

'It's OK, you'll be lookout tonight, and you'll have Con with you,' Tye told him. 'But since we've *got* those few hours . . .'

She spun a full circle on the ball of her foot and then launched herself into a formidable flurry of jabs and punches and high-kicks in his direction. Jonah jumped away, his wet feet skidding on the tiles.

'You know I normally wear glasses, right?' he joked.

'We'll start with a side kick.'

'All the best superheroes have them.'

'Stand with the right side of your body facing me,' she instructed. He did so, trying hard not to dwell on how good she looked in a swimsuit. 'Now pull your right knee up towards your left shoulder, and bend your left knee just a little as you kick in my direction, 'K?'

He took a stab at it. She slapped her palm against the sole of his foot. 'You want to hit me with the outside of your foot or your heel – it'll hurt me more and do less damage to you.' Jonah tried again. 'Better. Now with your other leg.'

'Is this kickboxing?' he said, giving it a try.

'Uh-huh. It's cool, gives you a total body workout. And it's great for getting out all your anger and frustration and stuff.'

Jonah kicked out at her a little harder. 'You get angry and frustrated a lot? Does that come from Coldhardt making you take all the risks while he sits around at –'

'Will you kick me like you mean it?' she snapped, grabbing his foot and pushing him backwards towards the pool.

'Sore point?' he asked.

'If you'd like one, I'm happy to oblige.' With that Tye performed an expert side kick, planting the edge of her foot in his stomach. Jonah doubled up and staggered back into the pool with an ungainly splash.

'Thanks for the lesson,' he croaked as he broke the water's surface.

Tye dived gracefully into the water over his head, barely disturbing the surface. She fired herself through the water like a torpedo, only resurfacing once she'd touched the other side, covering the length of the pool in just a few seconds with a powerful front crawl.

'See what I mean about the outside edge of the foot?' she said, bobbing up beside him, smoothing black plaits away from her eyes.

'You're doing nothing for my delusions of adequacy,' he told her, with a weak smile.

'Feeling nervous about tonight?'

'Well, I . . .' He nodded. 'Yeah. For one thing, I don't know why I'm even coming along. You don't really need two lookouts, do you? And I think we just proved that I can't do much else to help out.'

'You're seeing how we work,' Tye told him. 'You've got to know what it's like if you're going to be a part of it.'

Jonah nodded, doubtfully. Him a part of all this? It seemed like fantasy land.

'I was kind of like you are,' she said awkwardly. 'You know, when I joined up with Coldhardt. Motti and Patch were already set up together and I was the outsider – like you are now. I found it hard to trust anyone.'

'What did you used to do, before Coldhardt?' asked Jonah casually.

'You don't know?'

'No.'

At once her pretty face hardened. 'I think you do.'

Jonah sighed and looked away. 'Motti told you we talked about you and Con?'

'He didn't have to. I find it hard to trust, Jonah, 'cause I can see people telling so many damn lies the whole time.' Her dark eyes burnt into him. 'I read body language. And when I asked you outright you hunched a little, licked your lips, glanced at the exit. Classic signals. Your body gave you away three times over in a second.'

'You're good,' Jonah admitted. 'Patch told me no one could get stuff past you.'

'Did he now,' she said quietly, a bitter smile flitting across her face. 'You know I was a smuggler back in Haiti.'

'And that's all I know.'

'Ran stuff between the islands and South America for five years. If you can't tell between those you can trust and those who're trying to sell your ass down the river, you don't last long. And if you get canned for running out there, the prisons make your cosy little detention centre look like the teddy bears' picnic. I used to hope that if I was ever caught, it was by one of the gangs. At least they kill you neater.'

Jonah swallowed, unsure what to say. 'How old were you when . . .?

'When I started? Eleven.' Tye looked up at the cloud of flies and their endless circling. 'There was this guy, sixteen . . . He told me stuff, made me feel special. Said these guys would kill him if I didn't help him take this shit through.' She looked at Jonah. 'Yeah, you could say I learned about lying kind of young.'

'Didn't your parents . . .?'

'My mum ran out on my dad and me when I was five. Dad went to pieces. She was English, made documentaries. He used to love the sound of her voice, you know? So he spent every cent we had on English and elocution lessons for me, so I could grow up sounding just like her. He'd just sit there drinking and make me say stuff . . . to kid himself she was still there.' Now it was her turn to look away. 'I'm sorry. I know you didn't have it easy yourself.'

'Next to yours, my life's been a dream.'

'Liar,' she said with the ghost of a smile. There was real sympathy in the look she gave him. 'The photos Coldhardt put up on the screens in the hub . . . That was mean of him.'

'Not really. He wanted to show me he had power. That was a good way to do it.'

'How can you be so cool about it?'

'Analytical mind, I s'pose. What landed me here in the first place.' He shrugged. 'Anyhow, I wasn't so cool in those pictures, was I?'

'Want to tell me what really happened?' She tilted her head to one side. 'I'm good with secrets.'

'I guess you have to be.'

She half-smiled. 'And just so you know, this head on one side thing is a vulnerable gesture, hardly ever used by people who are lying to you.'

'Can't be good for your neck.' He reached out to straighten her head, but she flinched away just slightly. It was an awkward moment, and he found himself talking to fill it. 'So, you remember that company I helped my foster dad set up, selling secure payroll systems? I worked my butt off doing it 'cause I liked him, and I wanted our family to do well. We'd been together eighteen months; it was kind of a record for me. My foster mum was kind, I even thought I could maybe love her . . .' He stopped to rub at his stinging eyes. 'Sorry, it's the chlorine,' he mumbled.

'Uh-huh. Go on.'

'Well, anyway, I found out Derek, my foster dad – he was seeing some other woman. Found out he was planning to move in with her. Leave us. And I didn't want to lose another family . . . you know?' Jonah looked away, filled his ears with the uncaring growls and chatter of the traffic outside till he could speak again. He'd come this far, he might as well let it all out. 'So yeah, I broke into the encrypted accounts of one of Derek's clients. Transferred about five hundred grand to my account. I thought with that kind of money, me and my foster mum could just leave the bastard. We could go away somewhere, start a new life without him.'

'But you didn't tell her first,' Tye said softly.

'And when I did she freaked. She didn't know Derek had been playing away from home, and I handled the whole thing like a . . .' He snorted, cringing at the memories. 'She must have shopped me in seconds.'

'You've got a new family now, Jonah,' said Tye. 'If you want it.'

'I didn't steal that cash because I wanted to become a career crook,' he told her. 'I'm just an ordinary bloke.'

'No. You're a talent.'

'All I want is an ordinary life –'

He broke off, unnerved by the strength of Tye's gaze.

'Liar.' There was a sudden, fierce compassion in her soft features. 'Jonah, from what I know about you, your childhood stank. You lived through years of messed-up crap. You think an ordinary life's ever going to make up for that?' She shook her head. 'No way. Whatever cards you get dealt, you're gonna be turning that analytical mind on them – is my life normal enough yet? Hmm, you know, I think things could be a little more ordinary round here.'

'OK, you don't have to take the –'

'And *you* don't have to take this opportunity, Jonah. Before, I almost wished you wouldn't. It's dangerous, it's tough – it sure as hell isn't ordinary.' Her voice softened. 'But you know, I think you've got this big picture in your head of how peachy perfect a normal life would be. But like it or not, you *aren't* normal, Jonah. You've got a gift.'

He ducked his shoulders under the water, trying to stop himself shivering. 'What, and so I should give it to Coldhardt?'

'*Sell* it. You saw those pictures, Jonah. You're known – some big people out there, they've been watching you, close-up.' She pushed out her chin, defensive. 'If Coldhardt hadn't come for you, someone else would.'

'How do I know he didn't take those pictures himself?' Jonah argued. 'Trying to scare me. Like you are now.'

'Life with Coldhardt can get ugly sometimes, yeah. There's danger. But at least we belong.' She paused, took a small step towards him. 'For us, this *is* ordinary life. The risks are a little bigger, but then so are the rewards.'

'And I suppose you can stand there in your fancy castle and your designer gear with anything you want at your fingertips and say, look how far I've come. Look how far away that bad old life I used to have is now.' Jonah glared at her. 'But is it, Tye? Is it really?'

'Yes,' she hissed.

He realised they were both breathing shakily, just a little out of time with each other.

'Now who's lying?' he said slowly.

The doors to the pool kicked open loudly. Jonah and Tye splashed as they sprang apart almost guiltily.

'Jesus, Patch,' Tye complained. 'You scared the crap out of us.'

He bounded over, a sly smile on his face as his one eye flicked between them. 'Sorry to interrupt your swim, but Motti wants to run through the plan for tonight.'

Tye nodded, pulled herself out of the pool without

another glance at Jonah. 'Find any surprises?'

'Nah.' Patch shook his head. 'Looks like it should be smooth. Nothing we can't handle.'

'Fine. I'll catch you both later.' She picked up her towel, headed briskly for the exit. 'And take your eye off my butt, Patch, before I come back and slug you.'

The doors echoed shut behind her.

'How did she *know*?' Patch sighed. He turned to Jonah. 'Everything all right, mate?'

'Oh yeah,' said Jonah. 'Everything's just . . . normal.'

Patch gave him a baffled little smile. He held out his hand to help Jonah up and out of the pool.

Jonah took it.

Tye drove the car down a side alley a few blocks from the museum and killed the engine. It was 2.45am. No one spoke, they just sat listening to the passing blare of horns and stereos, of distant arguments.

She kept replaying her argument with Jonah. Why had she even started that conversation? It wasn't like she wanted to be his special friend or something. She had learned all too well back in Haiti that if you opened up to someone, they could get inside and trash you. Did she really want to go through that again?

There he was in the rear-view, all nervous and trying not to show it. With his fair hair, clear skin and blue eyes, Jonah should've looked like an overgrown choirboy – if not for his smile. That seemed a long way from angelic . . .

'OK, it's time,' Motti announced. 'Move out, people.'

At once, Tye swept her head clear of idle thoughts, forced herself to focus on the only thing that mattered right now – getting the job done.

They got out into the moonlit street, all dressed smartly but simply in black. A lone flower seller stood in filthy robes on the corner, waving wilted roses at the heedless traffic. Music thudded from a cellar club nearby. A group of young men laughed and smoked beside a van stacked high with boxes.

Jonah shook his head in quiet amazement. 'Doesn't this city ever sleep?'

'Just hope it's quiet round the back of the museum,' said Con.

Patch nodded. 'Least there's no night watchman. What a shame museums round here get such crap funding.'

Motti had thought it safest to walk the last stretch to the lock-up – five teenagers in a BMW might have attracted attention, whereas if they played the part of late-night revellers staggering home through the dusty, rundown streets, no one would look twice at them. He'd detailed Con and Jonah to wait around up front and stage a distraction if anyone came too close. Con instantly suggested they could play lovers, just to see Jonah blush.

'This is the place,' said Motti quietly.

They broke off into their two groups. Con and Jonah lounged against a lamppost, talking in low voices, while Tye darted down a back alley after Motti and Patch.

She pulled a slim torch from her jacket pocket and bathed the two of them in its steady, yellow glow.

Their chosen entry point was an alarmed steel fire door. Motti traced a small gadget over some wires above the frame, searching for a critical point, while Patch produced a pick and torque wrench and practised his own brand of keyhole surgery.

'You ready?' Motti whispered. 'The alarms should take a three-second scramble without going off. So we gotta be quick.'

Tye and Patch both nodded.

He pressed his gadget to the wires, clicked a button. 'In!' he hissed.

Patch flicked his wrists, and Tye kicked the door open. She was first through, then Patch, then Motti, who swung the door back closed behind him.

They stood, their shaky breathing loud in Tye's ears.

Motti looked murderous in the sinister torchlight. 'That was a long three seconds. Can't believe nothing went off.'

'We got away with it,' said Patch. 'That's all that matters.'

'Can we get going?' Tye prompted, shining her torch up the concrete stairwell. Mica dust caught in the beam like a sinister mist. She had a bad feeling about this place.

'Lock-up's on the third floor.' Motti's long skinny legs took three steps at a time, and Tye and Patch jogged to keep up. 'Should be no real security till we reach it.'

Patch soon fixed the door that led on to the third floor. As it swung open, Tye swept her torch around. The beam lingered on thick, clouded Plexiglas, on dusty pots and plinths, on a row of light switches set into a rusty metal plate. Then she froze as a small red oblong of light flicked on in a corner of the room.

'Motion sensor,' she hissed. Patch and Motti froze beside her.

'Gimme that,' said Motti, taking the torch. He soon illuminated a security camera in the corner, and Tye swore. 'Be cool,' he told her. 'It's not CCTV, it's bogus – just an empty box. It's a sham, like the motion sensor.'

'Thank God for that,' said Patch. 'That was a big brown-trouser moment.'

'I *told* you there was zilch security up to this level,' said Motti, acting like he'd never been bothered. He led them through the priceless exhibits to a heavy looking door, a well-worn plastic keypad beside it. 'And not much more now we're here,' he scoffed, passing the torch back to Tye. 'So much for the secure area.'

Patch peeled back the leather over his missing eye. Then he plucked out the glass ball between finger and thumb.

Motti cringed. 'Goddamn it, freak!'

'I'm wearing the patch, ain't I? You should wear one on your mouth.'

'That's a sick, sick place to keep your tools.'

'Oi! I'm disabled, OK? Might as well make the most of it,' Patch retorted. 'Just 'cause you're so squeamish you can't even put in contacts.' He unscrewed the eyeball, which came apart in the middle like some twisted Russian doll. Then he pulled a tiny make-up brush out of it.

'Wait!' hissed Tye. She put out the light. 'Thought I heard something.'

They strained to hear in the darkness.

'You imagined it,' said Motti.

Patch looked less certain. 'Tye don't imagine stuff.'

'Stop sucking up. She ain't gonna lay you any more than Con will.'

'Can we just get this over with?' Tye whispered, flicking the torch back on. Patch kept fingerprint powder in his glass eye, and now he brushed it over the well-worn keypad. Purple stains rose like bruises on four of the buttons.

'These schmucks can't have changed the code in ten years,' gloated Motti. 'And I bet you it's sequential order, nice and easy for the knuckleheads to remember.'

Tye played the torch beam around the doorframe. 'Think it's alarmed?'

'Magnetic switch.' Motti carefully extracted a length of thin wire from the arm of his glasses. 'Magnet in the side of the door holds down a switch, completes the circuit. Open the door, switch comes up – the circuit breaks and alarms go crazy.'

'Yeah, I know. So you use your gadget to screw up the systems for a couple of secs –'

'No need,' he said, retrieving the torch from her. 'The cables are already exposed here, see? I can trip the circuit with this bit of wire once I've stripped the insulation –'

'Already stripped,' said Patch. 'Look.' He pointed to a shallow gouge beside the frame. 'Bloody switch has been dug out from the plaster.'

Tye felt suddenly sick as the realisation hit home: 'Someone's been here before us.'

A sudden scrabbling from behind the door.

'Scratch *before us*,' hissed Motti, 'they're still *in there* –'

Then the door to the lockup flew open. Patch yelled as the edge cracked into his face, knocking him backwards.

For a split second, Tye caught a dance of dark shadow in the torch beam, figures swooping out from inside. Then the light was knocked from her hand and bony fingers clamped around her throat.

CHAPTER NINE

Tye didn't struggle. She used her attacker's momentum to her advantage, falling back as he charged forwards. She landed on her back, brought up her leg against his stomach and flipped him over her head. He crashed into something that smashed noisily, but Tye was already back on her feet, running for the light switches she'd seen earlier across the room.

She slammed them on. An awkward flicker of light as the fluorescents warmed up. It was almost like a strobe effect: in snatches she saw Motti wrestling with a masked black-clad figure, saw the man she'd brought down in the debris of a large earthenware jar, saw someone else racing for the door that led on to the stairwell, dodging exhibits with ease.

'Stop them!' Motti yelled, like she needed telling.

As the lights strengthened into noisy, humming life, Tye hurled the torch at the fleeing figure. It was a woman, wearing a black veil like a dupatta – Hindu maybe? The woman staggered as the torch cracked against her skull, lost balance for a moment. Tye was already sprinting after her when she realised the woman was clutching something, some kind of jar . . .

The lekythos. Whoever these people were, they wanted it too.

The woman assumed a fighting stance as Tye approached. Though the black veil shrouded most of her face, her hooded eyes showed through, cold dark stones. Though her speed and agility suggested someone in the flush of youth, there was something ancient in those eyes that made Tye shiver.

In her other hand the woman held a stiletto. Its tapering blade gleamed. Tye clocked the tattoo that coiled up from the woman's wrist to her knuckles – a distinctive blue snake. Then she swung up her leg in a high front kick to knock the stiletto away.

The woman swung the knife out of reach, then lunged forwards. Tye jumped back but knocked against the edge of a display case, gasping as she felt the sharp corner bite into her spine. Caught off-balance, she couldn't deflect a kick to her stomach, and with a gasp she went down.

In a second, Tye's assailant was crouched over her, one hand holding the lekythos up and out of reach, the other ready to plunge the knife down into her chest.

Then, suddenly, the old Greek vase seemed to explode. The woman cried out.

And in a shower of fine black dust, a glass eyeball plopped out of the lekythos on to Tye's chest.

'Lousy bloody shot!' wailed Patch, still clutching his head.

Tye used the distraction well and punched her attacker hard in the jaw. But the woman fell backwards, rolled over and was back on her feet in a second. Still clutching the remains of the vase tight to her chest, she turned and ran for the door. Patch was knocked to the ground as Motti's attacker followed her to the exit. The man Tye had tackled first must already have made his getaway.

'Patch, is Motti OK?' Tye snapped.

'I'm fine,' Motti shouted, though his nose was pouring blood and his glasses were smashed. He staggered over to help Patch up. 'Get after them! Go!'

Tye nodded and ran to the exit. The sound of pounding feet echoed all around the concrete stairwell. She charged down the steps, swinging herself round the rickety banisters, driving herself faster, faster. Finally she shot out into the alleyway.

To find someone was taking a swing at her with a makeshift bat.

She twisted away desperately but she was going too fast to dodge the blow. The plank broke in two over her shoulder, and she cried out with the sickening, jarring impact. It was the same masked man she'd thown into the earthenware vase, waiting for her. She spun round, aimed a roundhouse kick at his knee – but he caught hold of her foot, threw her back against the alley wall.

The man raised his arm to deliver some kind of karate blow, but she jabbed her knuckles into his sternum as hard as she could. He staggered back, cursing in Arabic. Tye punched him in the face, once, twice – but on the third swing he ducked and landed a crashing blow to her bad shoulder. The pain almost blotted out her senses and she fell to her knees. She wasn't sure how long she stayed like that, clinging on to consciousness, but when she opened her eyes again the man was gone.

'Tye?' In a haze of stars she saw Con, running down the alleyway towards her from the main road. 'That bastard nearly knocked me flying. Did he hurt you badly?'

'There were two others with him,' she muttered. 'Man and a woman, already inside the lock-up.'

'We saw them. First the woman, then the man.'

'They were after the same thing we were.'

'Did they get it?'

'Kind of. Where's Jonah?'

Con pursed her lips. 'He went after them.'

She stared, appalled. 'You let him?'

'He just took off. He wants to prove himself, yes? You know boys . . .' Con shrugged. 'Don't worry, he'll never catch them.'

'But that guy who did this to me might catch Jonah!'

Con shrugged. 'I was more worried about you guys.'

'Check Motti and Patch are OK,' Tye told her. 'They're hurt, I dunno how bad.'

'And how bad are *you*? You look terrible.'

'Thanks.' Tye shut her eyes, fighting a wave of nausea. It felt like a load of termites were trying to eat their way out of her head, and the buzz of the distant traffic seemed sickeningly loud.

She staggered off towards the main road to see if Jonah was OK. She only hoped she didn't black out before she got there.

* * *

Jonah came staggering back up to the lamppost outside the museum, his lungs burning, saliva thick in his mouth. He spat on the pavement, gasping for breath.

Tye stumbled out of the shadowy mouth of the alleyway. She was obviously in a lot of pain.

'You OK?'

She nodded, wincing as she did so.

'What happened back there? Those people in black –?'

'They got away?'

'I'm crap, I'm sorry.' He coughed noisily. 'This other guy came after me, and I had to duck out of the way. They were all so fast!'

'Tell me about it,' she said. 'They sure sped that vase away.'

'They did?' He chewed his lip. 'Well, it may not be a total disaster. They had a car. I got the number plate.'

She just nodded. Jonah felt slightly hurt that she wasn't more impressed. 'Whoever they were,' she said, 'they had the jump on us. Totally.'

Now Con came out of the alley, Patch leaning on her for support and Motti lagging behind. He and Patch looked like they'd been chasing after parked lorries and hadn't stopped in time.

'Let's get out of here,' Con said. 'There must be cops on the way after all that.'

Motti was glaring round wildly. He was holding his broken glasses in his left hand, and his eyes seemed small and watery without them. 'Washout,' he snarled, wiping his bleeding nose on his jacket sleeve. 'We screwed up big time.'

'They were better informed than us,' said Tye, as they started as quickly as they could down the street.

'Local knowledge?' Con suggested.

Tye shook her head. 'I reckon they must have had inside help. One of the museum staff, maybe.'

Motti frowned. 'How'd you figure?'

'They'd already taken care of the alarm on the fire exit. They knew the layout of that floor of the museum so they could move fast even in the dark.'

'And they must have known the combination to the lock-up,' Patch added. He had a livid bruise rising over his good eye. 'They didn't knacker the keypad, did they?'

'So then why bother to screw with the magnetic switch?' said Motti. 'They coulda disabled the alarm easy.'

'Maybe that was for show,' Patch said. 'Fake calling card. Like, "Hi, we're regular burglars!"'

Tye agreed. 'If it looked too much like an inside job, cops would start asking the staff questions.'

Patch gave a theatrical groan and leaned more heavily on Con, managing to nudge his head against her chest.

'You're not hurt so bad,' Con told him, shoving him away. 'But keep that up and you will be.'

'OK, so they had some help.' Motti stared down angrily at his smashed glasses. 'But that don't let us off the hook. We screwed up big. Coldhardt ain't gonna be happy.'

'Don't write us off yet,' said Tye, gritting her teeth. Jonah offered her his arm to lean on but she pulled away.

The distant grizzle of police sirens sounded. As one, the group quickened their step. The car wasn't far away now.

'Come on. Let's pool what we know,' said Tye. 'Did you see that snake tattoo on the woman's hand?'

'Can't see nothing without these.' Motti dangled his crushed glasses in her face. 'But jeez, man, fists of fury . . . That guy whupped my ass. Didn't even have time to pull my blade.'

'Like you'd really use it,' Tye muttered.

'I've told you, Motti,' Con complained. 'You should wear contacts!'

'Don't start telling me what I should –'

''Ere, *I* saw that bird's tattoo,' said Patch quickly, heading off the row. 'What do you reckon, Tye – some kind of gang marking?'

She nodded. 'Or a cult, maybe. Some kind of religious thing, from the look of that veil she wore.'

'So we got us a religious broad and two body-guards,' said Motti.

'If someone at the museum *was* helping them, we could maybe try and find out who tomorrow,' Jonah suggested.

Motti looked at him like he was about to have a go. Then he just nodded, dabbed again at his leaking nose. 'Good thinking.'

They'd reached the BMW. Tye fumbled in her pocket for the keys. 'Jonah got the number of the car that picked them up, too,' she remarked, crossing round to the driver's side. 'Probably stolen or false plates, but it might turn up something.'

'If only they hadn't got the lekythos,' sighed Con.

Motti gave Patch a kick up the arse. 'If only he hadn't smashed it to bits.'

Jonah frowned, and Con mimed Patch picking out his eye and lobbing it like a grenade.

'That bitch was gonna kill Tye!' Patch complained. 'I was aiming for her head, all right?'

'And he saved my life,' added Tye, smiling at him as she freed the keys. 'Thanks for that.' She hit the button on her key fob and the car unlocked, flashing its side lights.

'Anyway,' said Patch, reaching into his own trouser pocket. 'At least we got to take *some* of the stupid thing away with us.'

He pulled out three large fragments of the funeral vase. A black, crumbly powder coated the pieces. Patch started brushing it away on to the filthy pavement, but Jonah stopped him. 'I'm guessing that black stuff was inside the vase and not in your pockets?'

'I just had these jeans washed last week,' said Patch indignantly. 'That stuff's all over my eye, too. Should've cleaned it up better.' He scratched the skin beneath his patch, grimacing. 'It's all gritty now.'

'Would you quit with the eye stuff?' Motti warned him.

Jonah took two of the pieces from Patch. 'So was it the vase or the grit they were after?'

'Got to be the vase, innit?' Patch argued. 'Who'd fight like that over some grit?'

'Over two and a half thousand years, whatever was stored inside could have decomposed,' Con reasoned. 'This black stuff is all that's left. We need to get it studied properly.'

Patch grinned. 'So we didn't come out with nothing but bruises after all.'

'Maybe more than you think,' Jonah realised as he held together the fragments like two pieces of a jigsaw. 'That description of the lekythos on the list – "engraved characters, obscure" – remember? I thought they meant like *cartoon* characters. But look here.'

'Could we just get inside the damned car?' said Motti, looking round shiftily.

Jonah ignored him and held up the pieces to Tye across the car roof.

'It's like writing,' she said.

'I think it's a cipher,' said Jonah slowly.

'You mean it could be the Amrita prescription?' Con breathed.

Patch laughed. 'And *we've* got it, they don't!'

'We've got *part* of it, anyway,' said Jonah more cautiously. 'Let me see those other pieces –'

'Back at the hotel,' Motti instructed. 'Get in the car. You got to drive us back to the hotel, geek.'

'Me?' Jonah blanched. 'I told you, I don't drive!'

'Well, I can't see a damn thing without my glasses,' Motti retorted. 'And Tye can barely move that shoulder.'

'It's not so bad –' she broke off, gasping as she tried to open the driver's door.

'It *is* so bad,' Motti told her. 'And Con won't drive us nowhere.'

Patch was watching her as she got in the front passenger side. 'Grand Theft Auto is my game, guys. Maybe *I* should try!'

'You know you can't judge distance good with just

one eye, man,' Motti said with surprising tenderness. 'Geek, it's down to you. It's only a couple of miles.'

Tye handed Jonah the key.

He got into the driver's seat, tried turning the ignition. The car lurched into life, strained forwards before the engine died.

'Needs to be in neutral,' Tye told him.

'What's neutral?' said Jonah nervously.

'That's it, I'm walking,' Con announced. 'No way am I going anywhere in this car.'

Motti sighed. 'Look, I could sit up front and work the gearshift if you'd just –'

'And I'm not going in the back, either,' she snapped.

'OK, let's not stress over this,' said Tye wearily, shifting in the seat, trying to get more comfortable. 'We'll just have to hang here in the car for a while and hope the cops don't find us. There'll be a bus or something when it gets light.'

A tense silence settled over them.

'This is bollocks,' said Patch at last. 'Five so-called talents and we can't even drive a car between us!'

'I know.' Motti gave a grudging snigger. 'We're like, total crap!'

'Totally.' Patch tittered, dabbing his eye.

'It's not funny,' Con said hotly. 'Coldhardt will be expecting us to call in.'

Motti nodded seriously. 'We could maybe tell him we were stuck in traffic.'

This time he and Patch dissolved into guffaws of laughter. Con turned away and looked grumpily out of the window.

Tye yawned. 'Welcome to the family, Jonah.'

He nodded, half-smiled, looked down at the fragments of pottery in his hands. Pondered the characters and curlicues scratched beneath the glaze, and the secrets they were keeping.

Jonah woke with a start, a dull stiffness in his neck. He was still in the car, a whiff of stale sweat now about the expensive upholstery. The drone of the traffic that had lulled him to sleep had risen to a low roar, and the sun was a fat orange perched on the boxy horizon.

Motti lay snoring softly in the back, a grisly sight with his face and goatee caked in dried blood. Otherwise the car was empty.

Suddenly his door was opened sharply and he jumped.

It was Tye. 'Morning!' she said.

'I s'pose it must be.' He rubbed his eyes. 'You feeling better?'

'Good enough to drive, I think,' she said. 'Just been stretching my legs. Took a walk with Patch and Con back down to the museum.'

'Back to the scene of the crime?'

'Since we're here. Working day's beginning. Thought I could check out the reactions of the people working there, watch their body language. See who knew more about the break-in than they were letting on.'

'And did you?'

'Didn't have to. The chief janitor's freaking out there 'cause his early-shift assistant hasn't shown, and he's got so much crap to clean up. Seems it's the first day this guy's missed in almost a year.'

'Coincidence?'

'Con got the address out of the janitor. It's local, so her and Patch, they're going to check it out.' She looked at him meaningfully. 'Now do you want to shift over? I need to see what I can do with this shoulder. I've got a plane to fly.'

'Stiff, is it?' Jonah shifted into the passenger seat. 'Need a massage?'

She looked at him warily. 'No thanks.'

'Then how about you give *me* one?'

'I'll give your head a massage with this gear stick if you don't watch it.' She got awkwardly into the car. 'But Patch said to give you these.' She passed him some more red-brown clay fragments. 'Cleared out his pockets. The last bits of the vase he picked up.'

'More parts of the puzzle. Cool.' He took them and arranged them on his lap. While Tye slowly flexed her arm, breathing deeply and calmly, he picked up some of the black crumbs and placed them inside an old sweet wrapper. Only one of the fragments showed any more of the cipher – if it even *was* a cipher. The rest showed only bits of people. One showed a man's head, thrown back in grief like he was wailing.

'You have no idea,' Jonah muttered.

The district was called Faggala, though Patch reckoned 'Fag End' might be more appropriate. It was a slum neighbourhood, with a diesel reek about it. Prayer recordings blasted out from crumbling mosques, a wake-up call to the masses, warbling through rusting loudspeakers. Panicked chickens ran about in the soiled gutters as traffic rumbled through. Somewhere in the rooftops, a cock was crowing over the din.

It was the kind of place people did their best to believe did not exist – a sick, smelly dumping ground for life's unluckiest victims.

Patch glanced at Con, who was attracting more than a few glances in her figure-hugging black. 'Glad we're just visiting,' he said.

Con strode through the decay, aloof. 'Some nights I used to lie awake and wonder if I'd end up in a place like this.'

Patch was surprised by the confession. 'What, when your parents died you mean?'

'Each time I was packed up and shipped out to the next relative on the list, I was sure . . . Sure that this time the trick would be played,' she shrugged, 'and I'd be here.'

'We *are* here.' Patch stopped, checked a street sign. 'This is the Rue Kamel Sidqi. The bloke we want is somewhere down here.'

In Arabic, Con asked a dumpy woman in a flowery shawl and djellaba if she'd heard of a man named Muneeb. She waved to a second-storey apartment a little way up the road. Patch led the way till they reached the gaping doorway, and an odour of piss and orange peel. Then he stepped aside so she could go first.

Patch followed her slowly up the creaking wooden steps, which felt like they might give way beneath him at any time. The gloomy atmosphere was oppressive.

The sounds of the street were muted in here, the prayers reduced to a low, deranged jangle.

The door stood ajar. Patch watched Con tense herself and put on her biggest smile, ready to waltz in and charm the Egyptian pants off Muneeb.

But as she stepped inside, he heard her gasp. Peering over her shoulder, he saw the body on the crumpled bed.

The man lay on his back, clearly dead, his sightless eyes fixed on the cracked ceiling. His dirty white nightgown was stained almost black with blood. A wound gaped in his neck like an obscene smile.

'You'd think he'd have called in to work and told them he was ill,' joked Patch weakly.

Con walked further inside the filthy room. There was a note on the bed, scrawled in Arabic on a torn piece of paper. She closed the dead man's eyes with the tips of her fingers, then picked it up.

Patch hovered in the doorway; he didn't want to follow her in. 'What does it say?'

'"A warning to those who would seek to follow us,"' she read.

'Love from . . . ?'

'There's no signature. Just a pattern of dots.' She folded it away in her pocket. 'Our friends from last night, I think, yes? They must have realised we'd know it was an inside job.'

'Poor old Muneeb.'

'He told them how to get inside,' Con agreed. 'This is how they repaid him.'

Patch glanced around the cramped, poky room but there was nothing else to see.

Con kicked a bedpost. 'Once again, they have got here ahead of us.'

'And that's what we can expect if we run into them again,' said Patch, drawing a finger slowly across his throat.

CHAPTER TEN

Jonah supposed there was nothing more to keep them in Cairo. Motti had used his flash mobile to call Coldhardt on speakerphone, told him the facts of last night's escapades just as they'd happened – apportioning no credit and no blame. Coldhardt had endured the telling stoically – even the news that a man had been murdered in connection with the stolen lekythos. Now he wanted to inspect the pottery and the powder they'd recovered. Jonah imagined he'd soon be working on the cipher fragments, and felt a tingle of anticipation.

But they weren't going back to Geneva. While they'd been gone, Coldhardt had relocated to his smaller base of operations in Siena – more convenient for the next stages of the operation, he said. He told them to fly there at once.

The plane had been berthed at a private airfield. Tye dropped the owner a stack of cash for the use of the facilities, for refuelling the King Air – and to keep him quiet.

'Coldhardt always move around so much?' asked Jonah, settling into the big, squashy chairs on board the plane.

'Standard security,' Motti told him. 'Plus it's closer to Samraj's place in Florence, the place we're turning over.'

'That's where she's meant to keep her part of the recipe for this eternal life juice, right?'

'Uh-huh. The Amrita.'

'You honestly believe in that immortality stuff?'

He shrugged. 'In this game it can be as dangerous to believe as to disbelieve, man. Me, I treat the unknown with respect. So should you.'

Jonah hadn't expected such a considered response from Motti. He felt a little shiver snake down his back. 'Sorry, I s'pose I –'

'Don't forget, Jonah, those tattooed types killed a man over this stuff. Killed him like it was nothing – maybe just to scare us away.'

'And to think I went chasing after those people.'

Motti sniffed, dabbed at his bruised nose. 'Something big is going down, all right.'

'And will Coldhardt *let* us be scared away?'

'What do you think?'

Jonah dwelled on the thought for a time. Then for the sake of his gooseflesh, he decided to change the subject. 'So, anyway, Samraj's house . . .?'

'Big mansion, well-protected,' said Motti. 'Gonna be a real challenge, but I think I got it taped for the most part.'

Jonah raised an eyebrow. 'Already?'

'Sure, already!' Motti grinned. 'What did you think I was studying on the flight out to Cairo, geek?'

'I thought you were working out how to crack that museum.'

'That was, like, five minutes!' The amusement faded from his face. 'But this place . . . it's a whole other league. Some *serious* security.'

Jonah looked out of his window, at the sea of cloud stretching out to the distant blue horizon. It looked so solid you could stand on it.

'This whole thing has got a bit serious for me,' he murmured.

Tye landed the plane at a small airfield in Siena where a car was waiting to collect them. Jonah stared out of the window at fields of wheat and poppies, at sleepy Tuscan villages nestling on hilltops beneath the faultless blue sky.

None of the others gave the surroundings more than a glance.

The base here was no less opulent than the Geneva headquarters. Coldhardt owned his own medieval castle overlooking fat sweeps of countryside. Huge palm trees flanked the front gates, towering above a line of sculpted topiaries like they were trying to peep over the castle walls.

'Don't people think it's weird,' Jonah wondered aloud, 'people like us rolling up to a place like this?'

'Pretty much the whole area is given over to tourist accommodation,' said Con. 'People think the castle is a luxury conference centre. And the neighbours change every couple of weeks so no one gets suspicious. It's perfect.'

Certainly the driver didn't even blink when his ragged passengers got out and trailed into the magnificent grounds of the twelfth-century *castello*.

Jonah was shown to his room, an apartment in a converted farmhouse in the shade of a sprawling mulberry tree. It was like some luxury holiday home – and certainly for now he was strictly a tourist, as the others were summoned to Coldhardt without him. Presumably they would brief the big man on Jonah's performance, such as it was, as well as handing over the bits and pieces they'd managed to collect in Cairo.

Jonah was too tired to worry or care much about it. It was weird how fast you adapted, he thought. And it was hard to worry about the future when it was so sunny and warm and the pillow on your four-poster was so soft . . .

He caught up with the others later that afternoon in a quiet courtyard, the centrepiece of which was a fabulous outdoor pool. Con was sprawled on a sunlounger wearing a tiny red bikini, which probably explained why Patch was lying on his front to watch her. Regardless of the blazing sunshine, Motti was wearing his usual black jeans and T-shirt, reading a magazine through dark glasses. Tye was in the water, wincing as she exercised her bad shoulder.

'How'd it go with Coldhardt?' he wondered.

None of them seemed eager to talk about it.

'It went OK,' said Tye. 'Considering.'

'So can we pick up the self-defence class again?' Jonah asked brightly. 'With your shoulder out, I might stand a chance of beating you.'

'Yeah, right,' drawled Motti, turning a page. 'You couldn't beat an egg.'

'He took *you* down,' Con reminded him. Ignoring

the finger he raised in her direction, she looked at Jonah over her shades. 'Tye's still too sore for a workout. But I could show you some moves, yes?'

Jonah smiled nervously. 'You could?'

She got up slowly, teeth bared in a sharp smile. 'Sure. I've got some great moves.'

Motti glanced over at Patch. 'Don't you dare start humping that sunlounger again.'

'You know, maybe I'll pass,' said Jonah, with a brief smile at Tye. 'I think I was kicked into the pool enough times yesterday.'

Con's flirtatious smile cooled a little. 'It's not all play here, Jonah. Coldhardt wants you trained up. I'll meet you in the gym at seven tonight for a proper workout.'

With that she strutted slowly away from the poolside.

'Jonah!' Patch moaned. 'What d'you go and do that for?'

'To save you from going blind?'

Motti laughed. Encouraged, Jonah sat on a chair between the two. He felt the familiar urge to try and impress, to fling himself at them puppy-dog fashion in the hope of affection and acceptance – and as usual, heard the cynical voice in his head that told him he hadn't a hope.

I don't need this, he told himself.

Tye's voice in his head: '*Liar.*'

He noticed her looking his way for a few moments before she returned to her exercises, making slow, circling movements with both arms.

'Con's a bit of an ice queen, isn't she?' Jonah

observed. 'Or is she secretly warm and cuddly underneath?'

'She's been through some tough times,' said Patch.

'Yeah, right. Haven't we all?'

Motti turned another page. 'Her parents were killed in front of her when she was eight,' he said casually. 'Family outing. They hit a truck, their car musta rolled over ten times. Con was smashed up in the back, pretty bad. Had to watch the medics cut Mommy and Daddy from the wreckage before they could even get to her –'

'OK, OK, I take it all back!' Jonah held up his hands. 'God, that really *is* tough.'

'You could say that,' Motti agreed.

'It's why she won't ride in the back seat,' added Patch.

Jonah grimaced. 'I'm surprised she'll get in a car at all.'

'Took her a long time,' Tye remarked. 'But she knew she was useless to Coldhardt if she couldn't travel, so she gave herself some hypnotherapy.'

'*Mesmerism* therapy, you mean.' Motti winked at her. 'Sounds cooler.'

Jonah half-smiled. 'So Con was the last person Coldhardt recruited before me, right?'

'Must be nine months ago, now,' said Patch. 'We needed her for that crypt job in Lima.'

'She kept half the shanty town off our backs while we got hold of that crystal,' said Motti, his admiration plain. '*There is nothing to see here,*' he mimicked crudely. '*Nothing to see.*'

Patch chuckled. 'Yeah, we're just nicking the object

you've been worshipping for hundreds of years!'

Jonah laughed along with them, though he didn't find it so funny. 'So I'm guessing Motti, you found the place, and Patch, you got them inside –'

'Place was crawling with traps,' Patch shuddered. 'There were these big swords, right, rigged to spring out of the walls . . .'

'Nice. What about you, Tye? What was your job?'

'I took the curse off the crystal,' she said simply.

Jonah raised his eyebrows. 'Curse?'

'Tye's the voodoo lady,' Motti murmured.

'You're joking.'

Motti turned another page. 'Some things you don't joke about.'

'*Then* I had to smuggle the thing out to Coldhardt's buyer in Colombia,' Tye went on. 'Solo – while these assholes went off on a Caribbean cruise.'

'You did tell us it would be safer if you worked alone,' Patch reminded her.

'Safer for you lot!' Tye retorted. 'It was after that little experience that Coldhardt agreed to get the plane.'

'He could afford it after a sale like that,' Motti remarked. 'A cool million in one hit.'

Jonah whistled. 'Coldhardt sells these relics to the highest bidder?'

'Unless he's specially hired for an assignment like this one,' said Tye. 'He works out what – and *who* – he needs to get the job done, and just gets on with it.'

'And the first kid he recruited was Motti.'

'This time around,' Motti agreed.

A cloud drifted over the sun. The pool's clear water

lost its glitter for a few seconds.

Jonah frowned. 'So there were other Coldhardt's children before you? What happened to them?'

Motti shrugged. 'Had enough and moved on, I guess.'

'Or maybe one day their luck ran out,' said Jonah, 'and something happened to them.'

Motti put down his magazine crossly. 'Yeah, something happened to them all right – they got rich enough to retire, so they split. Nothing lasts for ever. Coldhardt woulda known 'em well enough by then to let 'em go without any comeback.'

'Yeah, that makes sense,' said Patch, nodding vigorously. 'I bet they all set themselves up in some luxury home somewhere. Coldhardt probably helped 'em invest the cash so they could live off the interest.'

'Yeah, that sounds like a nice, likely happy ever after,' said Jonah, making no attempt to hide the sarcasm in his voice. 'Does he send them Christmas cards each year too?'

'Aw, who cares what happened in the past?' Motti argued. 'Right now, it's the present – and life is sweet. Gotta enjoy it while you can.'

Jonah was about to argue that history often repeats itself, but he bit his tongue. He was trying to fit in here, not piss everyone off. From the worried look on Patch's face, he had already put a dampener on things. Why *did* he spend so long looking on the black side? He thought of the losers and no-hopes he'd been stuck with inside, what they would be doing in the YOI right now. And then he looked again at the clear blue pool, the pristine gardens, Tye in her swimsuit . . .

Maybe Motti had the right idea.

'Come on, Patch,' he said. 'Race you six lengths in the pool.'

'I'll slaughter ya!' Patch beamed and launched himself into the pool, splashing Tye. She splashed him back, kicking up her legs at him.

'Mind your arm, Tye!' Jonah called.

'It's cool, I'll stop 'em fighting,' Motti announced. 'Incoming!' He cannonballed into the water, creating a miniature tidal wave. The three of them squealed and shouted. The water churned like it was full of piranhas.

Jonah grinned and jumped in beside Tye, joining her in her splash-struggle against Patch and Motti. Their laughter and splutters echoed around the silent courtyard under the sun.

And even through the taste of chlorine, Jonah found that life had never tasted so sweet.

It was the next afternoon before he saw Coldhardt again.

Jonah found the time passed quickly, enjoying his new-found social life. He'd had a good workout with Con in the gym. Not only did she look great in a leotard, but she was a good and patient teacher. She really made you feel you could do it – Jonah came away from the two-hour session with a couple of quite slick moves under his belt.

He'd wanted to say to her, 'I'm so sorry about your parents.' But even in his head, the words sounded hollow, beyond inadequate. He'd never known a proper mum and dad, but to have had them and then lose them both . . .

Jonah wondered how much money it must take before Con felt better.

After a sauna and shower he was ready to chill with Motti and Patch in the castello's hangout. They held a pinball tournament, which Tye crashed for a while, until she'd soundly trounced all three of them. Then he and Motti joined Con in sampling some of the local wines, bluffing that he could taste the differences between them. It didn't really matter – they all tasted good with the fantastic pizza Coldhardt had ordered in from the local trattoria. He slept well that night – no sleeping pills required.

For most of the day he'd been net-surfing in his room. He'd scoured a dozen sites and hacked into a few more trying to learn more about early Greek and Spartan ciphers, but had learned little he didn't already know. And as his mind wandered, he found himself imagining who might have stayed in this beautiful room before him, and what had happened to make them leave.

Give it a rest, he told himself. What was the use of obsessing over it?

The doorbell roused him from his thoughts, and he pounced on the distraction. It was Con, soberly dressed in black trousers and a high-necked top.

'Coldhardt's called a meeting,' she announced with a smile. 'I will escort you, yes?'

'It would be a pleasure,' said Jonah, though he felt his insides twitch and tickle in grim anticipation. It was a kind of stage fright, he supposed. Would Coldhardt expect him to crack the lekythos cipher on the spot?

Con led him through the old, impressive passage-ways of the castello. She had to stand in front of a retinal scanner to activate the hidden lift. As in Geneva, a section of floor sank smoothly down into the hidden depths before discharging its passengers into a brightly lit antechamber.

This version of the hub was smaller but otherwise nearly identical. Coldhardt sat at his desk, just as he had the last time Jonah had seen him. He smiled in greeting, but the gesture stopped short of his eyes. Con fared little better, despite the major-league dental dazzle in her boss's direction.

Tye, Motti and Patch were already seated. Jonah was glad to see the skin round Patch's good eye was now a lighter shade of purple and Motti's nose was less swollen – he wore a new pair of glasses, identical to the old. Tye waved her stiff arm and flexed her fingers in what might have been greeting, or might have been physio – he wasn't sure which. But she looked a lot more relaxed. Twenty-four hours' rest seemed to have done all of them some good.

'Welcome, Jonah,' said Coldhardt. 'You enjoyed your first field trip, I hope?' That roguish touch of Irish in his accent made the enquiry slightly mocking.

'It was an experience,' Jonah answered, evenly. For a fleeting moment, he felt like a fly caught in the dead centre of some immense web.

'Sit down. Look at the screens.' There were only four of them on the walls of this junior hub, each of them plain blue, devoid of signal. Coldhardt sat at the head of the table and tapped a remote. The screen top left kicked into sudden life. It showed an obscure arrangement of yellow points scattered over black.

'I recognise that pattern,' said Con. 'It is the same as the ink spots on the note I found in the Egyptian's room, no?'

'The *dead* Egyptian's room,' Patch added, in case they needed clarification.

'The resemblance is striking isn't it?' To reinforce the point, Coldhardt put an image of the ink spots on the screen top right. 'The points of light represent a constellation that sprawls across 948 square degrees of sky – a part of which falls within the plane of the zodiac between Scorpio and Sagittarius.'

Con looked at Tye. 'It's the constellation of Ophiuchus. Like Demnos said.'

Coldhardt nodded. 'Yes, Ophiuchus. The only human being in history to be granted a place among the stars.'

'So that chick who trounced Tye in the museum,' said Motti, 'she was, what, a stargazer with attitude?'

'From the serpent tattoo Tye described and her attire, I would say the female belonged to the Cult of Ophiuchus. An ancient secret society supposed to have died out centuries ago.' He smiled, his rich voice shot through with a measure of ice. 'Like the man himself, blessed with a long, long life.'

'So what – these people are his fan club?' said Jonah uneasily. 'They hold Ophiuchus conventions and stuff?'

'They practise his teachings,' said Coldhardt. 'Follow the ancient texts. It was long believed that his acolytes could recite every prescription by rote. One reason for the cult's believed extinction was that from the Middle Ages onwards, certain unscrupulous types tortured many of the cultists to death in their efforts to extract the recipe for Amrita. None of them gave away so much as a syllable.'

'Devoted,' said Tye.

'Idiots,' Con muttered.

'Fanatics,' Coldhardt corrected them both. 'But it seems they were not destroyed by this persecution. Merely driven underground.'

'So why come sniffing around the surface now?' Patch asked.

Motti cracked him on the head with a pencil. 'Because shit is going down,' he said simply.

'Your birthday is on December 2nd, Jonah.' Coldhardt was looking at him expectantly. 'Is that not so?'

'Yeah. What're you gonna get me?'

'Remind me, that would make you in astrological terms . . .?'

'You want me to say the obvious, that I'm a Sagittarius,' said Jonah. 'So I'm guessing that I'm really an *Ophiuchan*, right?'

If Coldhardt was impressed, he didn't show it. 'Quite correct. From November 30th until December 17th the sun passes through Ophiuchus. There are thousands born under the Ophiuchan star sign, if they only knew it.'

'So why does everyone make out there are only twelve zodiac signs?' asked Tye.

'Twelve months of the year,' Con suggested.

'It's neater.'

'There's more to it than that.' There was a wintry gleam in Coldhardt's eyes. 'The origins of astrology can be traced back to 3000 BC. As an art it was pioneered by the Chaldeans of Babylonia, but the ancient Etruscans, Egyptians, Hindus, the Chinese – they all held that the movements of the heavens affected not only their crops and the seasons, but the fates of all humankind.'

'Like believing comets were bad omens,' said Tye.

Coldhardt nodded. 'In the fourth century BC the science of astrology was practised in Ancient Greece. And around that time, a presence of evil was linked to the constellation of Ophiuchus. A kind of hysteria appears to have set in – and soon, no mage would cast horoscopes for that sign.'

'Why?' asked Jonah simply.

'The documentation is frustratingly sparse,' Coldhardt admitted. 'It seems that even the act of writing about this evil was considered enough to bring a curse upon the author. However . . .' He paused, his expression growing more severe, his voice dying to a theatrical whisper. 'Some imply that Ophiuchus's long life eventually corrupted him. That his thirst for knowledge led to his possession by unspeakable forces and a terrible fate. That since he refused to travel to the dead land . . . its dreadful denizens travelled to him.'

'Just stories,' Con argued, looking round at the others for support, and finding only grave faces.

'And yet despite this evil about him,' said Tye, 'these acolytes, they still guard his powers, his prescriptions?'

Coldhardt nodded. 'So it would seem. The few who are left, anyway.'

'So just what was in that vase?' asked Jonah, a now-familiar tingle travelling along his spine. 'A secret they were willing to kill for?'

'Not enough of the black powder was recovered to be analysed properly,' said Coldhardt. 'All I've been able to ascertain is that it was organic in nature. Such a complete cellular degeneration is highly unusual. However, there –'

'What about the pottery fragments that Patch –?'

'*Do not interrupt me, Jonah.*'

Jonah instantly opened his mouth to apologise, but there was something in the old man's eyes . . . some dark strength there that Jonah couldn't fathom. His mouth dried. The room fell crypt-silent.

For a moment, those eyes seemed almost inhuman.

Then the moment passed, as Coldhardt spoke more softly: 'I will come to the fragments in due course.'

'Of course,' Jonah said. 'I – I'm sorry.'

'Now, as I was saying. There may yet be a result forthcoming on the substance that was stored and sealed within the lekythos all those centuries ago . . .' Coldhardt smiled wanly. 'From Samraj Vasavi.'

Con frowned. 'Her? How can she help us?'

'Those people who stole the funeral vase ahead of you all . . . the registration plate of their car in Cairo, as recorded by Jonah, was naturally a false one.' Coldhardt smiled, his earlier outburst apparently forgotten. 'However, by allying myself to certain . . . *agencies*, I was able to track down the manufacturer and fitter of that fraudulent plate. The car in question was a black Chrysler – registered to Serpens Biotech.'

'Samraj's multinational,' breathed Tye.

A third screen flicked into life, this time showing a large, white concrete edifice against a deep blue sky. 'This morning, that Chrysler was seen parked outside this Serpens facility in Jordan.'

'So is that where Samraj is based right now,' Tye wondered, 'or is she home in her mansion in Florence?'

'I really couldn't tell you,' said Coldhardt, matter-of-factly.

There was a pause. Then Jonah noticed Tye look down at the table, as if troubled.

'What's an acolyte of some ancient sect doing running errands for the head of a big genetics firm?' asked Motti. 'Makes no sense.'

'Or if you look at it the other way round,' Con argued, 'why does Samraj's high-tech multinational company need the help of an ancient, superstitious sect?'

Coldhardt nodded. 'Strange behaviour on both sides, wouldn't you say?'

'Only one of those guys we came up against had the tattoo,' Patch pointed out. 'Maybe she's retired from the cult.'

'Membership of the cult is for life,' said Coldhardt. '*Long* life. Jonah, those pottery fragments you mentioned earlier – the others tell me you think it's a cipher.'

Jonah shrugged. 'It's like nothing I've come across, but yeah. I do.'

'Perhaps you could set up a likely program to crack

the code? Regretfully, we have less computing power here than in Geneva, but while the solution is slowly assembled . . . I have another use for you.'

Jonah raised an eyebrow. 'Oh yeah?'

'Indeed. We're pleased with your progress. You're being kept on.'

'That's generous of you. Cheers.'

'It's my hope that as you learn to drop your guard a little, you'll be able to curb your facetious tongue.' Coldhardt smiled again. 'As for my generosity . . . you'll find an indication of it in your room here.'

At once Jonah was buzzing with curiosity. But he played it cool. 'This "other use" for me you mentioned . . .'

'Our employer, Mr Demnos, is most upset that we were – shall we say – beaten to the punch in gaining possession of the complete lekythos. Yes, we have a part of the lekythos cipher, but the other part must surely now be in Samraj's possession.'

'So it's like the prescription for the Amrita,' Con reasoned. 'They both have a part of it, but neither has the whole thing.'

'Will Samraj be able to translate the cipher without Jonah?' asked Patch, rather touchingly.

'Oh yes,' said Coldhardt simply. 'She will go to any lengths to secure the information she needs.'

Jonah glanced at Tye again, but she was still look-ing down at the table. He sensed that something was wrong, but didn't have a clue what it might be.

Con, meanwhile, briskly summed up the situation: 'So now we must find her bits of the lekythos as well as her fragments of the Amrita prescription, yes?

That is, if she really has them.'

Coldhardt smiled enigmatically. 'Oh, I am quite certain they exist.'

'How come?' said Motti.

'I know Samraj of old,' was his only answer. 'But Con is right. Which is why we now have *two* priority assignments. First, we must steal, or at least photograph, the scraps of prescription she keeps at her house. Jonah, you will accompany Motti and Patch to Florence.'

'And help them break into that mansion?' Jonah wavered. 'It's one thing breaking into a museum or something, but when it's someone's home . . .'

'If it helps ease your conscience, I believe Samraj stole those fragments in the first place. It is very doubtful that any police force will involve itself in this affair.'

Jonah didn't have to look at Motti to know a *told-you-so* stare was being tossed his way. 'So are we meant to be looking out for the other bits of the lekythos too?'

'No.' Coldhardt steepled his fingers. 'Wherever Samraj is, she will be having them tested, examined . . . pored over in detail.'

'So me and Tye take the second assignment, yes?' said Con brightly.

'You will take the plane and travel to the Serpens building in Aqaba that our cultist friends so recently frequented.' Coldhardt filled the fourth and final screen with a map of the area – Aqaba was situated at the top of the fat boot of the Middle East, very close to the border of Egypt. 'You will . . . *explore* the premises. See if you can find what's happened to the lekythos, where it might have gone. Join me here at 1800 hours for a full briefing. Motti, we'll run over your strategy for the mansion job at 1900.' He paused. 'In the meantime, I have one or two private calls I need to make. Jonah, return here in thirty minutes. I want you to give me your first thoughts on a strategy for cracking the lekythos cipher.' He smiled round at the table. 'You may go, my children.'

Tye rose and crossed quickly to the door. She hesitated in the doorway, glancing back at Coldhardt as though something was still bugging her. But he was staring at his screens, apparently lost in thought.

As she slipped from the underground room, Jonah quickened his step to catch up. 'How's that shoulder now?'

'Better, thanks,' she said.

'So what else is up?'

She looked away. 'What are you on about?'

'I saw you in there,' he persisted. 'Something's wrong. Care to share?'

'Yes, you look glum, sweets.' Con had joined them in the lift, Motti and Patch close behind her. 'What is it?'

'It's nothing,' Tye muttered, with just the tiniest warning look at Jonah. 'I could just really do without another long-haul to the Middle East, that's all.'

'It's not Coldhardt's fault the cultists took the funeral vase to Aqaba,' said Con as the lift pushed them serenely upwards to rejoin the castle corridor. 'If we'd done our jobs properly in Cairo –'

'Oh, if *we'd* done our jobs, huh?' said Motti,

rolling his eyes. 'Poor ol' Con, shown up in front of the old man. I suppose if I'd let *you* go into that lock-up, the lekythos would be all ours, right?'

'I never said that.'

'No, you didn't have to.'

'Oh, just stop it,' Tye snapped, 'all of you.' She pushed past Jonah to get out of the concealed lift, stalking off down the castle corridor. The patches of late afternoon sun through the lead-glass windows were like spotlights tracking her progress, and she put on a good show: aloof and weary. But Jonah couldn't help feeling that this *was* about more than just tiredness, whatever she said. That something *was* up.

The question was: what?

CHAPTER ELEVEN

Jonah wandered the grounds by himself till it was time to return to the planning room. Part of him wanted to go rushing to his room like a kid on his birthday, eager to see what Daddy had bought him. Another part of him dreaded to think what gift might be waiting – and what his acceptance of it might signify. He felt uneasy, out of his depth.

When it was time, he returned to Coldhardt's junior hub feeling like a schoolboy summoned to the headmaster. But the old man seemed in a chipper mood, and greeted him warmly. One on one, he was a different person. He had a way of making you feel you were the centre of his world, worthy of all his attention. Jonah could well understand how the others had fallen under the spell of this man.

Unfortunately, he found he didn't have much he could tell Coldhardt about the cipher. With the age of it, he guessed it must be character substitution like the Spartan scytale, but he didn't recognise *any* of the characters this time. It didn't appear to be any kind of alphabet – at least not a complete one.

'I'll run a couple of algorithms on it in combination,' Jonah said. 'Maybe in 24 hours we'll have something.'

'Well, if anyone can crack this,' said Coldhardt, 'I believe you can.'

The affirmation made him uncomfortable. It tapped into the way it had been with his foster dad when they'd been setting up the business. Talking Derek through each step he was taking, swapping clever ideas for pats on the head . . .

'Can I believe in *you*?' Jonah asked.

Coldhardt looked at him. 'If you find it hard to trust me, then trust my acumen. I invest my time and my money very carefully. And I look after the things that are valuable to me.' He smiled. 'You have entered my family now.'

'I'm not a child. I'm seventeen.'

'We don't outgrow the need for family, Jonah. Call it whatever you want, but you have a home with us here.'

The words were beguiling, but Jonah set his mouth, said nothing.

'You've been made to feel worthless your whole life,' said Coldhardt with sudden fervour, 'by petty people with small minds and no ambition.'

'And *you* have plenty of ambition,' said Jonah quietly. 'Enough for the two of us, right?'

'Yes, I do. I've achieved so much in my long life. And yet there is still so much more to accomplish, before . . .' He glanced back at the sinister statuette on his desk. 'You're a good investment, Jonah. I know you are. Now, go and get some sleep.' He gestured to the door with a charming smile. Jonah got up to leave, gratefully.

'And Jonah . . . All I ask is that you give of your best. I shan't fail you in return.'

Against his better judgement, Jonah turned in the doorway. 'The experts you had before us. What happened to them?'

Coldhardt fixed him with his wintry stare. 'You can never plan the future by the past, lad.'

Jonah nodded, awkwardly. Then he left the room, without a backwards glance.

More walking, more deliberating. Picturing what might be waiting for him in his room. Money? Another computer? Jonah watched the setting sun soak the lustrous sweeps of the Tuscan hillsides with brilliant golden light, until it had all but ebbed away and night was impatient to fall.

When he returned to his room, he found a black velvet pouch on his pillow. He picked it up warily. It felt empty – no, something was there, small and hard. He shook the pouch into the palm of his hand.

A single diamond fell out, winking and gleaming in the dappled sunlight through the window. Jonah stared at it. He hadn't imagined anything like this. It was like no gemstone he had ever seen. A scintilla of darkness seemed trapped inside it, a gauzy, glittering skein of mist. The gem had to be worth a small fortune. Or a massive one, for all he knew.

'So you got it, then?'

Jonah jumped, turned to find Tye standing in his doorway. He hadn't heard her come in. 'It's a diamond,' he said, shell-shocked.

'Kind of. It's a smokestone. Incredibly rare.

Incredibly precious.' She smiled. 'We've all got one. Coldhardt's way of telling us we've proved ourselves to him.'

'And I guess *he* has proved himself to *you*?'

'Ten times over,' she said flatly. 'Anyway, I just came to say it's been agreed – things kick off tomorrow. We're having dinner at ten, in the big hall. Motti wants to talk over this mansion job with you right after.'

'OK. Fine.' Jonah stared down at the diamond in his hand. 'How'd *your* briefing with Coldhardt go?'

'Seems a straightforward job. Find the lekythos, find the Chrysler, see if we can dig up anything on what the acolytes were doing there.'

'No more bad vibes from the old guy, like earlier?'

She sighed. 'Will you drop it, Jonah?'

'*Were* there?'

'No.' Tye sighed. 'Not really. It's nothing I can put my finger on. I'm just a little on edge.'

He crossed over to her. 'Tell me about it?'

She looked into his eyes. 'When I asked him about Samraj this afternoon, about whether she was in Jordan, or at home in Florence . . .'

'He told you he didn't know,' Jonah recalled. 'Which is kind of weird. I mean, if he could follow the Chrysler with fake plates, then surely he should have known where Samraj –'

'He didn't say he didn't *know* where she was,' Tye interrupted him. 'He said he really couldn't tell me.'

'Same difference, surely?'

'Is it?' She looked troubled. 'Coldhardt's good with words. He needs to be. I'm the walking lie detector,

143

right? So maybe he *really* couldn't tell me. It was like he was . . .' she struggled for the words. 'Like he was deflecting the question. Like he didn't want to get drawn into the whole thing about where she was.'

Jonah nodded. 'Because you might know he was lying.'

'Maybe.' She sighed. 'Or maybe I'm just ultra-paranoid. I'm tired as hell, I know that – I'm probably worrying when there's no need.'

'I hope so.' Jonah smiled ruefully. 'You're not exactly making me feel better about tomorrow's little assignment.'

'Don't worry about the job. Coldhardt wouldn't send us into anything he didn't think we could handle.' Tye half-smiled, closed his fingers round the jewel in his palm. 'Whatever else he might be, he's no fool. Like smokestones, we're not easy to replace.'

'But you reckon he has a fair idea where Samraj is, don't you?' said Jonah. 'He just doesn't want to tell us.'

Tye nodded.

'Why, for God's sake?'

The look in her eyes reminded him of the smoky glitter of the diamond. 'I have no idea,' she whispered.

The next day, Jonah learned why Tye was usually designated driver.

Motti was a maniac. His idea of driving was to floor the accelerator, aim the silver-grey Merc down the middle of the *autostrade* and hope for the best. He had some gadget built into the dash that picked up on speed cops and cameras, and so every now and then he would stamp on the brake, sending Jonah and Patch halfway through the windscreen before their belts locked. Patch barely reacted, too absorbed in his Game Boy Advance SP.

'Once I start I can't stop,' he explained, eyes glued to the little screen. 'Or else I puke.'

'You're gonna puke anyway,' Motti retorted, razzing past some startled senior citizens in a minibus. 'You always hurl.'

Jonah grimaced. 'Why don't we cut back on the puke-talk?' But at least his fears of flying upchuck and horrific car-crash injuries were taking his mind off the burgling field trip that awaited him.

Coldhardt had marked the mansion on the map. It stood on the outskirts of Florence, in the exclusive, sought-after hills of Bellosguardo. They squealed to a halt about a mile away, in some quaint little hamlet overrun with big hire cars. Once Jonah's legs had stopped shaking and Patch had paused to throw up on the bonnet of a Daimler, they made their way like wide-eyed tourists through orchards and olive groves until they had a good view of their target – or the perimeter of the place at least. The actual house lay entirely hidden beyond high walls, just as Motti had said.

'Good job we're superheroes,' said Motti, unfolding a plan of the place from his rucksack.

'But we're not going in till tonight, right?' said Jonah nervously.

'Jeez, geek, I thought I made it clear enough. How many times do I need to go over it?'

'I just want to be two hundred per cent certain of

whatever I'm doing.' Truth was, his recollection of Motti's after-dinner briefing was coloured with a mild red wine haze – an attempt to take the edge off his nerves. In hindsight, he'd probably sanded them down to dust.

'Go easy on him, Mot,' said Patch. 'It's his first time.'

'So I'm taking the geek's cherry. Perfect.' He glowered at Jonah. 'This is just the recce. Confirming what we got, fixing what we can. Remember, I don't like no surprises.' He pulled out a small, sleek pair of binoculars from the rucksack, wandered over to a tall, broad tree and started to climb. 'This'll be our approach area. First thing we gotta do is fix the PIRs.'

'Passive Infra-Red sensors,' Jonah recalled.

'Second they pick up our body heat, they'll light up the whole of the grounds like it's the Fourth of July. Set off the alarms too.' He pulled himself nimbly up into the gnarled, leafy branches. 'Photo-electric sensors tell the little beauties when it gets dark, and that's when they kick in.'

'So how do we get past them?' Jonah called up.

'Shh, man,' Patch told him. 'Samraj could be listening out, sunbathing the other side of the wall. Topless,' he added dreamily.

Jonah frowned. 'Have you ever even *seen* this woman?'

'She's got boobs, don't she?'

'You sad man. She's old enough to be your mother –' Jonah broke off. 'Sorry, I s'pose your mum's not the best subject to –'

'Forget it.' Patch looked away awkwardly, his hand straying unconsciously to the leather over his missing eye and rubbing it. 'Anyway . . . see, Motti's got this laser light thing, holds a solid beam over long distance. If he can shine it right at that sensor, it won't be able to tell when night falls. It'll go on thinking it's broad daylight, and it won't kick in. We can do what we want.'

'Clever,' Jonah admitted. 'But even if he can get a clear shot at the sensor from up there, he'd have to hold that beam so steady . . .'

The high-pitched whine of a power tool started up. A few birds clattered away as Motti drilled carefully into the trunk of the solid, spreading tree. Then he took a tiny metal cylinder from between his teeth – the laser torch, Jonah guessed – and fixed it into the hole.

Patch smiled. 'Sneaky little bastard, ain't he?'

Motti scrambled casually down from the tree. 'Should take care of that. Now, let's go see if we can't do something about the vibration sensors in this damn wall . . .'

Patch set off after him like an obedient puppy, and Jonah followed on, the long, nerve-jangling day stretching out before him like a desert.

It was hot and humid in Aqaba, the sun so scorching you could almost imagine its flames licking the azure sky. Tye was grateful for the air con in the hired Lexus. Stopping at lights, she took in the view. Through the shimmering heat haze she could see the mountains of Eilat looming orange and purple from across the Israeli border, and traced the red sandy desert as it gave gradual way to the blossoming colour of the Great Rift Valley. Con was spending more time eyeing the cool young Arabs hanging out in the bustling pavement cafes, dressed in Versace, smoking Marlboros, laughing and swearing in American English.

The Serpens Biotech offices were located on a modern industrial estate out on the coast road to Saudi. The massive concrete edifice was ugly but easy to spot with a green snake logo scaling its topmost storeys.

'There's a hotel on the estate with a good bar,' Con reported, checking over some literature she'd picked up from a business centre. 'Has a happy hour. Popular haunt for the workers gearing up for the weekend.'

'With loose tongues,' Tye agreed. 'We hope.'

'Excuse me,' said Con, embarking on an imaginary conversation with someone, 'can I buy you a beer? And did you notice a sinister tattooed acolyte with a couple of heavies dropping off a broken vase full of black flakes to your boss a couple of days ago?'

'I wonder if Samraj is still here,' Tye muttered. 'Coldhardt didn't seem to know.'

'Well, if she *is* here, we'll keep out of her way. And if she's in Florence, Motti will not even wake her. Yes?'

Tye nodded. 'Whatever.'

As the offices emptied of staff one by one they had no problem finding people to talk to. Some of the men gave them unwelcome hassle but there were all sorts there – Americans, Israelis, Africans, many of them bright young things lured to Serpens by the promise of cutting-edge research and good funding.

Con coaxed conversations on gene splicing and DNA mapping and God-knew-what. Sexy stuff, Tye supposed, for these young super-brainy types. But she got the impression that the Aqaba branch of Serpens was more a starting point for the career-minded or a dead end for the career-stalled. It was all agricultural labs, plant yields and GM food testing – none of the *really* hot and juicy research.

'This place must just have been a dropping-off point for the vase thing,' said Tye, extricating Con from the attentions of two eager and sweaty young men. 'Don't you think?'

Con nodded. 'I think they came here because it was the nearest Serpens facility. From here, Samraj could take the flakes and fragments anywhere in the world.'

'Another Middle Eastern wild goose chase,' sighed Tye, draining her cranberry juice. 'Total waste of time.'

'Maybe not total,' Con suggested, returning a smile to a good-looking Indian man who sat with two friends and a bottle of wine in an ice bucket. 'We can check to see if the Chrysler with the false plates is still on the premises. And someone here has just *got* to work in the post room.'

Tye saw what she was driving at. 'You think Samraj sent the lekythos on somewhere? But she'd never trust the regular post!'

'Of course not,' Con agreed coolly. 'But she might use a special courier, yes? And that might have gone through the post room.'

'Might.' Tye pulled a face. 'First we have to find someone who's willing to show us the company dispatch log.'

'Relax, sweets.' Con popped the melting ice cube from her glass into her mouth and smiled. 'By the time we're through with them, they'll show us any damn thing we want them to. First one to find a post boy gets first crack at the hotel mini-bar. Deal?'

'OK.' Tye smiled despite herself. 'Deal.'

Jonah stood in the Florentine orchard, holding his breath. The break-in had begun.

It was a warm, fragrant night, but he felt so cold that if he ever breathed again it would gust out like steam. Someone would see, the alarms would go off . . .

Motti's fierce whisper carried over the cascading chirrups of the cicadas. 'Right, Jonah, one step forward . . . Hold it.'

Their luck had held so far. The floodlights remained off, the PIR this side of the house successfully stymied by Motti's work. They'd got past the vibration sensors in the perimeter walls, too, climbing up high-suction footholds at a point where the wall changed direction at 90 degrees. The corner was the least sensitive part of the structure, since it was harder to press the co-axial cable that worked the system into the corner crevice.

'Patch, forward one . . . and hold it.'

Now they were performing Motti's patented way of beating the seismic detectors he was convinced lay buried in the garden. *'These systems usually rely on the intruder not knowing they're there,'* he'd told them. *'The processor studies the weight and frequency of the impact – if it recognises, say, a couple of footsteps in a thirty-second period, it hits the panic button. But if you keep it real soft and real slow . . .'*

So here they were, creeping through the beautiful

moonlit gardens at zero miles per hour, one person at a time and no more than one little step every 45 seconds. The agony of it was that they were in full view of several windows, and the lights were clearly still on behind the heavy drapes. If Samraj or one of her staff looked out they'd find three fellas frozen red-faced in the grounds. Probably set the guard dogs on them . . .

Please, God, let them not have guard dogs.

Finally the long slow-mo traipse through the lavender-scented night came to a quiet end. Motti declared they were out of range of the innermost sensors and could walk normally again. He led the way over to an opaque glass outhouse attached to the main building. Jonah felt a flush of achievement that they had made it this far; not because he'd contributed anything much, but because he hadn't messed up.

Now it was Patch's turn to shine; his job, as ever, was to get them inside. He pulled off his shoulder bag and laid it carefully on the floor.

Jonah became aware of a low rushing noise, like a fan heater. He saw there was a vent built into the frosted glass near ground level, spewing cold air out into the night.

'What's in here?' he asked quietly.

'It's a glasshouse,' grunted Motti. 'Gotta be plants, right?'

'Attached to the main house?' It didn't sound likely to Jonah. 'If cold air's coming out, it must be pretty warm in there.'

'You want us to strip off? Is this some faggy play to see me topless, geek?'

'Would you keep it down?' said Patch indignantly,

kneeling on the ground. 'I'm unleashing my genius here.' He removed two rolls of thick duct tape from the bag and handed one to each of them. Jonah and Motti tore off long strips and handed them to him. Carefully, Patch started covering the lowest window with the tape.

'*The outhouse is a fairly new addition,*' Motti had explained. '*The glass was ordered from a security firm. A line of metallic foil makes a circuit, stretching round the perimeter of each pane – so fine that if the glass so much as cracks, the foil tears, the circuit breaks and the alarms go off.*'

Jonah had decided he might as well ask the obvious so Motti could tell him: '*So how do we get inside?*'

But it was Patch who'd explained, and here he was putting his proposal into practice.

He'd taped up a fair portion of the window, leaving a clear square of glass in the centre – enough for someone small to crawl through. The tape would now act as a shock absorber, so Patch could deal with the exposed glass with less risk of tearing the foil.

Now he pulled out his glass eye and unscrewed it at the middle. Motti muttered under his breath and turned away, white-faced, but Jonah was intrigued to see what looked like a diamond inside. Swiftly, Patch removed the jewel and pushed it into the 'pupil' of the fake eye. Then he used it to score a square in the glass, just within the thick duct tape frame.

'Glass cutter,' Patch explained proudly. 'Diamond-tipped. Coldhardt sorted me with a whole lot of cool stuff like this.'

Motti obviously disapproved. 'Batman has a utility

belt, *Butt-kid* here has utility eyes. How dumb is that?'

'You want me to take my patch off and wink atcha? Just keep talking.'

Motti shut up and Patch continued to cut his crawl space. Jonah stared round nervously for any signs of approaching security guards. Motti watched Patch work, tutting and shaking his head now and then like he thought he could do better.

'Should be worn thin enough now,' Patch concluded a couple of minutes later. 'Mot, get the newspaper.'

Jonah watched as Patch started pressing a thin layer of clay against the window and Motti produced the *New York Times* from the shoulder bag and started pouring water all over it. For a moment, he thought they'd lost it.

'The clay deadens the sound of the glass hitting the floor,' Patch explained, 'stops it smashing everywhere. He took the dripping newspaper from Motti, placed it over the square, and started tapping with his knuckles. 'This muffles the sound of me tapping at the glass to knock through the –'

With a dull crack, and a heavy thud, the square of glass jumped away. Patch bit his lip. Jonah held his breath. The noise was deafening to his ears, however muffled it was supposed to be.

But no alarms went off. All Jonah could hear was the cicadas, invisible in the night.

And a strange, sibilant hissing sound.

'What the hell's that?' whispered Jonah.

'We ain't got time to worry,' said Motti. 'Jonah, get inside.'

'Why me?'

'It's your first time.' Motti grinned. 'You wanna make it special, right? So treat that hole real gentle.'

Jonah ignored their quiet sniggers, swallowed hard and crouched down in front of the hole. The hissing was definitely coming from inside. Some kind of gas heater maybe? It was horribly humid in here . . .

He wriggled slowly, cautiously through the crawl space, into the fetid darkness. Was this carpet? Felt almost springy, like AstroTurf or something. 'How about some light?' he whispered, when he was halfway through. 'I can't see a—'

He froze. Something brushed against his back.

Then Motti flicked on a torch. It cast a hazy light, sending Jonah's own shadow bobbing thickly about on the wall ahead of him, and some kind of weird reflection back into his eyes too.

When he saw where he was, it was all he could do to stop himself screaming at the top of his lungs.

There were snakes in here. Everywhere around him, fat hoses of flesh, coiling, stretching, writhing.

This was no hothouse. It was a *reptile* house.

And he'd emerged not into the viewing area, but into one of the crowded enclosures.

CHAPTER TWELVE

'Jesus, Motti, get me out of here!' Jonah tried to push himself back out through the narrow crawl space. He shuddered as a length of scaly flesh started to slide round his neck like a noose. 'It's full of snakes! They've built enclosures up against the walls!'

'Hold still,' Motti snapped. 'You'll slice yourself to ribbons on the glass and you'll set off the alarm. Plus, you make any sudden moves and one of those critters could bite you. Either way you could end up dead.'

'Thanks for the good news,' Jonah murmured, clamping his eyes shut.

'So it's an enclosure, right? Like a big fish tank. You've got to pull yourself all the way inside and then push up on the lid. That's the only way you're gonna get out.'

'I'm getting out the same way I got in!' Jonah informed him.

'Hold *still*, Goddamn it!' Motti whispered hoarsely. 'Come on, Jonah, you can do this. You got your smokestone, didn't you? We need to know we can count on you.'

Jonah said nothing. He could feel the sweat oozing all over his body. He knew the longer he was in here, the more likely he'd be bitten or gash himself on the sharp glass like Motti said – and then what would he do? Ask Samraj for a plaster?

Slowly, carefully, he pulled himself into the cage. Kneeling now, he felt a squat head push itself against his cheek, felt the tickle of its tongue, held absolutely still for a few moments. When the head pulled away he reached cautiously up, felt the glass lid of the cage. 'Please,' he murmured, pushing with all his strength, trying to ignore the tail that slithered round his wrist. 'Please . . .'

With a quiet crack, the lid gave way. Forcing himself to keep his movements slow and controlled, he eased away the heavy glass panel and straightened up. The cage stood as high as his hips.

Placing the lid quietly on top of the neighbouring enclosure, Jonah started to pull himself clear. 'All right, we've got a way in. Now could one of you help me get this bloody great python off my ankle?' A few seconds later he felt a pair of hands forcing their way under the reptile-flesh, coaxing away the weight. The second he thought it was safe to do so, Jonah pulled his leg free and clambered out of the enclosure. He stood shaking and sweaty in the humid, fetid atmosphere, listening to the sibilant hissing all around him. In the gloomy glow from the torch, he could see it was a real Snakes-R-Us, packed with reptiles of all kinds and colours.

Motti joined him a few seconds later. He was breathing a little shakily but seemed otherwise unbothered.

'Didn't have this down on your plans, did you?'

said Jonah quietly.

'It's all custom built,' Motti observed. 'Explains why they've built against that outside wall. Still, I don't think the bastards are poisonous.'

'I don't think they're pets, either,' said Jonah. The walls and floor were tiled an antiseptic white, like a hospital or something. 'So many of them, caged in together? That's not right, is it?'

Motti scowled and shrugged. 'We'll write to the humane society when we get out of here, 'K?'

'Boo!' whispered Patch, clambering out of the cage holding some nasty-looking green snake over his head. 'Oi, Mot, think we can take him with us?'

'Think you'd enjoy my boot in your mouth? Come on, we've wasted enough time.'

Patch put back the snake almost sadly, and Motti led the way over to the door. It led on to a tiled corridor that again put Jonah in mind of something medical.

'Is that a lab?' Patch wondered, peering through a doorway. 'Motti, look here!'

Jonah looked too. It *was* a lab, all sorts of gear and gizmos hogging the workbenches. As Motti played his torch around the room, they saw a kind of operating table. A white sheet had been laid over it, flecked with spots of blood, covering something.

Motti pulled it back to reveal a small snake, incisions made down the length of its body.

'Gross.' Patch screwed up his nose. 'Samraj ain't just a bitch, she's a butcher. What the hell's going on here?'

Motti put the cover back over the mutilated body.

'Let's just find the fragments and get the hell out of here.'

'Will there be any more security?' asked Jonah.

'Doubt it,' said Motti. 'Lights are still on, must mean people are about – so the PIRs inside won't be set yet.'

'But we could walk right into Samraj or whoever!'

'You never hear of audacious theft?' he grinned. 'This is *bo*dacious, man. Now, the documents are supposed to be in a hidden safe in the drawing room.'

'How'd you know?' asked Jonah.

'He doesn't,' said Patch. 'Coldhardt does.'

Once out of the lab area, the house became more traditional. It was plush and opulently furnished as you might expect, if kind of oppressive with all the huge, dark oil landscapes and portraits staring out from the walls. Jonah saw large, bluff figures in bright military colours, slim, demure maidens with wide, dark eyes and uneasy smiles. It felt uncomfortably like the paintings were watching his progress through the house, and from the way Patch sent nervous looks in every direction, it seemed he was feeling uneasy too.

Motti, on the other hand, didn't spare the pictures a glance. He must have been acquainted with the layout of the main building, as he led them through it quite confidently. Jonah couldn't believe his nerve. Good thing there were no seismic detectors inside the place – never mind the footsteps, his pounding heart could set one off on its own.

'I don't know, Samraj . . .'

Jonah nearly hit the ceiling at the sound of the voice. It was a woman speaking, slow, stolid English with a strong accent, and it was coming from behind the door of the room they'd just passed.

Motti and Patch spun round at the sound too. Jonah pointed to the door. 'In there,' he mouthed.

'You're certain we are close to a breakthrough?' the woman's voice went on. 'After all this time?'

Jonah crept away, holding his breath. The thought of Samraj and her guest catching him here wasn't a happy one.

'Chill,' said Motti. 'If they're gassing away in there, we got the run of the place, don't we?'

He joined the others, moving swiftly but stealthily over the deep pile carpeting.

Their luck was in. The drawing room was empty. Motti made a beeline for some weird, abstract painting showing an angel with moth-eaten wings hunched over a filthy bed, and carefully removed it to reveal a small grey combination safe.

'Doesn't look like much,' Jonah observed.

'It *ain't* much.' Motti chuckled, putting down the picture. 'Gotta love these rich houseproud types. They blow a bomb doing big-time security on the grounds and they think no one'll get as far as the crap like this. This safe came out of the ark, man, just like Coldhardt said.'

'Probably the most valuable antique in the place.' Jonah watched Patch reach into his shoulder bag and pull out an old-fashioned telephone receiver. 'Unless *that* is. What're you going to do, phone a friend?'

'This is all you need to crack an old-time safe like this,' Patch explained, unscrewing the mouthpiece. 'The amplifier in here lets you hear the clicks of the safe dial like someone's snapping their fingers in your ear.' He fished out a small metal disc attached by short, coloured wires. 'You note down the numbers that set the tumblers clicking, then try out each combination of them till –'

'Get on with it, Cyclops,' said Motti, who was now keeping watch in the doorway.

Jonah felt a bit of a spare part. He crossed to the window, looked out into the grounds. Different darknesses of sky and shadow loured over the silent orchard. Nothing moved.

He started as the safe door opened with a noisy creak.

'We're in,' Patch breathed, putting down his phone.

'OK, geek, take over the watch.' Motti crossed back to the safe and reached gingerly inside. 'This has gotta be it. Could be rigged. Incendiary or . . .'

'Could be cursed,' said Patch.

Motti pulled a small cedar casket out of the safe, placed it on a writing desk and started muttering something quietly. His saturnine features looked almost demonic in the uplight from Patch's torch as the strange, arcane syllables tripped darkly from his tongue. It sounded to Jonah like some ancient prayer, but to what god or spirit he couldn't hazard a guess.

Slowly, Motti opened the cedar chest. 'We got 'em,' he muttered, carefully removing what looked like bits of old leaf that had somehow blown inside.

'The fragments,' breathed Patch, pulling a tiny camera from his shoulder bag. 'Lay 'em down on the desk and I'll get snapping.'

Jonah watched, fascinated by the speed and precision with which they worked. But then Patch caught him looking and frowned over his camera. 'The door, Jonah!' he urged him.

Jonah nodded, turned and checked for signs of movement outside.

His heart almost stopped as he saw a small figure across the darkened hallway, hunched up and half-lost to the shadows at the back of the room.

He ducked out of sight, but knew he'd been much too slow.

Motti and Patch caught the sudden movement.

'Trouble?' Motti demanded, gathering up the scraps of parchment and replacing them in the cedar chest.

'I saw someone!' Jonah hissed. Terrified, he peeped back around the side of the door, but the figure had departed as silently as it arrived.

'He saw me,' he breathed. 'Must have done.'

'You useless dick! You had one job to do . . .' Motti passed the little chest to Patch, who stuck it back in the safe. 'Which way did they go?'

'Back the way we came.'

Patch pocketed the camera and hastily hung the painting on the wall. He turned to Motti. 'So we gotta find a new way out?'

'It's OK. We ain't so far from the main entrance. If the alarms go off now, we got nothing to lose going out that way.' He barged Jonah aside from the doorway. 'Let's move it.'

Jonah felt sick with fear as he stumbled after the others. Any second now, the alarms would sound, steel shutters would slam down all around them, cutting off any hope of escape . . .

Only they didn't. The house stayed cloaked in a silence as thick as the shadows.

'You sure you didn't dream this figure you saw?' Motti demanded, his fingers hovering over a thick, heavy bolt on the massive oak door.

'I swear someone was there.'

'Only I don't hear no alarm bells . . .' Patch looked apologetic. 'And you've been pretty jumpy, Jonah.'

'Maybe they thought we were the cleaners,' said Motti sourly. 'Aw, this is bullshit.'

'I tell you I *saw* someone. Right when you were saying . . .' he shrugged, '. . . whatever it was you were saying.'

'Ancient Inuit prayer for protection 'gainst evil,' whispered Motti. 'Good all-purpose curse-buster, since Tye ain't around to work her voodoo.'

'Please say you're joking,' sighed Jonah.

'*Something* scared off your little shadow, right?' Motti started retracing his footsteps. 'C'mon, we should get the hell out of here. We are seriously pushing our luck.'

Jonah felt a mixture of relief and humiliation as he once again tagged on after the others. They wound their furtive way through the splendid halls and corridors. Somehow, the atmosphere seemed more threatening than before. Dark, accusing eyes stared down from the portraits. Suits of armour stood poised, ready to strike out at them without warning.

All three of them slowed down as they neared the room where they'd heard the woman's voice, but it was silent now, its door still firmly closed.

After what seemed like hours, they reached the

white, clinical tiles of the snake lab and the hothouse beyond. Jonah almost welcomed its stifling heat. It was a sign they were nearly out.

'Patch, you go first,' said Motti, 'clear the way of critters, since you like 'em so much. Then I'll go through with the bag. Jonah, wait till I'm well clear, then follow us through. We'll both help you out through the crawl space, but take it nice and slow, 'K?'

Jonah didn't argue. A little bruised pride was the least of his problems right now.

Patch shone his torch into the glass case through which they'd entered the house. There were no snakes there now – perhaps they had slithered outside? Jonah chewed his lip as Patch clambered into the case and twisted himself round ready to take on the crawl space. Once he'd vanished from sight, Jonah gave Motti a hand getting inside. Motti pushed his bag and torch through the hole first, then started to wriggle carefully after them.

For a moment Jonah stood alone, uneasy in the thick, hissing darkness, waiting for the all-clear.

'Leaving so soon?'

There was someone else there with him. A woman's voice, quiet and foreign. She sounded amused. Jonah swung round to see, but there was only blackness and shadow all around.

'Perhaps you are lost? I do not think you are where you think you are . . .'

Jonah scrambled inside the case, ducked down and shoved himself into the crawl space. 'Someone's here,' he shouted.

Motti shone the torch in his eyes, shushing him. 'Are you crazy?'

'It's no good! We've got to run for it!' He pushed forward, catching his arm on the glass as he tried to muscle through. A hard, sickening slide through his flesh, and the skin burnt hot. He gasped.

'Take it slow, Jonah,' hissed Patch. 'God, Mott, he's cut himself.'

'Hold still, you're gonna break the . . . Patch, help me with him!'

Jonah felt their arms gripping his, hauling him out. The glass scraped his shin through his jeans, caught on his shoe – but somehow it didn't break, the alarm didn't sound. The grass was sweet-smelling, cool against his hot face.

'Get up,' said Motti gruffly. 'Now!'

'Shit! He's bleeding a lot.' Patch sounded panicked. 'Can we carry him?'

'We gotta walk light to beat the sensors.'

'There was someone in there, I'm telling you!' Jonah whispered hoarsely. 'She'll hit the alarms! We have to run –'

'Jonah, you gotta hold it together, OK?' Motti's glasses were sliding down his nose, but he held Jonah's stare, as if willing him to calm. 'It's OK. Be cool. Breathe. It's OK.'

'I'm sorry,' Jonah croaked, getting a hold on himself. 'But I swear she was in there, Motti, watching us.'

'Like whoever that was watching us in the hall?'

Jonah squared up to him. 'I didn't imagine it!'

Patch laughed nervously. 'Maybe it was a snake?'

'It sounded like that woman in the room we heard talking to Samraj.'

'The dark plays tricks on us,' Motti said soothingly. 'You got a little freaked out in there, buddy, but you're OK . . . and now we gotta go.'

Jonah bit his tongue, nodded meekly. He supposed there would be time to argue the toss later – if they made it out in one piece. He stared down at his arm, which was starting to throb like hell, glad of the black clothes that hid the sticky wetness of the wound, the damage done.

Patch tore off some duct tape and wrapped it tight round his arm, a makeshift tourniquet. 'That good?'

'Hurts like hell.'

'Hell is what happens if we get caught,' said Motti quietly, cautiously leading them away from the house. 'You remember that.'

Their luck lasted as far as the outer wall.

The rubber footholds Motti had applied so painstakingly should have made the climb easy, and Jonah did his best to scale the brickwork as lightly and carefully as Patch and Motti had before him. But the cut in his calf was stinging sharply: he could feel sticky blood soaking his trouser leg, dribbling into his sock and shoe. Just as he was nearing the top he scraped the wound against one of the footholds and gasped with pain, gripped the wall to stop himself from falling.

And the goddamn alarms finally went off. The din and blare was incredible, even all the way out here.

Motti swore. 'Get the hell down from there, numbnuts!' Jonah threw himself down from the top of the wall, landed awkwardly and rolled over. Motti grabbed him by his good arm and hauled him up. 'What the hell did you do?'

'I'm sorry. My leg, I cut it on the glass . . .'

Patch slipped an arm round Jonah's back, tried to help Motti take his weight, though he was too small to be a lot of help. 'You did your leg in and you never told us?'

'I didn't want to make a fuss –'

'If we'd known, we coulda helped you,' Motti grunted. 'You don't get extra points for trying to be a hero.' He and Patch broke into a shambling run down the slope of the olive grove, half dragging, half carrying Jonah between them. 'God knows who's gonna come running at those alarm bells. But maybe if you're real lucky, there'll be a priest among 'em.'

'A priest?'

'Sure,' said Motti darkly. 'He can read you the last fricking rites once I've kicked your ass all over this goddamn olive grove.'

'At least it proves one thing that was bugging me, Mot,' Patch piped up. 'I was starting to think the alarms had been done before we got there. You know, like in Cairo. That it was maybe a set-up.'

'Well, hey, cool, guess the geek's done us a good turn,' muttered Motti. 'He's reminded us we're just the best there is. When we don't have a goddamn amateur screwing things up for us.'

Jonah listened to the deranged howl of the sirens. He didn't say a word. What the hell *could* he say?

When Motti judged that they'd covered a safe distance, they lay low in bushes for most of the night, awkward and uncomfortable. At one point a helicopter swooped in over the house like a UFO, blazing with light as it circled the area and then descended on the grounds.

'Think it's the cops?' said Patch.

Motti shrugged. 'Like I say. When someone like Samraj gets ripped off, it ain't just the cops she calls.'

When the helicopter departed, the dark countryside fell quiet save for the drowsy thrum of the cicadas. Jonah's arm throbbed in time with their song, and his leg was killing him. Sometimes he drifted into fevered catnaps, and each time he heard the woman's voice again in his head and woke with a start. He pictured her as some hunched and hideous witch, holding vigil in the shadows with her snake familiars, watching him through unearthly eyes.

As the morning sun began to warm the cold grey soup of cloud and sky, Jonah watched the beautiful Tuscan countryside resolve itself around him. Right now, he wished he could trade the whole lot for the hard, safe slab of mattress in his old cell.

'C'mon,' said Motti suddenly. 'I think maybe it's safe to move now. The car's another half-mile.'

'Is that all?' sighed Patch. 'What if they're still out searching for us?'

'We should see 'em coming now it's getting light.' He glanced at Jonah. 'You OK to walk?'

'Walk . . .' Jonah nodded to himself. 'Yeah, maybe it's time I did exactly that.'

'I'm . . .' Motti shrugged. 'I'm sorry for losing it with you, OK, man? I know it's early days for you. It wasn't your fault.'

'Yes, it was,' said Jonah. 'And I could have got you both killed.'

'Well, now you've learned for next time,' said Patch. 'Ain'tcha?'

'C'mon. Time to move on.' Motti struck out on to the path that led down into the sleepy hamlet. Patch followed him in silence, rubbing his fingers distractedly across the leather over his missing eye.

Jonah hung back a few seconds. Then he trailed along behind, like driftwood towed in their wake.

CHAPTER THIRTEEN

Jonah's elation at making it back to the car and escaping Bellosguardo soon bled away at the prospect of having to explain his foul-ups to the chief. Next to the crushing sense of humiliation he felt, his injuries were little more than scratches.

'Relax,' Motti said, burning rubber as they tore back up the autostrade. 'I'll square things with Coldhardt.'

'Yeah.' Patch was back hunched over his Game Boy. 'The important thing is, we got away with the stuff he wanted. The rest is just details.'

'I'll call ahead, make sure there's a doctor waitin' for you,' Motti added.

'Thanks,' said Jonah. 'I don't – I mean . . .' He sighed. 'No one's ever watched out for me like this before. You know?'

Patch actually looked up at him from his busy screen. 'Told you. We watch each other's backs.'

'Even after I screwed up the whole thing?'

'Will you quit beating yourself up?' Motti threw a grin back over his shoulder. 'That's *my* job! Just promise me one thing, geek.'

'What's that?'

'That you ain't bleedin' over my seats. 'Cause if you are, you're gonna know what bleedin' really is, right?'

Jonah smiled. 'Right.'

He slipped in and out of sleep. The journey seemed to take hours, even at Motti's breakneck speed, but finally the buzz of Coldhardt's gates woke Jonah properly. They were back in the grounds, but he felt no better. His failure weighed heavy on his mind.

'Tye and Con ain't back till this afternoon,' Motti reported, as he swung the car into a large, air-conditioned garage. 'So, unlucky – you got no nubile nurses to fetch you drinks and stuff.'

Jonah just grunted.

Patch staggered out of the car and threw up into an empty bucket standing beside a Land Rover, doubtless placed there for just that reason. 'You need a hand getting to your room?' he muttered, wiping his mouth.

'I can manage it,' said Jonah. He wasn't at all sure he really could, but he decided he'd already shown himself up enough today.

A suited doctor was waiting in his apartment in the castello grounds to stitch him up. He asked no questions, worked swiftly and in silence then got the hell away. Jonah felt the sudden urge to ask him for a lift out of here. *I can pay you*, he wanted to say. *I have this diamond, you see.*

He looked at it now, nestling in his sweaty palm. Then he hurled it into the cold stone fireplace.

Take it. It's worth a hell of a lot more than I am.

Tye wished Coldhardt would up the lighting a little

for these debriefs. She was dog-tired, both from the long flight back and the partying the night before – and they hadn't even had time to grab a shower before being summoned to the hub. Con sat beside her, a touch of pink about her skin from the sun they'd caught in Aqaba. Shame that was about the only thing they'd managed to bring back with them.

'You found no trace of the car with the fake plates?' Coldhardt enquired.

Con shook her head. 'A no-show in the car park, and no record of it ever having been there. Not in the visitors' log, anyway.'

'Oh, right, I can see them signing in to the building,' said Motti sourly. '"Name? *Masked Pseudo-religious Maniac.* Organisation? *Cult of Ophiuchus.* Car registration? *Shit, one of yours, actually –*"'

'Thank you, Motti,' said Coldhardt heavily.

Tye rolled her eyes at Motti, but she was smiling. He was always noisy after he got away with something. Like Patch, the buzz kept him going for days. Jonah, on the other hand, seemed quiet and withdrawn, staring at the blank screens on the wall like he could see something there. She doubted it was just the disappointment that, so far, his code-cracking programs had turned up nothing on the mysterious cipher.

'Tye,' said Coldhardt suddenly, 'what news of the lekythos?'

'It was there maybe twenty-four hours. Samraj's assistant booked a top level courier the morning after the black Chrysler showed up.' She glanced at Con. 'According to the dispatch boys, a "package" was transported by the courier to an address in Rome.'

'Well, well. I wonder why she kept it there for twenty-four hours?'

'I don't know. There was nothing special about the labs at Aqaba,' Con told him. 'Just boring foodstuff research. We think it may have been a drop-off point, the nearest Serpens offices.'

'The nearest by car, perhaps,' Coldhardt agreed. 'By plane, the Turkish and Italian facilities would be far easier to reach.'

'They might not get the vase through customs,' Patch argued.

'Yeah, and can you imagine their passport photos?' Motti snorted. 'Any distinguishing features? *Big black veil-thing over face.*'

'I think we can assume that their resources might stretch to bypassing traditional routes in and out of the country,' Coldhardt surmised. 'But since you're feeling so loquacious, Motti, please give Tye and Con your field report.'

Jonah stiffened.

Motti explained that they'd photographed the fragments as instructed, and went on at length about how his ingenious plan of entry had been executed. When he got on to the snakes they'd braved in the hothouse and the gory discovery in the lab, Tye turned up her nose.

'The fragments are of a manuscript written in Ancient Greek, unencrypted, allegedly from the pen of Ophiuchus himself,' Coldhardt announced. 'I've attempted a preliminary translation. "The root of the snake" is mentioned – possibly as an ingredient of the Amrita.'

Patch nodded. 'Is that why Samraj is torturing the snakes, then – she's looking for their roots?'

Coldhardt paused and smiled. 'She's doing many things in her quest for this secret. She is a first-class biologist.'

'First-class bitch, more like,' Con whispered. But Tye was more interested in the way Coldhardt had carefully evaded the question. What was it about Samraj that made him so secretive?

'Well, Samraj was there when we did the place,' Motti went on. 'Coulda turned us into one of her specimens.'

Coldhardt frowned deeply. 'You didn't mention this before.'

'Some woman was talking to her in one of the rooms we passed.'

'You *saw* Samraj?'

'No, the door was closed,' said Jonah, breaking his silence.

'Then it's possible you misheard,' said Coldhardt thoughtfully. 'I understand the atmosphere there was rather highly charged. Jonah, Motti mentioned you thought you actually saw somebody watching you.'

Jonah glanced at Motti, swallowed hard. 'Yes. I'm sure I did.'

'And do you believe, as he does, that it was this person who activated the alarms upon your attempted escape?'

Tye noticed Motti staring at Jonah, nodding his head a fraction, encouraging him to agree. You didn't need uncanny instincts to know that something bad had kicked off at the mansion, and that it involved Jonah up to his cute choirboy's neck.

'I don't know,' Jonah faltered, blushing. 'I s'pose it's possible . . .'

'All things are possible.' Coldhardt smiled, leaned back in his seat. 'The important thing is, you got away safely with a record of the contents of that safe, as instructed.'

Tye was watching Coldhardt closely. Motti wasn't the only one covering something up. Coldhardt didn't believe that Samraj was in that house for a moment, or that this mystery woman had hit the alarms – but for whatever reason, he had decided to keep his opinions to himself. She supposed that was his prerogative. A boss spared his workforce the details of how the business was run, and a parent didn't tell his children everything . . .

Why then did she feel so uneasy?

Once they were dismissed, Jonah walked back to the hangout with the others. But while the four of them chatted and caught up, he kept a stony silence.

Motti swung open the double doors into the hang-out and led the way inside. 'Hey, geek. How you feelin'?'

'The lengths some people will go to get out of train-ing,' said Tye.

Still Jonah kept silent.

'Hey, I'm talking to you,' said Motti, tapping on Jonah's head. 'Or did the doc stitch your mouth up along with your arm and leg?'

'Why'd you lie back there, Mot?' Jonah demanded. 'You know it was me who set off the alarms.'

Con frowned. 'You did?'

'I screwed up climbing the wall.'

'He was badly hurt,' said Patch quickly.

Motti nodded. 'Geek had some kind of panic attack –'

'Look, you don't believe me about seeing – *hearing* – that woman in the house,' said Jonah hotly. 'And yet you told Coldhardt that *she* was the one who hit the alarms.'

'So sue me.' Motti shrugged. 'I was just trying to save your sorry ass from a roasting. Anyways, it's done now, so forget it. Coldhardt don't care – we got what he wanted and got out ourselves. Next time it'll come easier, and you won't louse up.'

'There won't be a next time,' said Jonah quietly.

It was as if his words crushed every sound in the place. There was just silence and staring.

Motti glared at him. 'Say what?'

Jonah shrugged. 'I can't live my life like this. You're all brilliant at what you do, but . . .'

'C'mon, Jonah . . .' Patch looked at him uncertainly. 'You're still new to it. Mot'll tell you, I screwed up enough when I –'

'I don't want this,' said Jonah. He looked at Tye but she was staring at the floor. 'I should just go before I let you down again. I could have got all of us caught last night. It could have been one of you who got hurt, not me.'

'Let *us* worry about ourselves, Jonah, yes?' said Con.

'Yeah, come on, mate,' said Patch, smiling hopefully. 'You're just tired and upset. We had a rough old night – it happens. But we still got what we –'

'You just don't get it, do you?' Jonah rounded on

them, felt his cheeks flushing. 'I can't hack it the way you all can. I'm no good to you.'

Motti's face soured further. 'Aw, save us the bullshit self-pity!'

'It's not just that. I really like you guys, but . . .' He looked away from them. 'I never wanted to be a thief.'

'This is not about being a thief,' said Con. 'There *are* no thieves like us.'

'This is your only shot at being somebody, Jonah,' said Motti quietly. 'You wanna go back to how you had it in jail?'

'Your life isn't for me. I wish it was, but –' He shook his head, miserably. He knew he sounded like some whining little kid but he just couldn't help it. 'I don't want to talk about it any more. OK?'

Tye was looking at him. She looked like she was about to say something.

But then a vintage black phone rang close by, with a big old-fashioned ring.

'It's the Bat-phone,' said Patch, nervously. 'D'you think he –'

'This place is clean, man,' Motti told him. 'Coldhardt don't listen in on us.'

Con answered the phone. 'Yes, Coldhardt?' She listened for a few seconds, then put the phone down and looked over at Jonah. 'He wants to see you.'

Jonah raised his eyebrows. 'Well. I s'pose I want to see him too.'

'Don't tell him you're leaving us, Jonah,' said Patch. He rubbed furiously at the leather patch over his eye. 'We ain't never had no one leave us. It's – it's bad luck!'

'Aw, save your breath, man.' Motti gave Jonah a look that was part scorn, part pity. 'He ain't worth it. Let Coldhardt handle him.'

Jonah turned away. Told himself he didn't care what they thought. He was used to being on the outside. Used to not belonging.

Besides, this wasn't who he wanted to be, he reminded himself. This was a million miles away.

Just one more situation that hadn't worked out.

It seemed to take him an hour to reach the door. He felt the eyes of the others on his back, but nobody said a word.

Perhaps the ones Motti had uttered were enough.

'*Let Coldhardt handle him.*'

Jonah spent the whole way to the junior hub rehearsing his reasons for quitting. He was dreading what Coldhardt would say.

The old man was hunched over his computer when Jonah arrived. 'I think you've done it,' he announced. 'The cipher has been cracked. Look here.'

Jonah hurried over to the screen, a little excitement and the old attitude sweeping him along. *Please Coldhardt and he'll like you better. Make this work out for him and he'll let you go.* 'God, look at that! The message put up a hell of a fight – multiple encryption to disguise character frequency . . .'

'You mean the way that Es and As occur more than Zs and Xs.'

'Yeah. But this level of encryption, without a computer it would take you, well . . .' He shrugged. 'I s'pose they didn't have TV in those days – whenever

177

those days were, precisely.'

'Maybe they attempted to be too clever,' said Coldhardt gravely.

Jonah studied the legible words in between the garbled random characters a bug in the program still threw up. 'Head of snake, dog of the shepherd . . . hand before . . . the preceding . . .' He frowned. 'It's gibberish. Like that Spartan scytale you got me to decrypt – what was that again?'

'Catacombs . . . north . . . stars buried in patterns.'

'Doesn't give you much to go on, does it? What does any of this have to do with the Amrita prescription?'

Coldhardt looked at him, impassive. 'There couldn't be a glitch in the translation software?'

Jonah shook his head. 'Sometimes the order of the words gets a bit messed up – like, "hand before" could be "beforehand", I s'pose. But for this job I programmed the decryption engine to hack into ancient language translation databases when sorting out the characters.' He smiled – *Like me! Like me!* 'I targeted the best, put together by professors at Oxford and Yale, for academic use only.'

'Most impressive,' Coldhardt murmured.

Jonah peered at the results more closely. 'It came up with numbers too?'

'Indeed. My first thought was that they were co-ordinates. But with no reference point from which to start . . .'

'We could translate the words *back* into Ancient Greek, see if they correspond to any place names?'

'I have done so,' Coldhardt looked at him, his blue

eyes pale and chill. 'No match – not to any known geographical site on any map, from classical Greco-Roman well into medieval times.'

'These place names could be coded in some other way. Or based on local nicknames, not official ones.'

'And without that knowledge, we can't construct a key.'

Jonah nodded slowly. He felt a crushing sense of anticlimax. 'It doesn't make sense. Why encode information so carefully if the plaintext is meaningless to all but a few locals anyway?'

'The parts of the lekythos that Samraj now holds must contain further information,' Coldhardt surmised. 'We need to reclaim them from that address in Rome. That must be our next mission.'

'I . . . I need to talk to you about that.'

'Oh?' Coldhardt looked at him expectantly.

He couldn't meet the force in those icy eyes, looked down at the floor. 'I don't want to stay with you. I want to go back.'

'To what?' said Coldhardt, quite unruffled, like he'd been expecting as much. 'The Young Offenders' Institution?'

'If I have to.' Jonah paused, chanced his arm. 'Though if you don't want your rivals to know I'm back on the market, maybe you could place me somewhere a little less obvious.'

A soft, cold chuckle. 'Clever, logical and self-serving. I like that, Jonah.'

'I'm grateful for the opportunity you've given me,' he said carefully. 'But this life isn't for me. I don't belong here.'

'Are you so sure? I pride myself on my instincts in these matters.' Coldhardt paused. 'Perhaps I'm getting old.'

'I'd like to get old myself,' said Jonah. 'I can't see that happening if I live at your speed.'

'It's not only old that you'll grow, Jonah. You'll grow bitter, dissatisfied. You'll look back on this moment as the biggest mistake of your long, pointless life.'

'I've made up my mind.'

'You think you'll be safe back in your own world? You're a wanted man. You'll always be looking back over your shoulder.'

'It was a year-long sentence for theft,' Jonah reminded him. 'I hardly think I'm on the Most Wanted list –'

Coldhardt's eyes looked haunted. 'I'm not talking about the police wanting you, Jonah.' He turned to the marble statuette on his desk, the man and the demon locked in combat. 'And away from my fold, I can't protect you.'

Jonah swallowed. 'You're just trying to scare me.'

'We each of us have to face our own fears on our own terms.' His old, pale fingers caressed the unblemished marble. 'Resist the devil and he will flee from you, the Bible teaches. But that's simply not true, Jonah. He will return again and again. And each time, with a deal a little less fair than the one you refused the last time. Yet as the life you pursue gets harder, as second and third chances slip through your fingers . . .

there will come a time when you grasp that clawed, hot little hand in partnership. And you will have lost so much.'

'I'm not sure what you're saying,' Jonah admitted, 'but it sounds like you're speaking from experience.'

'When I was a young man, Jonah, a proposition was made to me as you would not . . .' Coldhardt tailed off, staring into space. 'But enough of this. If you feel you must leave us, so be it.'

'Just like that?'

'Please go to your apartment now. Don't tell the others what we've talked about here.' Still Coldhardt wouldn't look at him. 'I told you what would happen if you refused me. You'll be removed from here tonight and taken somewhere.'

'Where?' Jonah said uneasily.

'I doubt it will be anywhere you've heard of.'

'So don't I – can't I say goodbye to the others?'

'What do you care, Jonah?' The voice was a cold caress. 'You're not like us. You don't belong here, remember. Not in our world.'

'Have I earned anything for what I've done for you so far?'

'You've earned the right to walk away with your life,' Coldhardt whispered. 'No payment. This job is far from over, and your part in it unfinished. You'll leave here with the clothes you stand in, nothing more. Now, there are arrangements I must make. Leave me now.'

Jonah opened his mouth, to argue or to apologise again he wasn't quite sure. But there was nothing more to say.

He left the man, still tracing the outline of the cold stone with his fingertips.

Come two in the morning, Jonah lay fully dressed on his bed, alert to every sound outside.

Misshapen shadows danced about the room in the smoky light of the oil lamp beside him. He couldn't sleep, couldn't rest.

Where's the smokestone?

He'd searched the cold grate and fireplace for it. He'd decided that if Coldhardt would give him nothing for the risks he'd taken – well, then. He would take it and sell it.

Or rather, he would if it hadn't disappeared. It was either a fake and had shattered in the grate or, somehow, Coldhardt must have got it back. This was his workplace, after all.

The rules, and the terms, were his.

And that had set Jonah thinking. What if Coldhardt *wasn't* going to set him free? Wouldn't it be so much quicker and easier to have him killed?

No one will know I'm dead, he realised. *And no one will mourn.*

However he left here tonight, it would be alone.

He started as the twiggy tips of the mulberry tree scraped against the panes of his bedroom window, his thoughts chasing their tails. What could he do? Strike out now, make a run for it? How far would he get? No, he was panicking needlessly. Coldhardt would release him as arranged. He had to . . .

Then he heard a quieter scrape. A flurry of light footsteps in the bathroom.

Jonah sat up on the bed. 'Who's there?' he challenged, his voice cracking.

'It's just me.' Con came out of the bathroom. She was wearing a plain dress with a scoop neck, as white as her skin. The oily light made her look almost jaundiced, and her shadow danced ten times as large behind her. 'Hello, Jonah.'

'What's the matter?' said Jonah. 'Flush broken in yours?'

'I did not want to be seen coming here.' She looked at him, much as she had the first time she had come to him in his cell, half-knowing, half-curious. 'Is it true you're really going?'

He nodded, watching her warily as she walked towards him.

But she only smiled as she sat on the end of the bed. 'I couldn't let you go without saying goodbye, now, could I?'

'Coldhardt said I wasn't allowed to –'

'We don't have long.' Con started crawling along the bed towards him, the open neck of her dress gaping, leaving little to the imagination. Jonah looked up and into her eyes, which were fixed on his own. 'I had hoped we would grow to like each other properly over time. But life is too short to pass up opportunities, yes?' A look of sadness played around her face. 'Or so *I* believe.'

Then she was leaning in to him, her glossy lips parting as they pressed against his in a thick, smearing kiss. Their tongues touched, mouths opened wider. The fingers of her right hand coiled around the back of his neck, scrunched up his hair.

Then gently she pulled away. Her eyes were

shining. 'You will forget me, Jonah.'

'I won't,' he whispered, the taste of her lipstick on his tongue.

'Yes, you will,' she insisted. 'You will forget me. All of us.'

He shook his head, gave her a puzzled smile.

'It will be as if we did not meet.'

He leaned in to kiss her again but she shook her head softly, pressed her cold palm to his lips. Her eyes held his own, her voice calm and steady, soothing. 'For you, it will be like none of this has ever happened. You will forget everything. Everything that has happened since the date of –'

Jonah realised what she was doing, dragged himself free from her spell. He grabbed her hand and twisted it and she gasped. 'Bitch!' he hissed. 'Coldhardt sent you here, didn't he?'

'You know so much about us, Jonah,' she whispered, pulling her hand away. 'Enough to make you dangerous to us. And to make yourself a target.'

'So you mess with my mind? Take away my memories?'

'Isn't it better this way?' Her eyes were hard. 'You want to leave us, Jonah, remember? To turn your back on all we have offered you.'

'Like that kiss, like your friendship. It's all fake.'

'You want fake?' Her expression grew colder. 'You are right, I was sent here to reprogram you. But I didn't. If I'd really meant to, Jonah, you'd be out like a light by now. You'd be waking up somewhere foreign and strange with no clue how you got there, no money, no protection.' She looked away, eased herself off the bed. 'I can't do that to you, Jonah. So we fake it, yes?'

'You'd do that?'

'Go to the main gates and wait for the car. Take nothing. Say nothing.' The lamplight sputtered violently as she crossed back towards the bathroom. 'Act spaced when they come for you. Convince the driver, for both our sakes.'

'Con, wait –'

'Take care of yourself, Jonah Wish.' She disappeared inside the door.

He got up from the bed to follow her, but the rattle of the window told him she'd gone before he'd taken more than a couple of steps.

Jonah listened for any sound of her outside, but there was only the scrape of the branches in the warm breeze, tapping at the glass like they wanted to come in.

He waited five minutes, then he left the apartment. A fine rain was falling. Moisture ghosted on his face and he wiped it crossly away from his eyes. The grass dampened his trainers as he walked.

The moon was close to full, and Jonah glimpsed movement at the gates. Tye, maybe? He felt like such an idiot after what had happened with Con . . . It would be good to see Tye again, to say goodbye. Acting spaced, as ordered, at first he pretended not to notice. But then, with a twist of disappointment, he saw it was Patch.

'We had a bit of a collection for you, Jonah.' Patch glanced about quickly, clearly afraid he would be seen.

'Me, Tye, Motti. We didn't want you going with nothing.'

He held out a thick wad of euros.

Jonah hesitated a few moments before taking it gratefully. 'Thanks, Patch.'

'Con didn't chip in. She don't hand over money to no one if she can help it. But you still know who we are, don't you? *That's* what she's given you.'

Jonah nodded. 'I won't forget a thing. Not a minute of it.'

'I'm sorry it didn't work out, mate.' Patch heaved a sad sigh. 'Anyway, here's some extra. From me.' He held out a slimmer wad of notes.

'You don't need to.'

'Nah, go on, take it. I can afford it.' He closed Jonah's fingers round the money and gave him a conspiratorial smile. 'I been saving, see.'

'Yeah?'

'One day, when I've saved up enough, maybe I can get myself a real eye. A proper one, that I can see through and everything.' He smiled. 'And I'll find my mum and say, "It don't matter what you did to me, Mum – look. Look, you can forgive yourself now, I got my eye back again."'

Jonah just stared at him, pity and admiration all mixed up and choking his throat. The rain was falling harder, a summer storm. He pulled up the collar on his thin jacket. 'You know, I never thought to ask your real name.'

'Patch *is* my real name. Long time ago I used to be Patrick Kendall, no fixed abode. Used, abused, no offer refused.' He shrugged, pinged the black elastic on his face. 'That's why I'm happy to wear this thing, even when I got a false eye in. Reckon being Patch saved my life.'

A pair of powerful headlights swung into view, strobing past the railings of the main gate, illuminating the rain like a billion fireflies.

'Be careful, Jonah.' The boy gave him an awkward hug, and stole away into the darkness.

Jonah stood alone in the bright rain, slipped his money into his pocket out of sight. Here he was, ready to go off and face the unknown. Turning his back on people who could have been real friends. On maybe the biggest opportunity of his life.

The gates hummed open. The giant palms shook in the wind.

Jonah took a few stumbling steps towards the large, dark car. He paused and looked back through the rain, though there was nothing and no one to see in the bright-daggered dark.

Then someone got out of the car, took his arm, steered him towards it. Jonah leaned back heavily in the back seat, his wet clothes snagging on the leather upholstery. His eyes felt hot as the driver took him away into the night along its twisted, narrow lanes.

CHAPTER FOURTEEN

Tye viewed the washed-out grey morning through the window and wished she'd said goodbye to Jonah in person. She'd spent so much of her childhood saying goodbye. Goodbye to guys who took what they wanted and left. To friends, clawing their way out of the slums on to better things, or as they were lowered into the ground. To chances for change, when she'd jacked in school again or walked out on Dad – or when she'd been bullied, bludgeoned or blackmailed into one more run, one last time.

She didn't know what to say at goodbyes any more.

But she knew she was hurting somewhere – some soft, half-forgotten part she had little use for these days. As long ago as their exchange in the pool in Cairo, Tye had sensed she would be able to talk to Jonah in a way she couldn't with the others.

And that of course had been enough to scare her miles away.

She didn't want to open up. Didn't want to let in mess, to share anything more than her skill with the people around her. Of course she didn't.

'Liar,' Tye whispered miserably. She turned on her side, her back to the window.

* * *

The summons from Coldhardt came early, as she had expected. She sat beside Motti in the hub. Jonah's seat was empty, of course. Patch was staring at it morosely, so Tye was glad when Con slumped there with a cup of strong-smelling coffee. Though her make-up had been applied with her usual skill, she still looked tired, like she hadn't slept well. Tye supposed none of them had.

It wasn't like any of them even knew Jonah that well. But they'd told him he could be family, and he didn't want to know – threw the opportunity back in their faces. Tye knew that tapped into stuff for all of them, no matter how cool they acted on the surface.

Motti sniffed. 'Coulda made me some, Con.'

'Do I look like your slave, Motti?'

'Truth is, you look all-out gross. Even Patch would say no this morning, right, Patch?'

'Leave it, Mot.'

'Jeez, are we all on tippy-toes today just 'cause the geek cleared out? Does it have to be like someone died –?'

'That's enough,' said Coldhardt, looking up languidly from the head of the table. He was dressed in his habitual black, but somehow his manner this morning seemed a little more funereal. 'The cipher has been decrypted,' he announced, with no mention of the boy who'd cracked it. 'Unfortunately, it is inconclusive. We must locate and retrieve the rest of the lekythos. As Tye and Con have informed us, it was sent to the Serpens Biotech plant in Rome. And it is from there that we must recover it.'

'Why should the fragments still be there?' Con asked. 'Surely it was just another drop point, no? It's a genetics lab.'

'Which makes it the perfect place for testing that mysterious organic powder inside the lekythos,' Coldhardt said heavily.

'But what about the lekythos itself?' asked Motti. 'Y'know, I'm surprised we didn't find what's left of it in Samraj's mansion. I mean, it's just clay, man – got no call to be in a lab.' He looked at Coldhardt, smiling slyly. 'Hey, speaking of Samraj's place, how come you knew where that secret safe of hers was, anyway –?'

Coldhardt slammed down both fists on the antique wood of the table. 'You question *me*?'

The table jumped under the force of the blow. Patch quailed, covering his head. Con and Tye both stared at Coldhardt in shock.

'Was just impressed, man,' Motti said hoarsely.

'If you're not prepared to trust me you can walk out now,' he snapped, glaring round at them. 'Leave here for good. That goes for any of you.'

An oppressive silence shrouded the room. Tye knew that Coldhardt meant what he said. But she could also see a glimmer of fear in those proud eyes. When he saw her watching, he looked away, reaching for a slim briefcase.

'You will go to the Serpens building in Rome. I have here the plans and details of the security systems. A reliable source informs me that Samraj has hidden things of value in laboratories on the second floor – where no one would ever think to look.'

What reliable source? thought Tye, though she didn't dare say a word.

'It's likely that she'll be keeping the lekythos and the organic material there too,' Coldhardt went on. He pulled out a sheaf of files and CDs and pushed them across the table to Motti. 'I want your first thoughts on how we gain entrance to those laboratories by 1600 hours.'

Motti accepted the files without comment, nodding.

'Leave me now,' Coldhardt went on, rising and walking slowly to his desk. 'I must contact Demnos and update him on the situation. Tye, stay with me, please. I want you to witness the call.'

Tye nodded.

'He didn't mention Jonah once.' Patch looked pale and miserable as he followed Motti and Con to the door. 'It's like he don't feel nothing.'

I think he feels plenty, thought Tye, who'd noticed Coldhardt's statuette. It was lying half-pulverised on the floor behind his desk, but from here she couldn't tell whether demon or man had survived.

Tye moved to where Con had been sitting for a better view of the screens. Coldhardt had dialled the videolink from his computer, and a high-res image of Demnos soon rippled into view, enlarged over all four monitors so every nuance was clear for her to read. And one thing was obvious – Demnos looked terrible. His eyes were red-rimmed and puffy, his dark hair wild like a clown's.

'Forgive me, my dear Demnos,' said Coldhardt. 'Is this a bad time?'

The big man scowled. 'What is it you want?'

'I have obtained Samraj's fragments of the prescription, by covert means.' He smiled, paused for a few minutes. 'Would you tell me, please, does the phrase "the root of the snake" mean anything to you?'

A hopeful look spun through Demnos's crumpled face. 'That phrase is mentioned in one of my own fragments. The root, the essence of the snake – this is what I hunt for. But . . . was there nothing else?'

'I have studied Samraj's documents carefully. Mention is made of Ophiuchus's followers. Each of them possessed a particular type of funeral vase, with great treasure hidden within.' Coldhardt smiled to himself. 'That knowledge forearmed her. When the lekythos came to light in the Sakkaran tomb, she worked with members of the Cult of Ophiuchus to obtain it ahead of us.'

At this, Demnos stiffened. 'So. Some followers survived, after all.'

'You've had dealings with the cult?'

'I obtained my fragments of the Amrita prescription from a leprous peasant, drowning in the filth of an Indian shanty town. He claimed to be the last of the line. He died soon after the pieces came into my possession.'

'Retribution for sharing anything of Ophiuchus's secret has traditionally been swift and deadly,' said Coldhardt. 'Be assured, Demnos, his cult endures – and Samraj is linked to it intimately.'

Demnos nodded gravely. 'So the advantage is hers.'

'Not entirely. A cipher was etched in the lekythos, and we possess a vital part of it. It translates as "Head of serpent, dog of the shepherd, hand before the preceding" . . .' Coldhardt gave him his most urbane smile. 'Does this mean anything to you?'

'The head?' Demnos's face clouded. 'For twenty years, cell by cell I have torn apart the brains of almost two thousand species of snakes in search of the secret . . . Nothing.' His anger began to show. 'And now you talk of a shepherd's dog, a hand preceding? Preceding *what*?'

'We are in the process of extracting more information from the cipher. We hope to have more to tell you soon.'

Demnos's frown softened. He looked away from his webcam, staring into space. 'What does it matter now, in any case?'

Tye glanced nervously at Coldhardt, but his attention was fixed on the screens. 'What has happened, Demnos?'

'Two nights ago my precious Yianna was abducted from my home. I was away on business, and when I returned yesterday morning . . .'

'Who would abduct her?' said Tye. She felt Coldhardt's eyes on her, angry that she should speak out of turn. But she could see that Demnos was in great pain.

'I don't know. There were signs of forced entry. The alarms were tripped – but the police received a call from Yianna insisting it was a false alarm. So did my own security people.'

'The abductors forced her to make those calls,' Tye reasoned.

'Of course they did,' Demnos snapped. 'It is ironic, is it not? While I am paying you to steal from Samraj's house . . . unknown agencies invade my own mansion and take what is most precious to me.' His dark eyes were shining with tears. 'She is the reason I must have the Amrita. She is sick, born with a wasting illness. I watch her grow worse month by month, unable to save her . . .'

Tye risked a look at Coldhardt. He was watching the screens impassively.

'She is all I have to remind me of my wife,' he whispered hoarsely, wiping the tears from his face with his slab-like hands. 'I *must* find her.'

'You've received no demands from her captors?'

'Nothing. When I think of the pain she must be enduring, and the fear . . .' He shook his head savagely. 'I have promised her an end to her pain, and a new life. A life of health and happiness that will last for ever. The truth of the Amrita lies hidden in the serpents somewhere, I *know* it.'

'It looks like Samraj is experimenting on them too,' Tye told him. 'She must think the same as you.'

'For Samraj the Amrita is simply a means of gaining power,' Demnos sneered. 'For me, it is a matter of life and death.'

'Perhaps someone feels you're getting close to the secret,' Coldhardt mused. 'And that with power over your daughter you will give Amrita to them.'

Tye frowned. 'Samraj? I thought we just agreed she's the one with the advantage here.'

'Yes, perhaps so. Or perhaps a third party is at work,' he went on. There was a look in his eye she couldn't fathom. 'Yes, someone playing each of you against the other.'

Demnos looked straight at the screen again, a flicker of hope in his eyes. 'Coldhardt, you are a thief. Steal back my daughter.'

'I don't deal in human goods.'

'You *must* help me.' Tye took no pleasure from seeing this powerful man tremble. She doubted he had asked for help from anyone in his life. 'Find Yianna. Bring her back to me unharmed and I will reward you with wealth and treasures you can only dream of.'

Coldhardt's voice dropped to an icy breath. 'Be careful, Demnos. I have the most vivid dreams.'

'Please,' he whispered.

'Very well. I'll consider it. Put together a business plan as before, and submit it to me for consideration.'

'I will speak with you again,' Demnos vowed solemnly. Then he broke contact and his image vanished from the screens.

'He was telling the truth,' Tye said shakily. 'About everything.'

'I feel for him,' said Coldhardt, gazing into space. 'To lose a child is always painful.' He said the words simply but with a conviction that chilled. 'Even so, learning the truth about Amrita is our first concern, over and above everything else. Do you understand?'

Tye nodded. 'But if Yianna's going missing is linked to this stuff about the Amrita –?'

'The truth will out. Wherever she is, I doubt she will remain hidden for long. She has been taken for a purpose.' He mused pensively on this for a while, then nodded. 'You may leave me now. Make sure Motti is

195

fully engaged in finding a way into the Serpens premises.'

'I'm sure he will be.'

'We need to move fast on this.' Coldhardt looked back at the blank screens like he could see something there that Tye could not. 'By tonight.'

She wanted to protest, to insist that it wasn't enough time. But she didn't dare. Turning to go, she caught sight again of the smashed statuette.

Without looking at it any closer she hurried from the hub.

Tye drove them through the northern outskirts of central Rome to a business development park on the Via Fortuna. It was ugly and functional, the total flipside of the romantic, picturesque city with its thousand sights. At this time of night the area was more or less deserted save for a few unlucky souls arriving for the night shift.

It felt weird to Tye, just the four of them together again, sitting in the van while they waited for the hour to act. Or rather, the four of them and a mangy, grouchy black cat they'd found prowling around a building site. To Tye's surprise, it sat purring noisily on Motti's lap, perhaps recognising a kindred soul.

'I dunno,' said Patch. He was toying distractedly with his ceramic eye, unscrewing the two halves and then putting them back together, over and over. 'I've got a bad feeling about this job.'

'You're gonna have a bad feeling in your mouth when I smack you there,' growled Motti. Now Jonah had gone, Patch was first in line for his abuse. 'And would you quit playing with the eye?'

'I'll stop when you stop playing with the cat,' he retorted. 'Just 'cause it's the only pussy you can get.'

Con slapped him round the head. 'Don't be vulgar.'

'Yeah, don't be so vulgar, you little shit,' Motti agreed. 'And don't forget this cat is gonna save your ass tonight.'

Tye patted a bundle in a black bin bag. 'So long as the sight of the toy terrier doesn't scare him away.'

Patch shook his head, looking worried. 'I can't believe our plan depends on a clapped-out cat and a stuffed dog.'

'First rule – you gotta do different,' Motti argued. 'Gotta do something they won't expect.'

'We're rushing into this. We need more time to plan.'

Tye sighed softly. 'I think so too.'

'Coldhardt must have his reasons for wanting to move quickly,' said Con defensively.

'We'll be fine,' Motti agreed. 'The plan's OK. It won't be so tough.'

Patch blew cat hairs from his eyeball and popped it back under the leather. 'Wonder where Jonah is right now?'

'Who the hell cares? He's out of our lives. I don't give a damn if he's living or dead.' Motti looked quickly at Tye. 'And don't you start working your voodoo and telling me I'm a liar.'

'We don't need her voodoo to know that,' said Con dryly.

They sat in gloomy silence a while longer, listening to the rasping purr of the cat.

'Hamburgers when we've finished?' Patch suggested tentatively.

Tye smiled. 'Sounds good.'

'Fillet o' fish sounds better,' said Con.

'But it smells worse.' Motti tapped his watch. 'OK. Five minutes, people.'

'Say, "Synchronise watches", Motti.' Con batted her eyelids. 'You know I love it when you say "Synchronise watches".'

Motti glowered at Con, put on a bad falsetto French accent: 'Would everyone kindly confirm their watch is telling the same time as their neighbour's watch, yes?' He picked up the cat and reverted to his usual gruff tones. 'Then, if you're ready, Puddy-tat . . . we're going in.'

CHAPTER FIFTEEN

Con stubbed out the cigarette she'd hastily puffed at in the van, swigged from a beer bottle and gargled messily. She dabbed some of the dribble on her neck, then mussed up her hair and tugged her black leather skirt – or the wide belt as Motti had called it – to a wanton angle. Instant post-club chic achieved, she walked calmly towards the main gate. Lights still burned on the upper floor of the squat, boxy business unit. 'Here we come,' she whispered. 'Ready or not.'

She heard Motti's voice in her head. *Four security guards on the night shift, at least two in central monitoring. Good news is, they're outside contractors, not Serpens staff – if they screw up, they know they'll just get sent to work in some other place, so they don't need to play superhero if they find trouble.*

'Should be ripe for a distraction.' Con checked her watch, speeded up the walk just a fraction. It was three minutes past two in the morning.

Tye pulled on the leash of her dog on wheels, walking it like it was real round the perimeter of the Serpens unit. She took a moment out from counting her paces to check her watch: 2.04am.

'The fence ain't alarmed but it's tough,' Motti had said. 'We need to get through at the farthest point between the electronic field sensors in the grounds. Twenty-two steps from this point on the plan. That's where you gotta make the cut, but be careful. They got a camera trained there.'

She counted twenty-two and stopped with the dog, shaking her head impatiently . . .

On the dot of 2.04, Con reached the security monitoring station, all drunken smiles. It was a small room adjoining the main building, made from steel and glass. A bank of monochrome monitors dominated the wall behind a counter with a phone and a sign-in book. On one of the screens, Tye had just walked into view.

A blue-uniformed guard opened the door for her, obviously having seen her approach. He was a burly man in his forties with a thick, well-groomed beard. His younger buddy was bright-eyed and balding and stood behind the counter. Both carried guns in macho black leather holsters round their waists. Con guessed the other guards on patrol would be carrying too.

'May I help you, miss?' asked the bearded guard.

Con peered at his name badge. 'Hello, Marc. I need to see Lorenzo Issigri,' she began in perfect Italian, relieved to find both men's eyes on her legs and not the monitors, where Tye was now crouching between the fence and her slightly suspect dog. 'Can you call him for me?'

'Issigri?' Marc frowned. 'Doesn't normally work nights, does he?'

Con shook her head emphatically. 'Only those nights I go out and leave my bag in some idiot's taxi. My friend's meant to be crashing with me tonight, but I've got no keys, no phone . . .'

The younger man was already looking up the surname. 'I'll try him.'

'Thank you . . .' She bent forward to look at his name badge, giving him plenty of cleavage. 'Gian. That's a nice name.'

'Take a seat?' Marc suggested, no doubt keen to see if her skirt could ride any higher.

'Thanks.' She flopped down, popped a mint in her mouth like she was trying to hide the beer on her breath. Caught movement on the screen behind them and leaned in quickly, confidentially. 'You know, between you and me, I don't think Lorenzo's working late at all. I think he's got another woman.'

'What department?' asked Gian.

'I dunno. The last bitch he tried it on with was in Accounts.'

He laughed. 'No, I mean, what department's Lorenzo?'

She laughed too, threw her head back, stuck out her chest. 'I'm such a ditz!'

Tye had pulled out a poop-scoop and was crouched beside her dog-on-wheels. From inside the scoop she shook out some titanium wire cutters and, using the dog to disguise her movements, snipped quickly through the tough links.

Once she judged the split was large enough for two skinny boys to sneak through, she hurried away, yanking the stuffed dog after her.

'So, this guy . . .' Gian eyed her casually. 'He your husband?'

'Boyfriend,' Con corrected him. '*Ex* if he's not careful . . .' *And while you were trying to see my underwear, you just missed Motti ducking under your fence.* 'Anyway, you were asking – Lorenzo's in stem cell research, second floor. Tell him Maria's here, and she's mad as hell.'

'Will do,' grinned the guard.

Praying Con was on good form tonight, Patch ran up to the fence after Motti and slid himself under the flap of loose chainlink. With a steel peg he clipped the flap back in place so the break wouldn't show on the cameras, and sprinted to where Mot waited in the shadow of the nearby outhouse. It was 2.06am.

'OK.' Motti was trying to hold on to the wriggling cat he had stuffed up his grungy top. 'The quickest way through to our nominated way in – the east block fire door – takes us through the overlap of the two rotating cameras.'

Patch nodded, miming cameras buzzing slowly from side to side.

'Only they're just a tiny bit out of synch with each other. And I've worked out there's just one fifteen-second window coming up when they're both pointing away from our route.'

'So that's when we run like the devil's biting our arse?'

'Or like this damn cat's clawing it,' said Motti, still

struggling with the bulge in his top. 'We move in one minute forty. Of course, when we start running we're gonna set off the electronic field sensors . . .'

'Tell me something I don't know,' said Patch, checking his watch. 'But don't let the cat out of the bag till then.'

'No reply from your boyfriend,' said Gian. 'I'm only getting his voicemail.'

Con frowned, drummed her fingers against her thigh. 'Maybe he's in the men's room. Would you try him again in a minute for me?'

Suddenly a loud, intermittent buzzing sounded, a red light flashed on the console. Con could hear sirens sounding outside. The guards swore, checked their monitors.

'Are you having a *break-in*?' Con asked, acting thrilled at the thought. Then she smiled as a mangy black cat prowled unhappily into shot.

'Where'd that damn moggy come from?' Marc pulled out his two-way radio. 'Carlo? Control here. Don't freak – we've got a cat in the grounds. It just passed exit three – you're nearest. I'll reset the alarms. Let me know when you've shooed it out of here.'

Patch and Motti stood panting for breath, leaning against the outside of the building. Motti was rubbing his chest ruefully.

'Damn fleabag almost tore my guts out.' He set off quickly along the paved path, staying close to the walls. ''Course, the sensors wouldn't really pick up an animal as small as a cat. But these contract guards, they don't know jack about the security specs. They just hear a noise and go after it.'

Patch nodded, just behind him. 'You're sure we won't set off the alarms again, moving about?'

'They won't reset the sensors till they've got rid of Puss. In any case, we're beyond the range of the receptors now. These are the staff walkways. The guards patrol round here – when they're not running round after dumbass cats.'

Motti came to an abrupt halt. Patch swore as he almost bumped into him.

'OK, we're out of range of the revolving cameras,' said Motti. 'That's the fire door up ahead – our way in.' A static camera, a different kind from the others, was trained directly on it. 'Can you bust the lock in sixty?'

Patch bit his lip. 'It'll be tight.'

'We won't have much longer than that,' said Motti. 'This camera sends a digital image back to a CPU in security. The processor scans the video image twice a second looking for any change in the pixel pattern. When movement's detected, it sounds a warning for the night shift. If they see a Cyclops picking the lock, guess what? They blow the big alarms.'

'If we still had Jonah, he could hack into the CPU, freeze the internal clock or something,' said Patch gloomily.

'Yeah, well, Jonah didn't want to be in our gang, did he?' Motti pulled something from his pocket. 'So we have to do the budget version.'

'Could you try Lorenzo again for me?' Con asked Gian.

'Wait a second.' He swore, looking up at one of the screens. 'Now what's up with camera six?'

All that showed on the screen was a white blur.

'You've done something to the picture,' said Marc accusingly.

'I have not! That's something on the lens!'

Marc pulled out his radio again. 'Carlo, are you through with the cat? Looks like a technical on six, but you'd better check it out. I don't like this . . .'

'Good ole cheap squirty cream,' said Motti, surveying the dollop he'd squirted over the lens of the camera. 'Starts melting away to nothing the moment it's in the bowl. Why *is* that?' He put away the canister. 'If they're watching, guards'll think some bird came over and dumped its supper. But by the time they get here to clean it off, it's already gone. *Twilight Zone* time. What was that mysterious bird with the vanishing poop?'

Patch was already working on the lock. 'It's night-time, you prat. What birds come out at night?'

'Owls.' Motti was feeling round the doorframe for signs of the magnetic switch that would trigger the internal alarms if the door was opened. 'Owls are nocturnal.'

'Maybe so. But they drop pellets. Like little balls.'

'You ought to know all about little balls.' Motti grunted with satisfaction as he found the switch point. He pulled out his scrambler.

Patch looked at him. 'Lock's done. You ready with the pulse?'

'Just like in Cairo,' Motti warned him. 'We'll have

three seconds: one to open, one to get through, one to close the door behind us.'

'Not *just* like in Cairo, I hope,' said Patch. 'This time if we don't do it in time . . . the alarms *will* go off. And we're royally screwed.'

Con feigned anxiety when Gian's next phone call to Lorenzo was no more successful. 'Could you take me up? Let me see if he's there for myself?'

'I don't know . . .'

'The sooner I know, the sooner I can get out of your hair.'

Gian was still staring at the screen. 'It's clearing. Whatever was blocking six, it's more or less gone.'

Con peered round, wide-eyed.

The screen showed only a closed door.

'Probably a bird,' said Marc, miming a bomb falling and splattering on the camera. 'I'll walk blondie here up to the second floor.'

He led her out of the security station and into a sumptuous reception. The sleek chrome lift arrived in moments, and hummed smugly as they climbed up two floors. Con checked her watch again. 2.12am.

'So is it just the three of you on duty?' Con asked idly.

'Pieter's doing the lab walkround,' Marc told her. 'He'll soon tell us if your Lorenzo's been here tonight.'

The lift doors swooshed open. A large, uniformed black man lay sprawled on his back in the corridor.

'What the hell?' Marc crouched beside him, reaching for his radio. 'He's out cold.'

'Really?' Con karate-chopped the back of Marc's

206

neck and he keeled over without a sound. 'Looks like it's catching.'

Motti peered out from a nearby room. ''Bout time you showed up,' he hissed. Congratulations were a waste of time in his book. 'C'mon, let's lock 'em both away in here.'

'Take their keys and the radios,' Con told him as they dragged the bodies out of sight. 'Might buy us some more time if Gian or Carlo want to get chatty.'

'Meantime,' said Motti, once he'd found the key that locked the door, 'Patch has found a restricted area. Just round here.'

Con jogged along with him. 'Sounds promising. Any cameras?'

'No. Let's just hope he can get us inside.'

Patch was grinning at them beside an open door as they rounded the corner of the corridor. 'Did you doubt my genius for a minute?'

'Let's see what's so restricted,' said Con, leading the way into an impressive antechamber. Four neatly arranged workstations flanked a wide passageway leading to a set of double doors. The air carried a faint chemical tang, and the lights were bright and clinical. A wipe-clean board hugged most of one wall, the kind you found in hospitals with patient details on them. It was covered in scrawls that were just as hard to read.

She crossed quickly to the double doors. 'Through here.'

Then she stopped dead in her tracks.

It was like a small hospital ward, with six beds. But Con couldn't believe that the people inside them were there to get well. She walked slowly inside, studying the man nearest to her with a kind of horrified fascination. His looks were Middle Eastern, but he had no hair, not even any eyebrows. Only his head and left arm were visible – the rest was hidden beneath a mess of micromesh sheeting and scanners. The exposed skin was stuck with the tiny barbs of electrodes and needles and wires, trailing to a large monitor that flashed up the same four letters in endless combinations. They were chemical bases, Con realised. The precious, infinitesimal codes that made up DNA, the stuff of all life.

'Look,' said Patch softly, hooking away a wire to reveal a little of the man's hand. A faded blue snake coiled like an old, fat vein towards the man's knuckles.

Con stared at him, the hairs rising on the back of her neck. 'Cult of Ophiuchus?'

'They all got the snake,' said Motti, passing from bed to bed. 'What's up with them?'

'More to the point,' said Con, 'what about these fragments we're here to pick up?'

'Help me!' It was a girl's voice, weak and croaking in Italian. At first Con thought it came from one of the six acolytes. But it was coming from behind a screen at the end of the ward. 'Please, someone help me!'

Con gestured to the others to keep watch at the double doors. Slowly, gingerly, she walked over to the screen and pulled it back.

A thin, delicate looking girl with dark, sunken eyes and angular features lay stiffly on a hospital trolley beneath a starched white sheet. She stared up at Con with raw desperation.

Con recognised the girl at once.

It was Demnos's daughter, Yianna.

CHAPTER SIXTEEN

Con stared in disbelief. Tye had told them about Coldhardt's talk with Demnos, how the girl had gone missing – and the reward for her safe return. Now, as if conjured up from nowhere, she was lying in front of them.

'I . . . I know you,' Yianna said, frowning. When she spoke again it was in her heavily accented English. 'You were at the party they held for my father . . .'

Motti had wandered over. 'Who we got?'

'It's Yianna. The abducted girl.'

'Jeez, she looks rough.'

Yianna closed her eyes. 'I have not been treated well.'

'So,' said Motti, apparently unmoved. 'Samraj *did* take her.'

'Looks like it,' Con agreed. 'To get a hold over Demnos – her biggest rival for the Amrita.'

'Did . . . Coldhardt send you here?' Yianna whispered, licking her cracked lips. 'You are his people, yes?'

'His family.'

'Is he here also?'

'No. Just the three of us inside, and a girl waiting

out front to get us the hell away.'

'This is a gift, man!' crowed Motti quietly. 'Demnos offers Coldhardt a fortune to get her back, and here she is.'

Con turned back to Yianna, feeling oddly troubled. 'Can you walk?'

'I've been drugged,' she muttered, turning her head from side to side, her dark hair straggling over the crisp white sheets. 'Samraj is experimenting on these people . . . Wants to experiment on me. Wants the secret . . .'

Motti frowned. 'Who's that?'

'Samraj.' The word sounded scratchy and faint in her throat.

Con looked at him. 'What is it, Motti?'

'Dunno. Thought I recognised her voice.' He shook his head. 'Never mind. Where's Samraj now?'

'Back . . . Back in morning . . .'

'It will not be easy to get her out,' said Con quietly.

'We'll just have to carry her,' said Motti. 'Sneak down to the security station as planned, blow the phosphor caps and run out in the confusion.'

Con nodded. With big cash at stake, they couldn't afford *not* to take her with them.

'No one's moving out there,' Patch reported, crossing the ward to join them. 'What's going . . .'

He broke off as he saw Yianna, frowning like he was trying to place her.

'This is Yianna,' Con explained. 'Demnos's daughter.'

'That ain't all she is,' said Patch. 'I've seen her before, in a painting. A painting on the wall in

Samraj's house.'

Yianna stared at him in confusion.

'That's crazy,' Con argued. 'Why would her portrait be –'

'Wait.' Now Motti was staring at the girl with equal mistrust. 'The voice we heard behind the door when we broke in. It was *your* voice. You were there in the flesh at Samraj's house!'

'No,' Yianna protested feebly, 'you're wrong.'

'Guys, I'm telling you –'

Abruptly, Yianna sat up and kicked off the sheet.

She was holding a gun.

'Back off!' she hissed. 'Stand against the window, or I *will* shoot you.'

Con eyed Yianna evilly as they shuffled off to comply. It was clear from the wild look in the girl's eyes that she meant it. She was clearly unaccustomed to power; now, holding the gun, she seemed high on it.

'So much for Samraj's poor little victim, huh?' said Motti bitterly.

'I am helping Samraj with her experiments on the acolytes of Ophiuchus.' Yianna seemed proud of herself. 'They have helped us learn the secrets of the Amrita.'

'And in return you stick needles in them, yes?' Con was unimpressed. 'Demnos is an idiot. His dear, darling daughter wasn't abducted by anyone. You faked it – you went willingly with Samraj.'

'*Most* willingly.' Yianna's smile twisted into a leer. 'My poor, dear father rarely leaves me alone – so we seized the opportunity. I should really thank your friends here.'

'Don't bother,' muttered Patch.

'But I must. You made my apparent kidnapping seem so much more convincing.'

'What's that supposed to mean?' drawled Motti.

'You left so much incriminating evidence behind you.' Yianna nodded knowingly. 'The hole in the hothouse wall. The triggering of the perimeter alarms . . . Oh, and where is that blond boy, by the way? I couldn't resist teasing the little poppet, waiting all alone in the darkness.'

Motti and Patch stared at each other. Con saw the horror on their faces.

'Shall I spell it out for you?' Yianna's eyes shone darkly. 'That wasn't Samraj's home you broke into two nights ago. It was my father's.'

'You're crazy,' hissed Motti. 'We know it was Samraj's place.'

'You only *think* you know – because that is what Coldhardt told you. So easily duped – just like the police.' She smiled. 'Oh yes, when I found the three of you blundering about my home, I knew at once how I might turn your visit to my advantage. I called the police and told them the alarms were set off by accident . . . that everything was quite under control.'

Con sneered. 'And of course, they now believe that you made those claims under duress . . .'

'You must have seen the helicopter, boys, while you were hiding out in the area? You thought it was a police helicopter perhaps?' Yianna shook some stray hairs from her eyes – a swift, feral movement. 'It was Samraj coming to collect me, now our plans are almost complete. I used you, and now I have tricked

213

you all – just as Coldhardt has.'

'If you think you can trick us into doubting Coldhardt, you're crazy,' said Con fiercely.

'Coldhardt knows the difference between the two houses, even if you don't,' Yianna sneered. 'After all, he has been staying with Samraj as her guest, at her home here in Rome. While you fought for him in Cairo, he lay in bed with her.'

'You lying bitch!' Con hurled herself recklessly at Yianna, but Motti grabbed hold of her, hauled her back.

'She's still holding the gun,' he hissed at her.

'This may look like a hospital,' Yianna said, just the faintest tremble in her voice as she levelled the gun at Con's chest, 'but I know nothing of first aid. If I shoot you, you will bleed to death here.' Her eyes narrowed, the dark rings around them making her seem so much older. 'Samraj warned me intruders might come tonight. Having witnessed your bungled attempts at breaking and entry, I doubted you would make it this far – but now you are here, we may as well have you all. The girl is outside, you said – I shall have her collected. Where is the blond boy?'

'He's gone,' Motti snarled. 'Run away.'

'You expect me to believe that?' She moved the gun to cover Patch. 'I think this little one will tell me. Won't you, little boy?'

Patch raised his hands slowly, nervously. 'I may be little, but I'm ever so bright.'

Con took the hint, closing her eyes as Patch threw down a phosphor cap. It exploded in a blaze of light. Yianna cried out, staggered back. Motti slugged her in

214

the jaw and she fell sprawling against one of the beds, shouting as she became entangled with the wires and tubes hooked into the man who lay there.

'Out!' Motti snapped, leading the rush for the double doors.

But two dark figures were blocking the way. They looked like the men from the museum in Cairo.

'Like I said,' hissed Yianna, struggling to free herself, 'Samraj warned me intruders might come tonight. You think she would not give me protection?'

Motti reached them first, threw a punch at the closest cultist. But the man dodged aside and struck him in the throat. Patch yelled and threw himself at Motti's assailant, fists flying. The other man plucked him free and swung him round into the wall, head first. With a pitiful squeak, Patch went down in a crumpled heap.

Con assumed a fighting stance as both Yianna's bodyguards turned to face her. Patch was down. Motti was gasping for breath on the floor. She backed away towards Yianna, who was still struggling to get back up – where was the bitch's gun? The thought of using it terrified Con, but maybe she could bluff her way out . . .

But then the acolyte in the bed lashed out with his one free arm and gripped her by the throat. The skin on his arm came up short against the wires, stretched grotesquely like melted mozzarella. She struggled to free herself, but his grip was like iron. He stared up at her with cold, dark eyes like he felt nothing. Nothing but disgust for her.

The taller of Yianna's bodyguards loomed over

Con, a dark wraith in this sterile, frightening place. He took a firm hold of her, twisted her arm behind her back.

Yianna struggled up. 'The little one!' she shouted. 'Where is he?'

Con's heart quickened. Patch was no longer crumpled on the floor. He had gone.

'Get after him,' Yianna told her other bodyguard. 'Quickly! He'll be trying to get back to his friends.' She smiled darkly at Con. 'We should show him there's nowhere he can run to.'

Patch hared out of the restricted area and stabbed desperately at the call lift button. His head was throbbing, he felt sick. But he had to get out, tell Tye what had happened. She'd know what to do.

Together they'd rescue Motti and Con. No question.

The doors opened at once – but already he could hear running feet behind him. Patch threw himself inside, hit the ground floor button again and again. Finally the doors began to move.

But Yianna's minder was going to get to him long before they closed.

Patch scrabbled for his false eye, tugged it out and lobbed it at the dark shadow approaching. It cracked off the man's head, stalling him for a moment – long enough for the doors to close.

He grabbed the guard's radio from his pocket, struggled to remember the simple Italian phrases Con had taught him on the way over here. '*Uscita sei*,' he shouted into it as the lift doors opened again on the ground floor. '*Rapidamente! Intruso avvistato! Rapidamente!*'

The radio squawked back a moment later but Patch ignored it. Let security run around trying to spot intruders at exit six. He was too busy wondering which of these keys would get him through to the security station before the bodyguard could –

Too late. Patch swore as his faceless, implacable pursuer swept down the stairs and tore across the marble towards him.

'I'm in main reception! Open up!' Patch yelled into his radio. But English was no good. 'Uh, *ricezione principale, aprasi*—'

He threw the radio at the minder, knew he'd miss, didn't stay to see. He was running for the large marble reception desk, desperate to put something between him and his attacker. But the man leaped through the air and landed on top of the desk like this was some martial arts movie, completing the effect with a whistling kick that narrowly missed taking Patch's head off.

With nowhere left to go, Patch pelted towards the locked door – just as it opened to reveal a young security guard with a shaved head and a gun. His eyes widened in fear as Patch hurtled towards him.

'Get out of here!' Patch yelled. He brought down the guard with a clumsy tackle, knocking him back the way he'd come, through the doorway. The heavy door swung shut behind them, locking out the masked man.

The security guard tried to bring his gun to bear on Patch.

'Not me!' Patch knocked it away angrily and pointed

to the closed door. '*He's* the one you've got to worry about – *capite?*'

Suddenly the door shuddered under some great impact. Patch scrambled to his feet as a second blow almost smashed it off its hinges.

He helped up the dazed security guard. 'If I were you, mate, I'd find another job, pronto.'

The door began to splinter under another pulverising blow.

Patch let the guard run first. Then he followed him out through the security station and headlong into the night outside.

Tye was getting nervous, waiting in the van. She knew in many ways that she had the cushiest job as getaway driver, the least to lose. But just hanging around uselessly while the long minutes scraped against her nerves . . . wondering over and over if something had gone wrong, if this was the time that her friends wouldn't be coming back . . . It never got any easier.

Suddenly her stomach twisted as she caught movement in the rear-view. A security guard was sprinting down the dark, deserted road towards her, with Patch apparently in hot pursuit. What the hell was –?

Her mouth dried as she saw a dark figure steal out from between two parked cars close by. The guard was running blindly, he hadn't noticed. Not even when the moon peered through the covering clouds and lent a sheen to the stiletto blade in the figure's hand.

Tye opened her mouth to scream out a warning,

but too late. The figure swiped at the guard's back as he ran past. An arc of blood spat out. The guard tumbled to the ground.

Patch skidded to a halt as the dark shape turned its attentions on him.

'No!' Tye fumbled for the ignition key. The engine turned over.

Then she jumped as a dark, veiled face appeared up close against her window. A woman's hooded eyes bored soullessly into hers.

It was the Ophiuchus cultist she'd faced in Cairo.

Tye turned, catching a glimpse of movement through the windscreen – just as the glass exploded in on her, a thousand tiny shards tearing the air. A man's hand reached in to grab hold of her and she slammed the van into reverse gear, stepped on the gas, squealed away from her attackers down the road towards Patch. She had to get to him before the guard-killer did. And now she saw another of the lithe, shadowy figures had appeared outside the Serpens building, cutting off the boy's retreat.

Tye drew level with the guard-killer and twisted hard on the wheel, swerving to smash into him. She caught him a glancing blow but he rolled with it, somersaulted backwards and landed on his feet. He crouched into a fighting stance.

'That's right, Patch, get him!' she yelled, slamming on the brakes. As the man turned, ready to fend off an imaginary attack from his quarry, she jumped out of the van and kicked him where it hurt, following up with a judo strike to the back of his neck.

Before he'd even hit the asphalt, Tye was back in

the van. It lurched as Patch threw open the doors and jumped in the back.

'Hold on!' she yelled, flooring it in first, the night air cold on her face through the smashed-in windscreen. Two more sinister silhouettes jumped into the road to block her way. She screwed up her eyes and kept her course. At the last possible moment, the figures jumped clear.

'Where are they?' she shouted at Patch. 'Motti and Con?'

'They're caught inside!' he yelled back. 'Yianna's got them!'

'Yianna –?'

Tye stamped on the brakes and the van slewed to a halt. Patch was thrown forward, colliding with the back of her seat. 'Yianna's working with Samraj!' he gasped without missing a beat. 'We – we've got to get them out of there!'

'Are they hurt?'

'Motti was hit in the throat, I – I dunno how bad he is. Then there were these zombie cult people in the beds, wires and stuff shoved into them, and then Yianna had these two minders and they were the ones who mullered us in Cairo, I swear, and one of them grabbed Con when I –'

'Slow down,' Tye told him. She saw now just how awful he looked. He was white as a sheet. A huge lump on his forehead offset the bruise on his face. His patch was yanked down over his cheek, and she could see that he'd lost his false eye.

'This is all *my* fault. I let them down. I'm useless.' He gritted his teeth, started hitting himself around the head. 'Useless rubbish.'

Tye struggled to grab hold of his flailing hands. 'Patch, stop it.'

He went limp in her arms, started to sob. 'I tried to get us out, Tye. I threw a phosphor cap but it wasn't enough.'

'Listen to me,' she squeezed both his hands. 'Patch, you did everything you could. If you stayed you'd have got caught. Now we have to call Coldhardt. He'll tell us what to do.'

'Him?' Patch stared at her. 'Yianna said Coldhardt's been tricking us. That he's been seeing Samraj in secret, screwing us over for her. Said it was really *Demnos's* place we broke into while you were in Aqaba, not hers. And I didn't believe it first of all, but her painting *was* on the wall, see? I recognised her, that's how I knew who she was, and she was acting sick and sort of harmless till I gave that away, so it's *my* fault that she suddenly –'

'Don't start that again. I need you with me on this.'

'D'you reckon it's true about Coldhardt?' Patch looked at her beseechingly. 'D'you think he's been lying to us?'

'I think we need to get our heads straight, and some *facts* straight.' Tye swallowed hard, a sick feeling clawing at her insides. 'But the first thing we've got to do is get Con and Motti back. Right?'

He nodded.

'Maybe we can double back, try to –'

But then in the rear-view, she saw a black Chrysler turn the corner.

'Oh, God.' Tye floored the van again. 'They're

coming after us. We can't help Motti and Con if we're all in the same boat.' She pulled out her mobile and stuffed it into his hands as she took a corner at speed. 'Call Coldhardt. Tell him what's happened. Ask him what we do.'

'But what if he's –'

The Chrysler was picking up speed, looming larger in the wing mirror. 'Patch,' Tye shouted, 'whatever they say Coldhardt's done, he still cares about us. We know that. Right?' She realised with a sick feeling inside that she was asking him as much as telling him. '*Right*. So call him. Direct line to the Bat-phone in the hub.' She had the pedal pinned to the floor but she couldn't pull away from the big black car behind them. The night air blasted in through the empty windscreen. 'Do it! This could be the last chance we have!'

She heard him hit the call button, with a noisy sniff.

Then, suddenly, twin green eyes loomed out of the night ahead of them. Traffic lights. They'd reached the intersection with the main road.

'He's not picking up,' muttered Patch.

The lights darkened to amber, then to red. Tye saw the traffic on the right at the intersection strain forwards, ready to accelerate away at the first wink of green.

'Tye, he ain't answering!'

The Chrysler was still gaining. No way could she stop now.

The traffic started to move, metal animals let off the leash.

'Hold on, Patch,' she shouted.

The van ran through the reds and careened out into the oncoming traffic. Cars swerved and horns blared, a dozen tones at once. With no windscreen, the sounds seemed amplified, a deafening soundtrack as Tye spun the wheel this way and that. A huge oil truck almost broadsided them, slamming on its brakes at the last possible moment.

A sickening crunch of metal on metal carried to them as they cleared the chaos, and Tye sent the van screeching down the Via Gianicolense towards the city. She checked the rear-view and saw that the Chrysler had smashed into the side of a tourer, its doors flung open. She glimpsed black-clad figures disappearing into the night.

'Gee.' Tye glanced sideways at Patch with a shaky smile. 'You think they didn't have insurance?'

'I think we need to dump this van before it gets so hot it burns our arses.' Patch looked and sounded utterly exhausted, dropped the phone sullenly in her lap. 'Coldhardt ain't home. You think he's at his girlfriend's place?'

'I think . . .' Tye began.

But she found she didn't know what to think any more.

CHAPTER SEVENTEEN

Motti was shoved roughly out of the security station and into the cool night. There were more of Yianna's bodyguards out here – together with the tattooed bitch from Cairo. He knew that these guys did not mess, so he didn't struggle. His throat felt like it had been hit with a hammer, and he tasted blood whenever he swallowed.

He glanced at Con, subdued and quiet, allowing the black-clad minders to push her along without protest. He guessed she was thinking on what Yianna had said about Coldhardt. Well, so was he. And it was bull. It *had* to be bull.

Yianna was talking with one of her minders, her voice rising in anger. Abruptly she broke away and limped over to Motti and Con with the help of a gleaming chrome walking stick. 'Your friends have caused us some inconvenience.'

Motti coughed painfully. 'Y'know, they're always doing that. I been meaning to talk to them about it.'

Yianna's expression stayed sour. 'But we have you two. That should suffice.'

'Suffice for what?'

A Mercedes limousine pulled up beside the security

station. The back door opened ominously.

'We going for a ride?' Motti croaked.

'You're going to visit Samraj. Her *real* home.' She nodded towards the car. 'Put them in.'

'No.' Con snapped out of her trance as she was shoved towards the back seat. She looked at Yianna, wide-eyed. 'Not in the back. I can't go in the back.'

'No tricks,' she hissed.

'It's not a trick,' said Motti. 'She freaks out in the back of a car. Let her go in the front.'

'Pathetic,' sneered Yianna.

Con struggled fiercely in the arms of the black-clad figures as they forced her step by step into the car and manhandled her inside. 'No,' she kept saying under her breath. 'No, no, no.'

Motti hurriedly joined her in the back of the limousine. Another man slid in beside him so he and Con were bunched up in the middle. Con's eyes were tight shut, her breathing erratic. Sweat glistened on her forehead. Motti took her hand and she squeezed it tightly, her nails digging into his skin. 'Look, she's going to have a fit or something.'

Yianna got in awkwardly beside the black-clad driver, didn't even turn round.

The car pulled slowly away and Con shrieked.

'I'm telling you, she can't do this!' Motti saw the sides of Con's mouth were flecked with spit. She was rocking back and forth, moaning under her breath.

''S OK,' Motti whispered in her ear, trying to hold her. ''S OK, sweetheart, it ain't for ever. We're gonna get through this,' he kept whispering, over and over, though she showed no signs of hearing him. 'And then it's payback time.'

As Patch finished telling his sorry story Tye's mind was racing, trying to make sense of it all. Yianna was sick, she needed the Amrita. Samraj was more likely to get it than her own father – was that what had driven her to betray him?

And what about Coldhardt's betrayal?

She remembered the intimacy between him and Samraj at Demnos's party. Coldhardt's evading the question of her whereabouts – '*I really couldn't tell you*'. Because then it might have come out that she didn't even *own* a mansion in Florence? That the mansion was Demnos's property all along?

But why would Coldhardt order a covert raid on the house of his own employer? What was the point? And why mislead Motti, Patch and Jonah in their work? Tye would have known if he'd told an outright lie, but Coldhardt was a wily old bastard, he rarely slipped. He chose his words like his suits, tailor-made for the occasion.

She remembered the call with Demnos that morning, though it seemed a lifetime ago. '*Perhaps a third party is at work, someone playing each of you against the other,*' he had mused, and there was a look in his eyes she hadn't been able to fathom.

Now, with sudden clarity, she knew.

'It's you,' she breathed.

Coldhardt was working for both Samraj *and* Demnos – and ripping them both off at the same time.

For Demnos, he had used the talents of his children.

For Samraj, he had used his own.

'*I have obtained Samraj's fragments of the prescription, by covert means,*' he'd told Demnos just that morning. Not 'we'. *I*. She imagined him rising quietly from the woman's exotic bedside in the dead of night, sneaking away to steal the secrets of her part of the prescription. Just as he'd sent Motti, Patch and Jonah to steal the fragments that Demnos possessed – for Samraj's benefit. Perhaps Yianna had been unable to crack her father's safe. Or perhaps Samraj wanted to be sure that Yianna was not holding out on her.

But why hadn't Coldhardt explained to them what he was doing? He'd been playing a dangerous game, so why go it alone when they could have helped him? Was he trying to protect them, or did he simply not trust them enough?

Her pride stung at the thought. When she got back she would ask for answers. No. Whatever his temper, she would *demand* them.

But when the battered van drew up outside the castle at last, she knew at once that something was wrong. The gravel in the driveway was churned up, as though a car had left in a hurry. One of the great wrought iron gates stood ajar.

Patch had noticed too. He flung open the van door. 'Coldhardt?' he yelled, pelting out into the grounds. 'Coldhardt!'

She raced after him, catching him up as he stood panting and anxious in front of the retinal scanner. He winked into it, got the match, and they held hands as the lift descended, holding their breaths too.

'Oh, God . . .' breathed Tye.

The hub – Coldhardt's sanctum and sacred heart, wherever the location – had been trashed. While Patch lingered in the doorway, Tye walked slowly inside. Cabinets had been tipped over, spewing files and papers. One of the screens on the wall was cracked, another smashed right open. The table was over-turned. A bloody handprint was smeared on the wall.

'Someone's got him,' she whispered.

'How could anyone get in *here*?' said Patch.

'I don't know. But he's gone.'

Patch looked at her. 'Then . . . we're on our own.'

Tye stared at Coldhardt's desk. The computer had been swept away, and what was left of the smashed-up statuette was standing in its place. She advanced on it slowly. The demon crouched alone in placid marble, its human foe ripped away along with most of its scaly stomach.

She saw it had been placed on a piece of paper and a crumpled handkerchief. Gingerly, she tugged the paper free.

It was a note, scrawled in Coldhardt's hand:

MISS ME, Cx

Tye touched the paper to her lips, lost in harried thoughts. Kisses from Coldhardt? It seemed unlikely.

'What the hell are we gonna do?' Patch wailed, and Tye wished she had a good answer.

Motti's journey in the limo was mercifully brief, barely half an hour through the outskirts of Rome to some fancy villa on the fringes of the Janiculum. The quaint, picturesque streets were dark and silent, lending a kind of creepy fairy-tale feel to the journey.

Con was still clutching his hand so tightly that the bloodied skin was blue beneath. She was shuddering and shaking. Seeing her like this hurt far more than anything she could unwittingly do to him. He'd never seen anything like it.

As the big car turned smoothly into a courtyard and started to slow, he realised with a chill that, after tonight, he might never see anything ever again.

'This is Samraj's villa,' said Yianna with a smug smile. '*Now* you believe me, perhaps, that you were sent to Florence under false pretences?'

Motti didn't even look up, cradling Con's head, stroking her hair. 'Just let us out of here.'

The big bruisers bundled them outside and towards an intricately carved doorway. Motti kept a close hold on Con, scared she would collapse. She was staring round sightlessly, the real her hiding away in some secret, safer place. Sounded good – Motti wished he could retreat from reality too. Gargoyles peered down from the old stone walls, watching them approach with scuffed lichen eyes.

They paused at the doorway while Yianna caught them up, leaning heavily on her stick, her left foot scraping over the gravel. As she pulled out a phony stone in the wall, Motti saw a black plastic pad behind – a 'print scanner by the look of it. Once she'd placed her index finger against it, a green light winked on and a hidden bolt retracted, allowing her to open the door.

Motti half expected them to be taken to a cell. Instead, they were led into an opulent study done out in art deco style, all black and white, squared-off corners, geometric lines. At once, his attention was taken by the tall Indian woman, her willowy form flattered by close-fitting midnight blue, standing expectantly by a black marble fireplace. She looked about forty, the hard beauty of her face framed by thick, straight black hair. She wore a snake bracelet on her upper arm, the gold curling sensuously twice around the toned, dusky flesh. Its eyes were diamonds, and there was something of their cruel glitter in the woman's own.

He gave Con's hand a reassuring squeeze, though probably more for his own comfort than hers, and did his best to seem unflappable. 'So you're Samraj, right?'

'Very astute,' she said mockingly.

'Don't be so hard on the boy. I imagine he's had quite a night.'

Motti whirled round at the sound of the familiar voice. It was Coldhardt. He was pouring himself a drink from a crystal decanter. The liquid was the same rich, dark crimson as the gash on his temple. His usually immaculate suit looked a little crumpled, his steel-grey cravat was spotted with blood, but his blue eyes were as sharp and clear as always.

'What is this?' Motti breathed as Coldhardt sipped from his tiny glass. 'You seem pretty much at home, man.'

'So he should,' said Samraj. 'He has been here many times.'

Motti went on staring. He realised he was clutching Con to him like a security blanket. 'You sold us out?'

He could feel the blood pounding in his temples. 'Is *that* what this is about?'

'Don't be ridiculous, Motti.' Coldhardt looked irritated, swigged back his drink. 'I'm a prisoner here, just as you are.'

'Only because you choose to be so difficult,' Samraj purred. 'If you'd accompanied me quietly, I wouldn't have had to resort to such crude violence.'

Coldhardt inclined his bloodied head in rueful agreement. 'Just how *did* you gain access to my stronghold?'

She raised her arm until the golden serpent was staring directly at him. 'In one of the diamonds there's a miniaturised retinal scanner. When you kissed my hand at the party, you gazed directly into it – a lingering look I recorded for posterity.'

'And used to create an exact match of my retina to bypass the security lift,' Coldhardt concluded. 'Motti, I trust you'll introduce safeguards to ensure such a breach never happens again?'

'Oh, I'll make it my number one job,' said Motti bitterly, 'when your girlfriend here sends us back home.'

Samraj turned to him. 'I had hoped that you and your friends would be at the castle too. I wished to take you all together with a minimum of fuss – so I was delighted when I learned of your plans to enter my premises.'

Motti stared at Coldhardt. 'You told her?'

'Since none of you were there, it was obvious you were out on a job,' he replied calmly. 'And Ms Vasavi knows very well what we've been working on.'

'Yeah, well. Since this is all so chummy, you think Con could sit down? She's flipped out.' He nodded angrily at Yianna, who now hovered behind them with two of her bodyguards. 'Little Miss Beatch here wouldn't let her ride up front.'

Samraj smiled at Coldhardt. 'I told you I had your workforce in my power.'

'Only two of them.' Coldhardt shrugged. '*I* told *you* they would not be taken easily.'

'Two will do.' She turned to her bodyguards. 'At the first sign of trouble from Coldhardt – kill his children.'

Coldhardt's face didn't betray a flicker of emotion. He casually poured himself a little more to drink.

'So that's why we're here. Hostages.' Motti helped Con over to an antique chaise longue, looked at Coldhardt beseechingly, all efforts at cool exhausted. 'What's going on? What *is* all this?'

'Yes, do tell the poor dears, Nathaniel,' said Samraj agreeably. 'Tell them how both Demnos and I approached you, quite independently, to steal the other's fragments of the Amrita prescription. Explain how you accepted both our offers – and both our advance fees – while keeping your talented little helpers in the dark. Worried they would think less of you, perhaps? Or that they might suspect you would double-cross *them* just as readily?'

Con sat perched on the edge of the couch, staring into space. Motti was glad she wasn't hearing this.

'Don't mistake me, Nathaniel,' Samraj continued. 'You know I have always admired your audacity and daring. Why else would I have employed you so many times in the past to acquire my little treasures?' He raised an eyebrow, and she smiled seductively, turning Motti's stomach. 'Aside from *that* reason, of course. I can see how such a bold enterprise must have seemed irresistible to you.' The smile faded. 'But while I did not presume to underestimate your greed and ambition . . . you underestimated *me*.'

'I didn't suspect that Yianna was working for you,' Coldhardt admitted. He cast a measured look at the sullen, sickly girl. 'Why? Why turn against your own father?'

'He is a monster,' Yianna said quietly. 'He does not love me. All he sees in me is the ghost of my mother. *That* is what he wishes to preserve.'

Samraj nodded, her face the picture of sympathetic concern. 'He is a fool not to love you for who you are.'

'I can understand it,' said Motti darkly.

'You know nothing.' Yianna stared at him, her hooded eyes agleam. 'No one can replace my mother in his memory. Together, they made me. I am their legacy, his dearest possession. He . . .' She faltered, put a hand to her cheek. 'He set a surgeon to my face when I was only ten, so I would look more like her . . . The clothes he dressed me in were copies of her old clothes.' She stared into space, shaking her head, bewildered. 'Nothing is mine. Nothing is about Yianna. And it should be. That is only fair, isn't it?' She snarled at Motti. 'Well, isn't it?'

Motti said nothing, wondering if this was what Tye might have become if she hadn't left her father so young: bitter, emotionally retarded, twisted as all hell.

'Do not torment yourself, my dear,' said Samraj softly. But Motti saw no sympathy in the woman's glittering eyes. She merely found the outburst distasteful.

Still Yianna's glare was on Motti. 'He chops up his snakes and makes promises and vows to find the secret of the Amrita, to heal me and make me strong. So he can go on controlling me for ever.' He looked away. 'But Samraj will have the secret before him. She will share it with me. She will share her *life* with me. And we shall leave my father with nothing.'

Coldhardt gave her his wintry smile. 'Samraj and Demnos are old lovers and older rivals. Do you truly believe she acts for your sake?'

Yianna nodded firmly.

'Of course I do. I have seen what the old fool has done to her over the years. I care for her as I would my own child. I'm like you, Nathaniel.' Samraj smiled benignly at Motti and Con, who was still staring vacantly into space. 'We both take injured, unloved little things and give them something to strive for, to believe in . . . We teach them our own values.'

Motti felt his cheeks burning. He willed Coldhardt to say something, to shout her down, to let loose his icy temper and trash the place. But he only stood there, impassive. He didn't contradict her.

'Is that what you've done with the Cult of Ophiuchus – taught them your values?' he said at length, changing the subject. 'I understood they followed only their illustrious, long-living leader. And yet you seem to have them running about for you like errand boys.'

'Only Hela is a true adept of the cult,' Samraj corrected him. 'The others are simply hired muscle. The best that money can buy, naturally.'

'She's got a load more of those tattooed creeps over at the Serpens labs,' Motti told Coldhardt. 'A ton of wires and tubes sticking out of them – she's using them in some kind of experiment.'

'Hela and I are united in our vision to restore the cult of Ophiuchus to former glories,' said Samraj slyly. 'So yes, she is assisting Yianna and me in one way, while her brethren aid me in another.' She stalked slowly forward towards Coldhardt. 'You never understood, did you, Nathaniel? You skulked around my house in the dead of night, and yes, you found my precious scraps of paper, the clues and riddles relating to Ophiuchus and his great secret. I knew what you were up to, and I was prepared to tolerate your curiosity – after all, it was you who stole several of those relics for me in the first place.' She shook her head, mock-chiding him. 'But when I told you I kept the most precious manuscripts of all in my labs, I didn't mean more pieces of parchment.'

Coldhardt considered, then smiled. 'You spoke in metaphor. How pretty of you.'

She nodded. 'I was speaking of the real legacy that Ophiuchus left behind. A manuscript written in chemical bases – the *genome* of the cultists. Their every gene and chromosome, given up for me to map and study.'

'Why?' Motti demanded.

'Over the passing centuries, these adepts of Ophiuchus have lived in small, isolated groups,' Samraj told him, 'maintaining a strict, rarefied diet, breeding selectively. As a result they are not mere mongrels like us, walking bags of contaminated chemicals. They are genetically pure. Their bodies yield up proofs of an impossibly long life – some of them, many hundreds of years.'

'That's not true immortality,' said Coldhardt quietly.

'Far from it,' Samraj concurred. 'Today's world is polluted and poisoned – the food we eat, the soil we tread, the air we breathe. And the cultists' unique genetic make-up makes them extremely vulnerable to this pollution.'

'So what are you saying?' Motti challenged her. 'That the stuff you need to make the Amrita ain't pure enough no more?'

She gave him a withering look. 'Amrita is not some magic potion. It cannot be squeezed from a snake's head as that fool Demnos believes. It cannot be concocted from eye of newt and toe of frog, quaffed down to give everlasting life. Nothing in nature is so easy.' She crossed to join Coldhardt, her voice slow and earnest, as if she sought his understanding and approval. 'My experiments have shown me the truth. Amrita is a purifying substance secreted within the body, by the higher glands. It can only be produced when a perfect balance is achieved between mind and body – a union, if you will, between our basest desires and our highest principles. For each is given meaning by the other.'

For a moment Motti was put in mind of Coldhardt's statue, the man struggling endlessly with the demon. He saw a dark gleam steal into his mentor's eyes. It scared him.

'So *that* is the significance of the serpent and the healer imagery in the legend of Ophiuchus,' Coldhardt said softly.

'We have only to look to his constellation to see the endless quest for balance playing out,' she said. 'Some look at the pattern of stars and see Ophiuchus bearing a snake torn in two. Others see him presenting a two-headed king snake, a crown adorning each. But to the cultists, the patterns are a nightly reminder that the balance is reached only through meditation, self-denial, fasting and prayer.'

Motti grimaced. 'If that's immortality, you can stick it.'

'Ironic, isn't it? The only way to live for all time is to have no kind of life at all.' Samraj looked into Coldhardt's eyes. 'But soon, even that will not be an option for the cultists. As the human body grows choked by chemicals and poisoned by pollution, Amrita is produced in ever smaller amounts.'

'Throw muck into the well and you clog up the water.'

'That is why the cultists are dying out,' she said. 'And why Hela and her fellows have agreed to share their secrets with me alone, so that I might help them.'

'I thought they'd taken sacred vows and stuff to keep their mouths shut,' said Motti.

'Yes, to protect the secrets of the cult. But with the cult itself doomed to certain extinction, such sacrifice seems slightly redundant. Therefore, a faction of acolytes have chosen to break their vows so that their precious religion will not perish.'

'But you don't care about that, do you?' said

Coldhardt. 'All you want is the Amrita – for yourself.'

'For the good of all humankind, Nathaniel, naturally.' She paused, smiled wanly. 'But my efforts have been in vain. All my attempts to synthesise Amrita . . . to enhance it and adapt it . . . They have failed.'

He stared at her. 'Then that's it? The end of the road?'

'So it seemed. But thanks to Yianna, I have found a new path. One that stretches into the shadowlands of history, towards knowledge the civilised world has shied away from.' Samraj's smile grew crueller in triumph. 'In his long, long life, Ophiuchus learned many secrets. And at last I stand on the brink of uncovering the greatest and darkest secret of them all.'

CHAPTER EIGHTEEN

Jonah was fleeing for his life down a foggy street. He couldn't see who was chasing him, but he knew instinctively they meant to kill him. The buildings all around him were towering, ancient and stooped, full of snakes that hissed and rattled, whispered his whereabouts. Dark shadows detached themselves from the smoke-blackened stone to join his hunters, and Jonah pushed himself harder, faster. He had to find Patch and Motti. They were in trouble and it was his fault, but now an alarm was blaring. An insistent warning. *Get out of here*, it was saying, *before –*

His eyes snapped open, he pushed himself up on his elbows. A dream. That was all. He was in his hotel room in Pisa and the phone was ringing. He squinted at the clock. It was 6.30am. No one knew he was here, and he hadn't asked for a wake-up call, so who the hell . . .

The phone wasn't stopping. Irritated, he grabbed for the receiver. 'Hello?'

Nothing but silence the other end.

'Hello?' he said again.

There was a click as the phone went dead.

He frowned. Replaced the handset. 'Wrong number,'

he told himself, not believing it for a second.

Now somebody knew exactly where he was.

Cursing, Jonah scrambled out of bed, swiftly slipped on his jeans and denim jacket, trying to clear his head of the shadows in his dream. Coldhardt's man had dropped him in a quaint, quiet little town called Pontedera as dawn was breaking. From there he had hitched a lift to nearby Pisa, hoping he'd stand out a little less obviously while he tried to decide what to do next.

After a day and a night's soul-searching he was no closer to an answer. And while he had found a quiet and modest hotel along the Via Roma, not far from the famous leaning tower, he had found no peace of mind.

But had someone now found him?

He bundled down the stairs, crossed the deserted reception. They had his passport behind the desk somewhere – he'd have to come back and collect it later. The door to the street was unbolted. He looked round, suspiciously, then slipped outside.

The street was just as quiet. Jonah walked quickly along the uneven pavement, past the cars that lined the street bumper to bumper, towards the looming layer cake of the tower. Its solid presence, its gravity-defying tilt had proved a strange comfort to him yesterday; he'd sat on the grass in the Field of Miracles and hoped for one himself.

He glanced behind him, unable to shake a feeling of unease – and glimpsed movement. Early-bird tourists, he told himself, having a good poke about the back streets before the place started filling up. But he quickened his pace nonetheless. He'd seen a police car near the tower yesterday in the shadow of the Duomo; obviously he wasn't about to go to the law for help but the sight of police might deter anyone from –

Another scuffling noise behind him. He turned, caught a further flash of movement – someone ducking behind a nearby car. Jonah backed away nervously, getting ready to run. Then someone slapped a hand down on his shoulder. He spun round, brought up his fists.

And Tye slapped them back down.

'Glad we taught you to be paranoid,' she said. She looked tired. Her eyes were bloodshot and a little puffy. 'If you'd still been in bed after that call I'd be disappointed.'

Jonah stared, a slow smile spreading over his face. He guessed he should be angry but he was too pleased to see her. 'What's going on? How'd you find me?'

'I knew where you'd been dropped. Guessed you'd have to hand in your fake passport to get a hotel room. So I've spent half the night calling every single hotel within thirty miles of Pontedera, asking for Johann Sypher till I got lucky.'

'And if I'd travelled more than thirty miles?'

'I would have gone to fifty.' She glared at him. 'And beaten the crap out of you when I finally tracked you down.'

'Lucky I'm lazy then. Did you fly here?'

'Yeah.'

'I take it you didn't come all this way just to say goodbye?'

She shook her head. 'Afraid you don't get off the

hook that easy, Jonah Wish.'

'That's right. We need you, mate.'

Jonah turned to find Patch standing just behind him. He looked terrible, his pale, angular face bloodied and bruised.

'What *you* need is a doctor,' Jonah told him. 'What the hell's happened? Where are the others? Are they OK?'

Tye tilted her head back, watched him warily. 'You mean you actually care?'

'I . . .' Suddenly seeing them like this, he realised in a second what he'd agonised over for hours yesterday. 'Well, yeah. I s'pose I do.'

'Good. 'Cause if you didn't, Patch was gonna have to spike your breakfast so we could smuggle you back to Siena in your sleep.' Tye's tiny smile did nothing to allay his growing concerns that something was seriously wrong. 'And we don't have time for you to waste sleeping.'

'You're now officially the brains of the outfit,' Patch added.

'I'm what?'

'Motti and Con were caught on Serpens property. Coldhardt's disappeared. The castle's been trashed.' Tye shrugged. 'I know you quit, but like Patch said – if we're gonna get them back, we need you. We *need* you, Jonah.'

'Me?' For what felt like an age, Jonah could only stare at her. 'But . . . but you know what happened before. I'll let you down. I'm bound to.'

She looked at him. 'You going to let that stop you trying?'

He held her gaze until the long seconds of shock and shadow had passed.

'No,' he said. 'No, I will try.'

Patch put a grateful hand on his back. Tye smiled.

There was no need for more words as they hurried on their way.

Motti listened to Samraj go on with a mounting sense of unease. She was giving away all the big secrets. This could not be a good thing. She was doing what every supervillain in every comic book had done for decades – explaining the details of her diabolical plan so they could die knowing how clever she was. Any second now the speech balloon would burst from the crimson slash of her lips: *But now you know too much! Prepare to die . . .*

Except he knew that none of this was for his or Con's benefit. Samraj was speaking solely to Coldhardt. It was like she was making some big pitch to him, wanting him to understand where she was coming from – and where she wanted to go.

But Coldhardt had some trick up his sleeve. That was what Motti was desperate to believe: the chief was only pretending to listen, playing Samraj along while he dreamed up a way to get them out of here to safety. But from his look of rapt attention he was genuinely enthralled.

Con, on the other hand, still looked genuinely out of it, slumped on the uncomfortable couch, breathing fast and shallow. She moaned suddenly.

Samraj turned, but the flash of irritation soon left her face. 'The poor child is truly suffering, isn't she?'

Motti scowled. 'Like you care.'

'I am not quite the monster you think me.' Samraj turned to Yianna. 'Find Hela. Have her make up some of the cult's healing draught. It will help to settle the girl.'

Yianna looked quite affronted for a moment. Then she nodded, and hobbled from the room.

'Thank you, Samraj,' said Coldhardt quietly.

'The root of the snake,' she said, abruptly returning to her tale. 'It is mentioned in the scraps of manuscript in my possession, and when Yianna told me it was written in her father's ancient papers, I knew it must be of great importance.'

'I thought the snake stuff was just metaphors,' said Motti.

'And so it is.' She didn't spare him so much as a glance. 'According to Hela, over the long centuries Ophiuchus grew weary of keeping the balance within his body. Bored with his endless existence, finding only emptiness in his meditations, he sought to stimulate the Amrita through other means. He craved more extreme experiences.'

'Bummer they didn't have snowboards back then, huh?'

'Be quiet, Motti,' said Coldhardt, his hushed voice still somehow filling the room.

Samraj continued. 'He heard of cave drawings in the Sahara desert – images that were old when even he was young, predating the Stone Age. They showed strange gods festooned with mushrooms, men harvesting the fungus, offering it up in ecstasy.'

'The use of hallucinogenic mushroom rites is as old

as humanity,' Coldhardt agreed. 'Many cultures and religions use them still to contact "spirits" – or what their addled minds *perceive* to be spirits.'

'So you see, the "root of the snake" has nothing to do with reptiles,' Samraj went on. 'According to the cult of Ophiuchus, *snake-root* is the ancient name for a rare fungus that thrived only deep underground – also known as "flesh of the gods". Ophiuchus and his followers located the source and partook of it. They expanded their consciousness, explored the higher realms of reality.'

'So the big god-guy tripped out on some magic mushrooms?' Motti snorted. 'Wow, that really is extreme.'

Coldhardt stopped him with a single warning look. 'The black, organic detritus in the funeral vase . . . it was the remains of this fungus?'

Samraj nodded. 'Sadly it was so desiccated it was barely viable for study – even with all the specialist technology at my disposal.'

'That's why the lekythos stayed at the Serpens lab in Aqaba for twenty-four hours,' Motti realised. 'It's agriculture-based – all your plant specialists are there. You already *knew* there was fungus in that urn, right?'

'I knew that Ophiuchus's followers transported great treasure in special funeral vases. But only the cultists could tell me the whole story.' The gloating smile on her face faded. 'It seems Ophiuchus grew obsessed with the snake-root and the higher realities it unlocked for him. He and his most trusted acolytes hewed acres of dank, secret catacombs in which to farm the snake-root. And then the petty, ignorant people who had venerated him for so long turned on him. It was claimed that he and his followers were swayed from the true path of balance and fell into physical and spiritual decay. That Ophiuchus, his mind and body ruined with madness, finally entombed himself in those catacombs, together with enough flesh of the gods to sustain him for all time.'

'Yum,' Motti muttered.

'Popular opinion turned against Ophiuchus. His image was struck from the zodiac. History was rewritten to remove much of his influence. His cult of followers was driven underground.' Samraj sneered in disgust. '*This* is the supposed great evil now associated with his name! Superstitious, disapproving guff about his greed for knowledge undoing the state of perfect bliss. All lies!'

Coldhardt looked at her expectantly. 'And the truth is . . .?'

'I know your naivety is a front, Nathaniel. It was the men of power who rubbished Ophiuchus and his achievements. It suited them that the people obey *their* gods, not find ones of their own. They knew that if the snake-root became widely used, they could lose control of the population.' Her eyes flashed. 'Throughout history there have been so many fools who would turn their backs on knowledge because of the risks it might bring. Fools who dare not act for fear of upsetting the status quo.'

Motti looked at her doubtfully. 'So you don't think this fungus stuff was bad news.'

'I believe the matter should be carefully studied,' she answered. 'If it's true that Ophiuchus fell into physical decline and yet remained immortal, then perhaps the snake-root acted as a kind of catalyst for the Amrita, allowing it to refresh a polluted body.'

'Which is why you had that detritus forwarded to your facilities here in Rome,' breathed Coldhardt. 'Just in case it could help your cultists.'

'It can't,' she said simply. 'They need a fresh source.'

The door opened and Yianna came back inside with Hela, the black-clad acolyte hiding behind her veil. Motti had only glimpsed her in Cairo, but as she moved across the room, holding a pewter goblet in both hands, he could see how lithe and graceful she was. The skin around her eyes, though, was tinged grey, almost translucent. Motti's own skin began to crawl.

'Hey, what's in that stuff?' he asked Hela as she set the cup to Con's lips.

'She cannot understand you,' said Yianna. 'She speaks no English.'

'You better not be tryin' any tricks –'

Con screwed up her eyes as she swallowed down the brew, and coughed a little. Hela took the goblet away. A faint white foam moustache coated Con's upper lip, and Motti dabbed at it with his sleeve.

Coldhardt watched the acolyte leave the room. 'So, healing potions aside, Hela's people need a fresh source of the snake-root. And that's what *you* need, isn't it Samraj, if you are to develop your own, personal elixir of life.' He drained his own drink. 'Genetically modified Amrita. The means to live for ever while enjoying life to its fullest.'

'Precisely.' Motti could see Samraj was practically drooling at the thought. 'Alas, the snake-root has not been seen on Earth for at least a thousand years. And the Cult of Ophiuchus lost the location of the catacombs long before, during the persecutions of the Dark Ages.'

'The only written reference to the catacombs known to exist is in the Spartan cipher obtained by my father,' said Yianna proudly. 'Spartan soldiers stumbled upon them – and the secrets within.'

Motti remembered Jonah translating the cipher for them back in the safety of the hub. 'Catacombs, north, stars buried in patterns or something, right?'

Yianna nodded. 'That cipher proves that the catacombs must be located in a place of Spartan military activity in the fourth century BC.'

'But now, thanks to Hela's tip-off, we can be more precise,' said Samraj. 'Each lekythos used by Ophiuchus's followers was encoded with directions to the sacred location of the holy catacombs.'

Motti looked at Coldhardt meaningfully.

'We have nothing to bargain with, Motti,' he sighed. 'Samraj took our fragments from the Siena hub when she took me.'

'And once the complete cipher is cracked, the last piece of the puzzle will fall into place,' she said. 'I shall have found the catacombs – and the snake-root. The flesh of the gods.'

'Did it occur to you that the cultists may be lying to make you help them?' Coldhardt suggested. 'Telling you exactly what you want to hear so you play along?'

Samraj shrugged, apparently unbothered. 'I am

merely diagnosing their conditions at present. Comparing *their* chromosomes against ours. No treatment until I test the truth of their story.'

'And what if the snake-root no longer grows?'

'Even if it does not, there should be enough genetic material left behind to make a fuller study of its properties.'

'Well, then. There's just one thing I don't understand.' Coldhardt set down his half-empty glass. 'Yianna told you the secrets of her father's fragments, and presumably some time ago. You had no need to engage my services to steal them from Demnos. So why did you?'

'Can you really be such a fool?' Samraj advanced slowly on Coldhardt. 'I wanted to involve you in my affairs once again. I've already told you I don't care about your double-crosses. I understand you had an impeccable motive.'

She took his hands in hers. He didn't pull away.

'You weren't just stealing secrets for me or for Demnos,' Samraj said, and pressed a kiss softly against his lips. 'You were stealing them for yourself. It was never the money you wanted. You wanted the secret of immortality for yourself.'

'Is that true?' asked Motti.

'You can't understand, being so young,' said Coldhardt quietly, talking to him but still looking at Samraj. 'You don't know how it feels to reach my years . . . to know that time's running out.' Now he looked at Motti with the full force of those haunted blue eyes. 'To know what's waiting for you, when you die . . .'

Motti glanced around with a sick feeling. 'Reckon I'm gonna be finding out sometime soon.'

'This need not be the end,' Samraj told Coldhardt. 'I appreciate your value. And if I am to live for ever, I shall need a consort. A partner.'

Coldhardt smiled. 'And what must I do to earn this honour?'

'I need to know the location of the catacombs,' she said softly. 'That little boy you acquired – Jonah Wish. He can break the lekythos cipher, and quickly. Bring him to me.'

'No way,' snapped Motti. 'Jonah bailed. He's history.'

'It's true, he resigned,' Coldhardt admitted. 'But there are ways of getting him back.'

Motti stared at him. 'What, you're gonna sell him out?'

'It may take a day or so to locate him and to lure him here,' Coldhardt went on, Samraj his only focus. 'But he'll come. And I guarantee he can be . . . *persuaded* to help.'

'A day or so? Then we have some time to kill together.' Samraj all but licked her lips. 'And soon, all the time in the world. Imagine what we could achieve . . .'

'Perhaps we should discuss it,' Coldhardt agreed. 'Alone.'

'You cannot be serious!' Motti shouted, jumping up from the couch. One of Samraj's thugs advanced on him warningly.

'Let the children run along to bed,' said Coldhardt. 'Yianna, take them to the guest room. Do make sure they're snuggled up tight.' Samraj paused. 'Remember, Nathaniel. If you try to trick me, they'll be killed.'

Coldhardt shrugged. 'They're not important any more.'

The words were said so casually but fell like scalding water into Motti's ears. He bunched his fists, wanted to lash out, smash up the place. But then the bruisers' arms were gripping hold of him, bundling him away. He screamed and struggled. Con was dragged up from the couch, woozy, blinking in confusion.

Coldhardt watched as they were taken away, his face impossible to read, melting anyway in Motti's eyes as the first stinging tears welled up.

CHAPTER NINETEEN

Jonah strained to set right Coldhardt's computer on the desk, while Tye and Patch waded through the debris in the junior hub for any clue the abductors might have left behind.

But as he worked, adjusting cables and calibrating the screen, his attention kept turning to the note on Coldhardt's desk beside the hanky. 'MISS ME, Cx,' he murmured. Then he sat down in the plush leather office chair. 'There was a big struggle here, that's obvious,' he announced. 'Whoever did this was looking for something in particular.'

'Most likely those bits of the funeral vase,' Tye agreed, trying half-heartedly to straighten out a mad stack of parchments.

'And obviously, he couldn't write a note telling us what happened. It would be found and destroyed.'

'So he sends us a kiss?' Patch sat down awkwardly on a chair with one leg missing. 'He's flipped.'

'Nah. He's just a clever old sod, as well we know.' Jonah tapped a finger on the piece of paper. 'What if the C isn't for Coldhardt?'

'What else would it be for?'

'C is 100 in Roman numerals. And X is ten.'

'So, 110?' Patch frowned. 'What's that meant to mean?'

'I don't know,' said Jonah. 'But the Miss part could mean a woman.'

Tye leaned forward. 'Samraj?'

'And the "me" part . . .' Jonah tapped the computer. 'What if this was still on the desk and switched on when he scribbled out this note? Maybe he was trying to draw our attention to it.'

Patch had stood back up again, hopping from foot to foot. Either he needed the toilet or he was getting excited. 'So how do we find out what was on there?'

'I set an auto-recover going. Rebuilding his desktop as it was when the power was tugged out . . .' He clicked over the keys. 'Keep your fingers crossed.'

Tye and Patch came over to join him. Jonah's heart was beating out a wild rhythm as he waited for the computer's creaks and whirrings to resolve into a result.

Finally it did. A kind of electronic organiser appeared on screen.

'His contacts book,' said Tye quietly. 'That's normally top secret. He never leaves it open.'

'Probably had no choice,' said Patch. 'He must have been using it when they got in.'

'If he had time to write this note, he had time to shut down the address book.' Jonah was already clicking to entry 110.

It was headed simply, 'Her'. An address in Rome was listed.

'Samraj,' Tye muttered. Her hand brushed softly against the back of Jonah's neck as she self-consciously squeezed his shoulder. 'Jonah, I'm glad we found you.'

So am I, he wanted to say.

'But what are we gonna find when we get down there?' said Patch worriedly. 'Look at these notes!'

'Main gate, alarm code override . . .' Jonah read aloud. 'Study: photoelectric beam at knee height trips steel shutters. Kitchen: foiled windows, magnetic switch on outer door trips main alarm. Fingerprint scanners in use throughout villa . . .' He looked up at Tye, forced a worried smile. 'Thorough, isn't he?'

But Tye wasn't looking. She had picked up the handkerchief. She'd spied something there and was squinting to see. Jonah took a look himself and found a small filmy square, glistening beneath the fluorescent lights.

'Oh yeah,' she said, a slow grin spreading over her face. 'He's thorough, all right.'

Motti waited in the grip of Yianna's bodyguards as the lady herself shuffled slowly forward to open the door. Constantly stopping and starting to let her catch up, it had taken for ever to climb the stairs and reach this little landing in the east wing. At least it had given him time to swallow back his tears. No way would these bastards ever know he was hurting.

'You don't look so good, girl,' he observed. 'Does she, Con?'

Con didn't respond, still lost in her daze. So much for the healing draught.

'I am sick,' Yianna said quietly. 'Sick and tired.'

'You ain't the only one,' Motti assured her. 'Looks like your new mommy is coming on kinda strong to my boss. That don't worry you?'

'You cannot provoke me.'

'I mean, three's a crowd and all. Samraj has got what she wanted from you – and frankly it don't seem like much to me.'

'I trust her.'

'Yeah, well, I trusted Coldhardt,' said Motti bitterly. 'And look where it's got me.'

'*She* trusts *me*, too,' said Yianna, finally dragging herself as far as the door and pressing her index finger against the scanner to open it. 'You see? I have the run of this place.'

'Run? More like the zombie shuffle.'

She slapped him round the face, her sunken eyes shining. 'She is going to make me well.'

'What, by sending you all the way over here, just so you can walk back again?' He shook his head. 'She's playing with you, girl.'

'You wouldn't understand. She cares for me as much as she hates my father.' She smiled. 'My disappearance has already started picking at the stitches that hold him together. Together we will watch my father grow old and bitter and die while we remain unchanging . . . *perfect*.'

'Yeah, right, happy ever after,' sneered Motti. 'This ain't the movies.'

'Maybe not,' she said, caressing the stiletto hilt that protruded from her bodyguard's belt. 'But remember . . . I still say when we *cut*.'

One gesture, and Motti was shoved viciously into the room. Con was bundled through after him. He tried to break her fall but together they both toppled and hit the floor.

'That's a wrap,' he sighed, as the door swung back shut. He flicked on the light switch and glanced around. The room was empty save for a heavy wooden wardrobe and a double bed. The window was sealed, security glass, unbreakable.

Gently, he lay Con on top of the hard mattress. 'You OK?' he asked her, just on the off chance.

No reply. She just lay there on her side.

'You know, if Patch was here he'd be looking down your top and stuff. Dirty little bastard.' Motti lay on the bed beside her, stared up at the ceiling and sighed. 'God, I hope him and Tye are OK.' He paused, glanced at her. 'But if you ever wake up and tell them you heard that, you're gonna be back in a coma for the rest of your life. Got it?'

His mind raced in the silence. Too many questions, and only painful answers. He was hurting – not just his bruised throat but all over.

He imagined Yianna's bodyguards waiting just outside. Waiting for the order to come in and kill them.

Motti took off his glasses and rubbed his eyes. 'Con, I swear I ain't no perv or nothing,' he whispered. 'And I don't mean to freak you. But God help me, I'm scared to death here. So if you can hear me, somehow . . . could you maybe pretend I'm someone you like?'

He shuffled up on his side and spooned her, reaching over and fumbling for her hand. Once he'd found it, he held on tight.

It was probably his imagination, but he thought he felt just the tiniest squeeze back on his sweaty fingers.

*　*　*

Motti was woken by a sharp cracking noise outside, a bang on the wall. He rolled away from Con, reached for his glasses, jumped off the bed, suddenly awake and wired like he'd had a dozen espressos. It was daylight outside. How long had he been sleeping? He checked his watch but it was bust.

'Con, wake up,' he hissed. 'You gotta wake up. I think this is it.'

He looked around but there was nothing he could use for a weapon. In desperation he tugged at his leather belt with the heavy clasp. He could maybe use it as –

The door swung suddenly open. Motti yanked out the belt and wielded it fiercely.

'What're you gonna do, doofus? Drop your trousers and hope Samraj dies laughing?'

'*Patch?*' Motti stared in disbelief at the small, battered figure grinning in the doorway. And standing just behind him was – 'Tye! I gotta be dreaming!' He grabbed and gathered them both up in a clumsy hug. 'C'mon. You gotta help me with Con.'

'Is she OK?' Patch pulled away to see. 'Con?'

'She's been out for hours,' said Motti. 'Flipped out in the back of the car. They gave her this weird drink but I dunno if it –'

'Look out!' Tye shouted as one of Samraj's bruisers sprang up from nowhere and grabbed her round the neck. Patch bundled back through the door to help her.

Motti was quick to follow, but another thug kicked him in the chest, sent him staggering back inside the room. He swung the belt, but it was caught and snatched from his grasp. He heard a cry of pain from Tye, couldn't help but turn to look. A fist slammed out towards his face; he parried with his wrist but the impact still floored him. He landed on his back at the foot of the wardrobe.

'Get underneath it,' hissed a voice from behind him. '*Con?*'

She wasn't on the bed any more.

'Do it!'

The heavy wardrobe was raised on four elegantly carved legs. Motti used his own two skinny ones to push himself backwards, wriggling into the dark space beneath the wood. He heard his attacker start forwards to grab him –

And flinched as unexpected daylight dazzled his eyes. The wardrobe was toppling forwards, ready to fall. But before the great weight could crash down on his legs he felt someone dragging him backwards and up.

The bruiser was not so lucky. He screamed as the wardrobe smashed to the floor, pinning him there.

Motti meanwhile found himself in Con's arms. He straightened his glasses. 'You came back to us.'

'I slept on it,' she agreed. 'And I have decided I'm angry as hell.' She stuck out her tongue. 'What have I been drinking?'

'You don't wanna know,' said Motti, vaulting the wardrobe and crossing to the corridor. 'But I'm glad you're mad, 'cause something tells me we ain't getting out of here without a fight.' Tye and Patch were climbing to their feet. 'You two OK?'

'We got this one.' Tye nodded to the jerk in black

on the floor behind her. 'But the other guy went running for reinforcements.'

'He didn't get too far.'

Motti stared at yet another familiar face. 'You came back.'

Jonah had come round the corner of the corridor, shaking a set of skinned knuckles. 'I know I've missed some training – but how d'you guys hit people without breaking your fingers?'

'Family secret,' said Motti, shaking Jonah hard by his bruised hand, making him wince. 'Remind me to tell it to you sometime, man.'

Con joined them in the corridor, smiling at Jonah in a way that made Patch look down at his shoes.

'You're OK?' Tye asked.

Con shook her head. 'Things are about the worst they could be.'

'Where's Coldhardt?'

'That's what I mean. He's sold us out.'

Patch looked back up sharply. 'He what?'

Motti stared at her, a blush starting to colour his cheeks. 'Then . . . you heard all that stuff?'

'It was like I was a million miles away. So far that nothing could touch me, yes?' She shrugged softly. 'But now I remember everything.'

'Excuse me – what does a person have to do to get rescued around here?'

They all turned as one.

It was Coldhardt. His dapper suit was scuffed and a little crumpled, and the welt on his head was angry and red. But the Irish swagger in the voice, the stance and the smile were those of a man on top of his game.

'Hello, Jonah,' he said coolly. 'I imagine it was you who cracked my cryptic little note. Welcome back to the fold.'

'You don't seem surprised to see me.'

'I told you before. I pride myself on my instincts in these matters.' He smiled round at his children. 'In the same way, I predicted Con would be unwilling or unable to fully remove your memories.'

'Unwilling,' she retorted at once.

'And under the circumstances, Jonah, I decided it could do no harm for you to leave the fold for a time.'

Jonah frowned. 'What do you mean?'

'No one escapes me that easily.' He beamed suddenly. 'Tye, Patch, congratulations on making it this far.'

'Wasn't so hard considering what you'd left behind to help us,' said Tye coldly.

'Guys, this could be a trap,' said Motti, bunching his fists. 'Samraj wanted all of us together. And she needs Jonah.'

'She sought to influence me through you,' said Coldhardt. 'She now realises that isn't possible.'

''Cause you don't care for no one but yourself,' Motti hissed.

Coldhardt stared him down. 'I got bored waiting for you two to free yourselves. So I thought I'd better come get you.'

'So you can hand us all over to your bitch girlfriend?'

'Who at this very moment is trussed up in her bedroom with her own silk sheets.' He shrugged. 'I tried to keep her occupied for as long as I could to buy you time . . .'

Con's eyes had narrowed. 'Yeah, I'll bet you did.'

'And what's all this, "as long as I could" garbage?' Motti challenged. 'I thought you had all eternity ahead of you if you stuck with her and sold out Jonah.'

Jonah looked alarmed. 'What *is* this?'

'She needs you to crack the lekythos cipher,' said Con. 'She's got all the fragments.'

'And now *I* have a copy of the complete cipher myself.' Coldhardt grandly patted a pocket of his suit. 'The fruits of my final seduction.'

Motti sneered. 'You expect us to believe that?'

'So, you no longer trust me.' Coldhardt clicked his tongue. 'Not even you, Tye?'

She didn't answer.

'Well, rest assured that the occupants of this house will kill me for escaping as readily as they'll kill you.'

'We should just get out of here,' said Patch, wringing his hands.

'I'm telling you, it's a trap!' Motti argued. 'Tye, what you getting off him?'

Tye bit her lip. 'I *think* he's on the level, but I –'

Then suddenly there was a dark blur of movement at the turn of the corridor as two of Samraj's henchmen attacked. Coldhardt whirled round, jabbed one in the sternum while bringing his fist up under the jaw of the other. One fell straight to the floor, the other bounced off a wall first. Neither got back up.

For an old guy, Coldhardt still had moves.

'That was no faked demonstration,' he said gruffly. 'I find close-quarters combat so undignified at my age. If anyone wants to debate this subject further, they can wait until we've got the hell away from here. Tye – you still have the key?'

She raised her hand and gave him the finger. Then she turned it round and wriggled it at him. 'Samraj's fingerprint? Yeah, I've still got it.'

'How?' asked Con.

'When he kissed her fingers at the Gallery Rimbaud,' Tye explained. 'He slipped a little square of acetate on his lips first.'

'So while she was scanning your retina you were lifting her prints?' Motti smiled despite himself. 'Jeez, you two really are a match made in heaven.'

'We know a little of each other's security arrangements,' said Coldhardt dismissively. 'That's more intimacy than I usually care for. Come on, this way.'

He stepped over the fallen bodies and vanished from view down the corridor. Tye, Patch and Jonah exchanged brief glances, then followed.

Motti looked at Con. She started to set off after them when he took hold of her arm. 'So . . .' he said awkwardly. 'You remember everything?'

'Yes.' She gave him a fleeting smile, the closest he'd ever seen her come to self-conscious. 'And I like you plenty.'

He blushed. 'Yeah, well . . . Tell anyone about what happened in there and I'll break your arm, got it?'

'Got it.'

They hurried after the others.

Jonah knew they'd been lucky, and that they had Coldhardt to thank. With Samraj all tied up and unable to dish out the orders, their opposition wasn't focused. Two more bodyguards were standing guard at the top of the main staircase, with three more in the hallway below. Tye and Motti tackled one while Con laid into another. With a yell and a graceful high kick she pushed her opponent clear over the banister rail. The noise of his impact on the marble floor echoed like cannon fire. As soon as the other man had been wrestled to the floor, Patch moved in and punched him hard in the back of the neck, knocking him unconscious.

Jonah led them in a stampede down the stairs. 'Hallway looks clear,' he reported. He tried the front door. 'Tye, we need your magic finger.'

She was beside him in seconds, pressing her coated finger against the black pad beside the doorframe. Jonah tried the handle and the door opened easily. Con, Motti, Patch and Coldhardt piled outside.

Jonah looked at Tye. 'We did it. We actually *did* it!'

He could see she was trying not to smile. 'Don't get cocky. It's not over yet.'

'Get out here,' Motti hissed, 'and close the door.' Tye ran to fetch the car, while Motti worked on the fingerprint panel with a tool Patch passed to him. The black pad sparked and belched a puff of black smoke.

'That should hold them for a few minutes,' he said.

Jonah frowned. 'They'll just break the windows to get after us!'

'Bulletproof,' said Patch, Motti and Con in unison.

They all hurried off after Tye, and Coldhardt smiled thinly at Jonah. 'You'll learn to recognise it yourself after a few jobs.'

'I s'pose maybe I will,' said Jonah.

As they reached the end of the drive, Jonah felt eyes on him from somewhere, felt he was being watched. He turned, checked out the upstairs windows. At one of them, just for a moment, he thought he glimpsed Samraj and Yianna, staring out, watching them go. But the glass was blank now, reflecting the whiteness of the sky.

CHAPTER TWENTY

Jonah's heart was pounding as Tye brought Coldhardt's limo to a screeching halt just outside the villa's gates. There was still no sign of any angry guards in pursuit, but it couldn't be long now. Con jumped into the passenger seat. Motti and Patch piled into the back of the car and Jonah scrambled after them.

'We did it! We're back!' cried Patch, who looked like all his Christmases had come at once. 'I can't believe we're all back together again!'

'Me neither. But where can we go?' Tye asked shakily, accelerating swiftly away down the private road towards the main thoroughfare.

'Back to Siena,' Coldhardt instructed.

'Via McDonalds,' called Con from the front. 'It's way past lunchtime and I'm starving.'

Motti's face clouded. 'It's not safe to go back to the castle. Samraj knows how to get round the defences – her hoods can walk right in and take us.'

'We need the plane, and there is information I must collect,' said Coldhardt. 'Samraj may not have Jonah to translate the cipher, but she knew my betraying her was always a possibility. She'll have a contingency plan.'

'I'm telling you, man, her plan B will be to send her thugs round to kidnap Jonah and kill the rest of us,' said Motti, 'wherever we go!'

'Oh, I imagine she'll have something far more elaborate than a swift death in store for me. Eternal pain and damnation, perhaps.' Coldhardt half-smiled, staring into the distance. 'But I'd sooner face it in the next world than this one.'

'Tell you what – why not just pucker up and kiss her ass, and maybe she'll forgive you, huh?' Motti slumped back in his seat. 'And suddenly we're expendable again.'

'Easy, Mot,' hissed Patch.

'What's up, Cyclops? Am I spoiling your game of happy families?' He jabbed a finger at Coldhardt. 'It's him you should be talking to!'

'Why *did* you keep the truth from us, Coldhardt?' Con asked. 'Why not just tell us you were working for them both?'

'I didn't want you involved,' he said simply. 'You people are the only things on this earth she could use against me. And she corrupts the young most persuasively. Just take a look at Yianna.'

Con's voice softened. 'You were afraid that if she got her hands on us she'd turn us against you?'

Coldhardt turned his gaze on Jonah. 'Those photographs I showed of you – at your arrest, inside the police station . . . They were arranged by her.'

A shiver ran through him. 'She was after me even back then?'

'She had learned from Hela about the cultists' use

of the lekythos, and was aware that the location of the catacombs would be encrypted on its surface. So she thought to acquire a young expert with no ties or loyalties for the day a lekythos was discovered. Someone who could be killed cleanly with no fallout once he'd done his work, so no one but her would know of the location.'

Jonah stared back at him. 'So you knew she was after me, and got there first?'

His face remained impassive. 'I delivered you from evil, Jonah.'

'Right. I get it.' Jonah nodded slowly. 'And once I was on your team, Samraj knew the easiest way to get to me was through you.'

'So she cosied up to you,' Motti agreed. 'She clued you in on all her plans.'

'I may be an old man now, but I like to flatter myself my own charms played a part in securing her interest.' Coldhardt half-smiled. 'They always worked in the past.'

'But to prove your loyalty to her now, you had to hand over Jonah,' said Con.

'And as I have said, I would never allow that to happen.'

'Just how far back do you and Samraj go?'

'I care for you all, Con,' said Coldhardt, 'but I answer to no one.'

He didn't speak again for the rest of the journey.

Tye was detailed to refuel the plane and get it ready for flight, while the others helped Motti rig up some on-the-fly defences around the castle to buy them some time in case of an attack – which they all knew could come at any moment. She heard Motti talking about trip wires, motion detectors, PIRs, bad-tempered but in his element.

Jobs done, they all met back in the junior hub, which was looking a little more like the slick sanctum of old. It was a relief to have Coldhardt back at the head of the table. Tye just hoped that Motti's lash-ups would warn them of unexpected visitors coming to call.

The only one of them not yet in his place was Jonah. He sat instead at the computer desk, his eyes scouring the monitor screen as he factored in the remaining pieces of the cipher that Coldhardt had acquired.

'So what do we do first?' asked Con. 'Sell Demnos the info on his daughter?'

Coldhardt shook his head. 'You think he'll pay us for news like that? He wouldn't believe a thing without proof.'

'So sell him the truth about Amrita, then,' Patch suggested.

'Tell him he's wasted the last twenty years of his life down a blind alley – and that his daughter's known the truth for some time?' Coldhardt shook his head. 'Besides, if our own role in this affair becomes known to him . . .'

'Like the way you made us break into his place and not Samraj's, for instance,' said Motti sourly.

'We still have Demnos's down-payment,' Con reminded them. 'Enough to cut and run?'

'Once travel and operating costs are deducted . . .'

Coldhardt shook his head. 'It's less than satisfactory. And it won't remove the problem of Samraj.'

'While we've got Jonah, we've got something to bargain with,' said Con.

'Nice to feel needed,' Jonah called.

'I told you, she'll have a contingency plan,' snapped Coldhardt. 'I know she's been keeping a file on a prominent professor of antiquities and languages.'

Patch looked worried. 'Full of juicy blackmail stuff?'

'I don't know what she has on him. But she'll find a way to make use of his services, depend on it.' He smiled bleakly. 'The moment he's done his job, I imagine both his secrets and apparent suicide will be splashed all over the broadsheets.'

'She won't give up, will she?' said Con.

Patch sighed. 'And when she's worked out how to make Amrita, she'll have for ever to get us!'

'We have different home bases, we can stay one step ahead,' Tye argued. 'Can't we?'

But Coldhardt was staring into space.

'Guys. I've found something.'

Everyone looked over at Jonah, Coldhardt included.

'I've been tracing the code formulas, following the path the program took, processing the last parts of the cipher.'

'There was an error?' snapped Coldhardt.

'No.' Jonah shook his head, his eyes agleam. 'But you know how I told you it hacked into those ancient language databases?'

'As used at Oxford and Yale.'

'Well it didn't translate the words into English from the Ancient Greek like we thought it would,' said Jonah slowly. 'It translated from ninth-century *Arabic*.'

'Arabic?' Motti frowned. 'But why?'

'The lekythos was Greek – but it was found in Egypt,' breathed Coldhardt.

Patch nodded excitedly. 'And Ophiuchus had been known before as that Egyptian guy, what was his –?'

'Imhotep.' Coldhardt's long strides devoured the distance to his desk in moments. 'What happens if we translate the words back into Arabic?'

'Already on the case,' Jonah told him, standing up to allow Coldhardt to take his seat. 'Won't take long to get a result.'

They waited tensely.

'Ras Alhague,' Coldhardt read aloud, 'Cebalrai, Yed Prior, Sabik . . . I've seen those names, I'm sure of it . . .' He looked up at them, comprehension dawning. 'Of course. Of *course*.'

'Care to share?' Motti drawled.

'Stars! They're the names of stars – in the Ophiuchus constellation!'

Tye saw Jonah frown, as though he was slowly catching hold of something in his mind.

'Arabic astronomers had been cataloguing the stars since early times,' Coldhardt went on. 'Their names for the brighter stars are still often used today – Aldebaran, Betelgeuse, Sirius . . . And they are names that would have been far more familiar a thousand years ago.'

'So now we understand them.' Tye shrugged. 'But

how does that help us? Why print the names of stars on the side of the vase?'

'And numbers,' said Jonah. 'Co-ordinates, Coldhardt – that was your theory, right?'

'A possibility,' he agreed.

'It fits. But the question is, how do we calculate the scale?'

Tye frowned. 'Scale of what?'

'What's a constellation, anyway?' Jonah was concentrating furiously. 'Just a pattern in the sky. A dot-to-dot with stars.'

'And important to the cult,' Con chipped in. 'They marked the pattern on that warning note they left for us.'

'Go on, Jonah,' said Coldhardt quietly.

'Remember the Spartan cipher that kicked all this off? "Stars buried in patterns" – that was a part of it. Those soldiers who found the catacombs must have realised it too.'

Motti's frustration was boiling over. 'Realised *what*?' he demanded.

Jonah looked at Coldhardt, a grin slow-spreading over his face. 'I think the cipher's meant to show us how to transfer the dot-to-dot Ophiuchus pattern in the stars on to an area of land.'

Con stared at him. 'To mark the place where the catacombs are hidden?'

'Then the coordinates must relate to landmarks,' said Coldhardt. 'Things that could be seen from afar.'

'Or even from above,' Tye reasoned, 'if you had to cross mountains to reach there. '

'But which mountains?' said Patch. 'What area are

we talking about?'

Jonah shrugged. 'There's no mention. I suppose if we were true cultists carrying the lekythos, we would *know* which country it was.'

'Could be anywhere,' sighed Con.

'No. Like Yianna said, it's somewhere the Spartan soldiers campaigned,' Motti told her. 'Somewhere they fought in the fourth century BC.'

Coldhardt nodded. 'Today it'll be part of Europe or northern Africa . . .'

Jonah nodded. 'The cipher mentioned the "north", didn't it?'

'That's still a large area to track,' said Con. 'We must do some research, yes?'

'We'll start at once,' Coldhardt announced. 'We should be able to find evidence of Spartan military operations from that era online.'

'And then we'll need maps for all those areas,' mused Patch. 'Really good maps.'

'There's sat nav on the plane,' said Tye, 'including digital terrain models.'

'Brilliant,' said Jonah. 'Can we load the software on to here, too? I'll program in the pattern of the constellation as an overlay.'

'It won't be an exact aerial view,' Coldhardt warned him. 'It'll be from a vantage point as Tye suggested – a mountain pass or a plateau.'

Jonah nodded. 'With a bit of time I can scale it up or down, rotate it, skew it over each part of the map. See if it fits any features.'

'This is gonna take for ever,' sighed Patch. 'Anyway, we'd need maps for, like, a thousand years ago.'

Coldhardt shook his head. 'If these acolytes really could live for centuries at a time, they'd choose landmarks unlikely to change over hundreds, even thousands of years. But you're right – it will take time.' He started tapping at the keyboard. 'So let's start our history lesson at once, and narrow down the field.'

Motti sighed. 'I thought we were meant to be clearing out of here?'

'No.' The word dropped from Coldhardt's lips with the weight of a brick. 'There's no time to waste. And besides, Samraj will be expecting us to cut and run – it's the obvious move.'

'That's 'cause it makes sense.'

'Not when she may know the whereabouts of our other bases in Switzerland, Mexico, southern France . . .' He nodded gravely. 'She could be dispatching her guards to any one of those places in readiness for our arrival.'

Motti sighed impatiently. 'Well, if nothing else, she's bound to have this place under observation.'

'A fair assumption,' Coldhardt agreed. 'Let us leave the gates ajar, just as they were. And we must black out all the windows. None of you will use your rooms – you will restrict your movements to the hub and the hangout as much as possible.'

'What will you do once we've found the catacombs' location?' wondered Con. 'Sell it to Demnos? Let him fight over it with Samraj and lie low somewhere till the heat's died down?'

Coldhardt shook his head. 'We must get to the catacombs ourselves, before she does.'

'Why?' challenged Motti. 'So you can get one up on your ex? So you can get the secret of everlasting life all for yourself?'

'So *we* can acquire ourselves a great deal of money.' He looked at Motti coldly. 'This venture is about maximising profit now, nothing more. If those catacombs really are the place where Ophiuchus chose to bury himself alive, imagine what relics and rarities may be hidden inside – quite aside from the unique properties of this "flesh of the gods".' He smiled, a true rogue's smile. 'And since Samraj seems to be on the warpath, a haul like that should buy us a good deal of protection from collectors all over the world.'

'We could give her the best of it to get her off our backs,' Patch suggested.

'*Give* it to her?' Con was offended. 'Offer her a discount, maybe.'

'First we have to actually find the catacombs,' said Jonah.

Coldhardt nodded decisively. 'So let's do it.'

CHAPTER TWENTY-ONE

Jonah woke blearily to the sound of distant engines and the sharp patter of gunfire. He scrambled up from the soft couch he lay on, wide-eyed, disorientated. The hangout was dark. Motti's quiet breathing carried from a large beanbag beside the bar. Then Jonah noticed a pale blue glow was coming from one of the side rooms.

'Come on! Yes, yes . . . Come to Papa . . . *Gotcha*!'

It was Patch's voice. Rubbing his gritty eyes, Jonah padded through and found him sitting in a big squashy armchair in front of a huge plasma TV, playing computer games.

'You scared the hell out of me,' Jonah complained. 'Shouldn't you be sleeping?'

'Sorry mate,' said Patch, hitting the pause. 'Only, I've never finished this game, see? And, well, after what's been kicking off around here . . .'

'You think you might never get the chance?'

Patch shrugged and hit the pause again, let the room fill with the sound of engines, screaming and flying bullets. 'Anyway, it helps take my mind off what's really bugging me.'

'Which is?'

'The prospect of a sudden, violent death is bad enough – but dying a virgin? That really stinks!' He blew up a couple of out of control tankers speeding towards him. 'Hey, since I helped save Con's life, d'you think if I asked her extra-nicely –?'

'I wouldn't bother,' Jonah advised. 'Not unless you want that joystick inserted somewhere unpleasant.' He sighed and yawned, and then his watch alarm went off. 'Three-thirty am. Con should be coming off shift. I'd better go and relieve her.'

'It's not fair,' Patch grumbled, blowing up a munitions dump. 'She should be the one relieving me!'

Jonah smiled through another yawn and set off for the hub. After all he'd been through lately, he felt he could sleep for a year – and a trawl through about a million aerial views and cross-sections of European landscapes was no kind of substitute. He and the others were working in rotas, four hours on, four hours off. All except Coldhardt, who kept ploughing on through the possible locations. He didn't seem to need sleep, his eyes clear and strong regardless of the time of day.

The night outside was quiet and still. Jonah hurried through it, keeping close to the perimeter wall of the main building. Motti had spent more time improving the castle's defences than on the actual task in hand, but no one was complaining. More than thirty-six hours had passed since they'd started the search for the catacombs, and they were all becoming convinced that an attack from Samraj's guards sometime soon was inevitable.

One good thing: the threat was a powerful spur to

getting a result, and fast.

Suddenly, Jonah caught movement up ahead. He flattened himself against the wall.

'It is only me.' Con's voice.

Jonah breathed a sigh of relief. 'I was just coming to replace you.'

She crossed quickly to him, a tired smile on her face. 'You think I can be replaced?'

'Er – no! I didn't mean . . .' He cleared his throat. 'So. How're things?'

'I have a pain in my guts if you really want to know,' she told him, grimacing. 'Ever since we left Samraj's place.'

'Were you hurt in the fight?'

She shook her head. 'It's probably just junk food withdrawal symptoms. Get me some chicken nuggets and I'll be fine.'

She started to move past him, but on impulse he blocked her way. 'Er, Con . . . I've been meaning to say. What happened in my room the night I left –'

'It was nothing,' she said briskly. 'I thought I was saying goodbye.'

'So did I,' he said.

She just smiled. 'Then we forget it, yes?'

Jonah nodded, though it wasn't the kind of kiss you could ever forget. As she pushed past him with a quick pat on the shoulder, he knew that was all it had been – just a brilliant snog from out of the blue. And he felt kind of weird, because if he'd ever pictured himself snogging anyone round here, it would be Tye . . .

Oops!

Sleep deprivation gave you funny thoughts. He only

hoped it didn't make you hallucinate too.

A few minutes later, as he neared the hub, he heard Tye whoop for joy. He rushed inside.

There she was with Coldhardt, poring over some printouts. She looked up at him, a huge grin stretching over her face.

'Cracked it,' she said.

'So this is Macedonia,' murmured Jonah.

Barely six hours on, and he was sitting with Tye in the cockpit of the plane staring out over the rugged, mountainous terrain. Viewed from this height, the landscape took on a slightly unreal quality: the glittering grey of glacial lakes, the dramatic drop of the basins and valleys . . . Like all of this was some weird kind of dream.

And yet he knew that, for better or worse, nothing in his life had ever seemed more vivid than his time with Coldhardt.

After so long spent dreaming about life, Jonah felt the time had come to start living it for real.

'We're flying over the *Plakenska Planina*,' Tye informed him, checking her sat nav. 'That's the vantage point, right?'

'It's the most likely mountain pass that the faithful acolytes would have travelled, yeah,' he agreed. 'If we've got it right.' There were no guarantees. The Macedonian landscape was riddled with waterfalls, lakes, peaks and ravines and –

'*Poljes*,' Jonah announced, pointing down at what looked like a couple of enormous animal footprints in the broad sweep of land. 'I read about them online.

Water dissolves the limestone and it kind of falls away, see, leaving these depressions in the land, several miles across . . .'

'You're *such* a geek, Jonah.'

'Who died and made you Motti?'

'I just hope that after working for two days straight, we're not on the mother of all wild goose chases.' Tye yawned noisily. 'Then I'll *really* show you a depression miles across.'

'It's tough on you,' he said, 'having to fly on top of everything else.'

'Want to take over?'

'Nah. Don't want to crash your party. Or the plane, for that matter.'

She shook her head with exaggerated weariness. 'Look, this lake below is one of the points on our do-it-yourself constellation, right?'

Jonah felt a snap of disappointment as she nudged the conversation back to business. He was probably boring her. And yet he couldn't help feeling that maybe there *was* some small connection there, despite the gulf between their backgrounds . . .

Get you! came the familiar nagging voice in his head. *Projecting all this emotional crap on to Tye, just because she's the only person who's ever come after you, the only person who's wanted you back in her life. But she was only using you to get back her friends.*

Look at her. How could someone like that be interested in someone like you?

'Uh, Jonah?' Tye asked again, looking up at him again with those incredible eyes. 'The lake?'

279

Go jump in it, Jonah told his nagging voice. It wasn't like he really felt anything more for Tye than friendship.

That would be crazy.

'Moving swiftly on,' he muttered. 'OK, let's see now . . . That's Lake Prespa, yeah? That's our point for *Marlick*, the elbow. Which makes that waterfall . . .'

'Which waterfall?'

'That waterfall, next to the bigger one further back,' he pointed. 'That must be *Yed Posterior*.'

'Hey, geek!' Motti yawned noisily, called from the cabin: 'You talking about posteriors in there?'

'Ha, ha!' said Jonah. '*Yed Posterior*. It means "hand after".'

'Hey, Tye, you got a geek's hand after your posterior!' Motti called, and Patch sniggered beside him.

'Just get ready for your jump,' Tye yelled back at him.

Up ahead was a distinctive red-black boulder, like a giant's marble fallen from the sky and come to rest against some rocky foothills.

If they'd gambled right and this really was the place, then that boulder would represent the brightest star of the constellation: Ophiuchus Alpha, also known as *Ras Alhague*.

The head of the snake. The point of the pattern most easily accessible from land.

And maybe – just maybe – the entrance to a hidden underworld, which contained the secret of eternal life.

Motti was calmly slipping on a bulky coat and a parachute harness, getting ready to jump. Jonah watched the muscles in Tye's smooth, slender arms tense and contract as she pulled up on the stick and the plane began to descend.

With Motti dropped on target to scout the land, Tye set the plane down at a small industrial airport about forty miles away, a range of grey buildings like a poor imitation of the mountains spanning the skyline. Con worked a little magic with the airport officials; it might have been her fluent Greek or some mild mesmerism, but they accepted the group's bogus business credentials and even arranged a hire car with which to explore the outlying district.

Tye supposed they were going a little further than the officials might imagine. Con sat beside her in the 4x4, Jonah, Coldhardt and Patch in the back, as she rattled them over the rough terrain, up perilous tracks and down into ravines. Coldhardt had worked out a route that ought to be drivable, and Tye took it slowly. A punctured tyre, broken axle or sheared cable now could set them back hours – or even finish their journey for good.

'Doesn't look like anyone's travelled this way before us, anyway,' Jonah observed.

'So our own tracks will stand out a mile,' said Con.

'We should have stolen quite a march on Samraj,' said Coldhardt. 'It's a chance we'll have to take.'

No one spoke much as the tension slowly grew with the passing miles. Patch was looking green and clutching his stomach, his Game Boy Advance out of batteries. Con was sitting in the passenger seat hugging her knees and studying the map intently. She seemed to be having some tummy problems herself.

Only Coldhardt looked serene, both eyes closed, mindless of the jolts and scrapes and the grinding of protesting gears.

It took hours, but they finally reached their chosen rock by late afternoon. Tye untangled her aching fingers from the wheel and slumped back in her seat, accepting the thanks and praise of the others without comment.

'From here it's a hike on foot down into the gully,' Coldhardt announced.

She felt Jonah's hand press down lightly on her shoulder for a moment as he led the exodus from the jeep. The muscles there felt like they'd locked together with the long tension.

'Could you use a quick massage, sweets?' Con asked her.

'Thanks.' Tye looked fleetingly at Jonah. He was staring out at the sky, a darkening blue now as it made its first overtures to the night.

'It's OK,' Con said quietly as her hands kneaded Tye's bruised and aching muscles. 'I won't be offended if you'd rather ask him.'

Caught off-guard, Tye opened her mouth to make some retort – and found she couldn't think of anything to say.

'Hey!' Motti's voice carried distantly through the wilderness, instantly electrifying the silence. 'Come down here, quick!'

Con and Tye both jumped from the jeep and followed the others to the lip of the gully. Motti was the size of a termite far below, waving his arms in what seemed to be a mixture of welcome and warning.

What had he discovered?

Jonah watched Coldhardt as he led the way down to meet Motti, scrambling down the crumbling incline with a speed that belied his years. He supposed that adrenalin, a desire for revenge, and basic, dirty greed could come together to make quite an energy boost. Certainly they helped him make it safely down to the marshy plateau at the base of the gully.

Coldhardt was breathing hard, his handsome features florid with exertion. But Jonah noticed that while a few anxious looks were passed, no one asked if he was all right. No one wanted to provoke his temper.

Besides, what the hell were they going to do if he wasn't?

'You guys sure took your time,' said Motti tetchily.

Jonah shrugged. 'Didn't want to rush the expert at his work, did we?'

'Motti,' Coldhardt wheezed, 'what have you found?'

'I think I've sussed out an entrance,' he said, losing some of his dour demeanour in his excitement. 'About fifteen metres from the boulder, built into the base of those foothills. It's just a crack, and it's real silted up, but I reckon it's our way in. Maybe there's some kind of pulley mechanism behind it.'

Patch looked suddenly alarmed. 'Like the old crypt we did over in Lima?'

Motti nodded. 'So long as we can find the trigger mechanism, and if it's still working after all this time –'

'Please God, no swords this time,' Patch muttered.

'You must study the door for yourself,' Coldhardt told him. 'You are familiar with many of the ancient tricks of the trade.'

'Well, on paper, yeah, but –'

'C'mon, Cyclops,' said Motti, wrapping an arm round his shoulders. 'You know what they say – you ain't worth the room till you crack your first tomb.'

Patch allowed himself to be led away with all the enthusiasm of a condemned man going to the gallows.

Jonah frowned. 'There'll really be locks and alarms and stuff on some old catacombs?'

Coldhardt gave a ragged cough. 'People have found many ways to protect their property through the ages, Jonah.'

'What, the Indiana Jones stuff? Big stone ball tumbling through the tunnel? Hundreds of spears in the wall?'

'On the whole, their precautions are a lot less spectacular but a whole lot nastier.' He stretched and padded away, kicking his legs as if to shake the cramp out of them. Jonah watched him go, felt an unsettled feeling gathering like a cloud in the back of his mind.

'Are you superstitious, Jonah?' Tye asked.

'Motti asked me that on my first night.' He shook his head. 'No. I'm not.'

'Patch never used to be,' said Con brightly, 'until the crypt job. Now he sleeps with the lights on, did you –?'

'Yeah,' said Jonah. 'I know.'

'So if you're not superstitious, why do *you* sleep with the lights on?' She smiled coyly. 'Or was that just so I could find you in the night more easily, yes?'

Jonah felt himself flushing. 'I didn't know you were coming – I mean, I was just – well, I –'

Tye just laughed. 'Guys, could you keep it to yourselves?'

'Oh, Tye, nothing happened,' Con said quickly, a mischievous look in her eyes. 'Nothing much.'

'Whatever.' Tye shrugged, glanced back at Jonah. He looked away, embarrassed.

Coldhardt walked back to join them; with a few minutes' rest he looked more like his old unflappable self. He glanced round, saw the look on Jonah's face. 'No last-minute nerves, I trust?'

'He is fine,' said Con. 'Aren't you?'

'Fine,' Jonah agreed.

'Then let's go join the others and see what we're dealing with,' said Tye, leaving them to trail behind after her.

It would be night soon. Tye shivered a little, stared up at the darkening blue sky. Small violet clouds had gathered above as if spying on them. Her ears strained to catch the sound of distant engines, any sign that Samraj might be approaching.

Patch and Motti had been poring over the old stone for some time. Coldhardt looked in and offered a measured comment or opinion every time they seemed to be flagging. Now they were starting to argue about how much force they should use to get inside.

'We ain't archaeologists,' Motti was saying. 'Screw the gentle touch. If that *is* a door it ain't gonna give easily.'

'It's just some kind of plaster they slapped on to disguise the opening,' Patch argued. 'If we keep chipping away –'

'It was slapped on, like, a thousand years ago! It's hard as the stone. Now, time's running out, and I say we blow it open.'

'Well *I* say blow it out your arse!' stormed Patch. 'You don't know what was hidden inside this door, Mot! Projectiles, gunpowder, poisoned sand – could be anything!'

Motti held out his hands, a calming gesture. 'OK, fine, so we lay charges in the surrounding rock.'

'I don't like it.'

'I don't like it either, Patch, but Motti's right.' Coldhardt looked at Motti. 'Make it a small charge, hmm?'

'Tell you what, then . . .' Patch reached up to his glass eye and made to pluck it out. 'I got a little gelignite in this one. Detonator cap is in the pupil.'

'Leave that damn thing where it is!' said Motti, cringing. 'I got some plastic here. I'll lay it round the frame, multiple detonation . . .'

'Say the Inuit charm prayer first.'

'I'm saying every prayer I know, man.'

While Motti got busy, Patch wandered over and sat down beside Tye. 'This place is bad news.'

'Tell me about it,' she said.

'Got any more food?'

She gestured to her rucksack. Patch dug himself out a half-chewed chicken leg and pulled off some scraps. Then he gestured over at Jonah and Con. 'Those two had a row or something?'

'Something.'

Jonah was sitting alone on the scrubby grass, minding his own business. His back was turned to Con who lay half-reclined on a slab of rock, silhouetted against the sunset with artistic abandon.

'She's incredible,' sighed Patch.

Tye nodded. 'Never ceases to amaze me.'

Motti didn't take long with the explosives. He uncoiled the detonator wire and motioned everyone to shelter behind Con's plinth of rock.

It was weird, having Coldhardt there amongst them. He ensured an air of respectful silence held sway, but Tye decided it was a mixed blessing. It spared her any more of Con's small talk, but left her with too much time on her hands to mull over what had – or hadn't – been said.

Truth was, she would never have put Jonah and Con together. But then, if Con had come on to him, why the hell would he resist? She could reel in anyone, as she'd proved to Tye on a fairly regular basis. Jonah was no different.

And she couldn't help feeling disappointed about that.

'Here we go, people,' said Motti, hurrying to join them.

The explosion was crazily loud, the rumbles of the after-echoes mingling with the clatter of distant birds taking flight.

'Well, that'll bring the park rangers running,' muttered Jonah.

Motti was back on his feet and running to see before the smoke had even cleared. As he ran into the grey wisps, he whooped.

'We got us a doorway!' he yelled. 'It's solid stone, five-sided.'

'That's a warning in itself,' snapped Coldhardt. 'Echoes of the pentagram.'

'What's that?' asked Jonah.

'Five-pointed star,' Con told him. 'Occult symbol.'

'Black magic, you mean?'

'With me, Patch.' Coldhardt strode off into the clearing smoke, Patch at his heels, and Tye quickly followed them.

There was something about the crude, thick outline of the door in the blackened stone that sent an instinctive shiver down her back. Coldhardt was showing some circular impressions in the rock to Motti and Patch, who were nodding like eager students. How could they be so casual about it all?

She walked away, troubled. Growing up in Haiti, half the people had practised voodoo. Not the creepy, zombie undead stuff you got in horror films – almost all of them considered themselves Roman Catholics – they just believed they could commune with the lesser deities and messengers who travelled between God and the believer. Tye had turned her back on the spirits like she'd turned her back on so many things. But sometimes, normally in the darkest hours when sleep or rest seemed a thousand miles away, she liked to believe she could hear the whispers of kinder spirits.

Right now, she could almost feel those whispers like a scratch deep in her ear, warning her that the door, and whatever lay beyond it, was evil.

*   *   *

Jonah knew there were more important things to worry about, but found he couldn't help wishing Con had kept her big lip-glossed gob shut. He knew she'd used him to score a cheap, throwaway point against Tye, but she'd made it seem like a lot more had happened than actually did.

The worst thing about it was that Tye probably didn't give a damn – if he tried to explain what really happened, she'd think he was a freak. So instead an undefined awkwardness hung in the air between them like the smoke from Motti's explosions.

Jonah went over to join the guys by the door in the wall, where things seemed less complicated.

Wrong again.

'I believe that each of these circles in the rock is a cylinder, seen end-on,' Coldhardt was explaining. 'A kind of bolt securing the door, probably knocked through with a stone and hammer. One of them will open the door, the others are undoubtedly booby-trapped.'

'So how do we know which to release?' asked Jonah.

'We don't,' said Motti. 'Trust those dumb cultists to leave that part off the lekythos.'

'Probably obvious if you're one of them.' Jonah pointed to the topmost bolt. 'That bit of the Spartan cipher said something about the north. If it *did* include instructions about how to get in here, maybe they meant –'

'We have no way of knowing that,' said Coldhardt. 'No, Patch, I'm afraid the call must be yours. Think of each bolt as a key in a kind of lock, turning tumblers and mechanisms within the stone.'

'Except if you louse up, God only knows what's gonna happen,' said Motti quietly.

'He won't louse up,' Tye insisted, as she and Con came over. Jonah noticed Con was crossing her fingers behind her back.

Patch turned his stoic eye on the stone. 'Square holes in the top of each circle. Probably for holding a tool of some kind, to get it to open . . .' He started rummaging in his rucksack. 'Reckon a big torque wrench might fit it.'

'Start with the topmost bolt,' Coldhardt suggested with a glance at Jonah. 'It's the only clue we've got.'

'We're starting to lose the light,' said Jonah.

''S OK,' said Patch- as he carefully inserted the wrench and placed his ear cautiously against the stone. 'I'm gonna close my eye anyway. Gotta think myself into the lock.'

'Here comes the Jedi mind crap again,' Motti said gruffly, but there was no disguising the concern on his face.

'You guys better stand clear,' Patch whispered.

Coldhardt simply nodded, falling back to what he felt was a safe distance and gesturing that his children do the same.

'This could take for ever, couldn't it?' said Jonah quietly. 'Surely after all these centuries, that bolt's going to be stiffer than a corpse's –'

There came a cold scrape as the stone cylinder shifted a little way into its housing. Jonah broke off, held his breath.

'Craftsmanship,' whispered Coldhardt, a rapt look

on his craggy features.

'Patch, man, can you feel anything through that rock?' Motti whispered.

'Only thing I can feel is a trickle down my leg,' he joked. Another scrape. 'Wait. No. That didn't sound –'

Everything kicked off at once.

There was a rasping *shunk* as some ancient mechanism activated behind the doorway. Patch twisted aside. The wrench flew from his hand. A stubby arrow burst out of the door, nearly skewered him as it shot through the air.

Patch landed awkwardly, sprawled on his back. Motti was already on his feet, sprinting over to check on him.

'Wait!' Coldhardt shouted. 'There could be a second trap!'

'That's why I'm going,' Motti yelled back. The next second, Jonah found himself rushing to join him. Together they lifted the shell-shocked Patch and carried him awkwardly away.

'I'm all right,' gasped Patch, laughing weakly. 'I'm OK. Didn't get me. I felt something give inside the stone – guessed it wasn't good.'

Coldhardt regarded Jonah and Motti. 'If I give you a command I expect you to obey. You would have achieved nothing by killing yourselves.'

Motti nodded sullenly, then glared at Jonah. 'So much for the "north" clue.'

'Here's the arrow,' said Con, running back from the side of the gulley with the ancient projectile. 'I think it's gold.'

Coldhardt took it from her. 'Ebony shaft, gold head.' He turned it carefully in his gloved hands. 'Almost certainly poisoned. This alone must be worth a small fortune.'

'Next time I'll try to catch it,' said Patch shakily. 'How'd it fire through stone?'

'I'll bet it wasn't real stone in that part of the door, just more of that plaster stuff,' said Motti. 'They must've sealed the hole back up each time an arrow went off.'

'What are we going to do now?' asked Tye. 'Is Patch going to try every other bolt till he kills himself and one of us steps in?'

'P'raps I'll be lucky next time,' said Patch nervously.

Coldhardt looked round at his children. 'You want to leave now that we're so close? You want to lose the chance to hit back at Samraj?'

'We ain't giving up,' Patch declared, retrieving his torque wrench and moving on to the next bolt.

'For God's sake,' Con hissed, 'be careful, yes?'

Dusk was falling, and the landscape was taking on a strange, alien quality. It was eerily quiet, and a cool breeze was blowing across from the distant lake. No one spoke as Patch started to probe the next bolt, his gestures precise and unerring, his face pressed up to the scorched and blackened stone.

Until he suddenly dropped the wrench and threw himself backwards. Tye swore, Jonah jumped.

And with a grinding, grating noise, the great stone slab yawned slowly inwards, surrendering an entrance.

'See? Second time lucky,' said Patch happily, dusting himself down.

'Yes!' Motti yelled, grabbing him and swinging him round as the others clapped and cheered.

But the jubilant mood didn't last long. Jonah put it down to the entrance itself. It stood gaping like a great maw waiting to devour them. Or perhaps screaming at them silently to leave this place. To leave well alone.

But Jonah knew they'd come too far to turn back.

'Tye,' Coldhardt whispered, 'we'll need the torches.'

She'd already collected them from her rucksack, and pressed one into his hand. White, comfortless light flicked from the end of the steel tube.

Cautiously, Coldhardt led the way across the stony threshold and into the darkness.

CHAPTER TWENTY-TWO

The stone slab had been lowered by a primitive but effective wheel-and-pulley system. 'Knew it,' said Motti, his torch beam playing over the mechanism. 'It's good news. Means we can close the door behind us.'

Patch shuddered. 'That's good?'

'It is if someone else comes looking for us, numbnuts.'

'Leave it open for now,' said Coldhardt. 'We don't know what's up ahead.'

They were standing in a small cave. A wide crack in the back of it led to a narrow passage through the rock. After taking just a single step inside, it felt to Jonah as though the outside world was a mile away.

The glare of the torch beams made him nervous at first. It felt like the six of them were poking bright white sticks into each dark corner, and risked disturbing whatever might be hiding there. But the blackness seemed absolute, the torches could show no detail; it was as if something in the air was absorbing the light.

Coldhardt broke the silence. His voice came out dry and echoless as he moved warily deeper. 'In centuries past, Macedonia was known as *Catena Mundi* – the link between worlds. I'd always assumed that was due to its position on the ancient trade routes. But it's possible the phrase has a more literal significance.'

'What, connected to this place?' asked Jonah.

'If the rumours about Ophiuchus were true . . . If his experiments with the snake-root led him into planes of darkness beyond human comprehension . . .'

'The link between our world and the underworld,' said Tye softly. 'Like a kind of no-man's-land?'

'This ain't so much a link road as a dead end,' Motti pronounced. The passage had opened out into a semicircular cavern. 'No way through.'

Jonah jumped at a sudden clattering sound close by. In an instant, five spears of torchlight landed at Con's feet. But her own beam was playing on the yellowing skeleton she'd knocked against on the dark, silty floor of the cave.

As Jonah advanced he saw two human skulls leering up at him, eye sockets gaping like black screams in the bone, their mouths hanging open like they were laughing.

'I knew I should've brought a spare pair of trousers,' said Patch shakily.

'Why not borrow their uniforms?' Jonah muttered, blinking as a breastplate reflected his torchlight back in his face. 'They don't seem to fit them so well these days.'

'Spartan,' breathed Coldhardt. 'Part of the legion who created the cipher, perhaps. Who found this place and meant to prosper by it.'

'I thought the Spartans were big on self-denial and honour and all that,' said Jonah. 'How come they were trying to get themselves eternal life?'

'For their empire?' Con suggested.

'The Peloponnesian wars badly weakened Sparta,' Coldhardt informed them. 'By the time that cipher was written, her army was filled with helots and mercenaries. And their moral code was a little looser than the strict Spartan way of doing things.'

Motti chuckled in the darkness. 'Gotta love those helots and mercenaries.'

'Or maybe they didn't send that cipher just to tell their generals how to find this place,' said Jonah. 'Maybe they wanted them to send soldiers and destroy it, but the message never got through.'

'There's a door here,' Con reported, shining her torch into a shallow alcove in the cave wall beside the skeletons. 'Look.'

Jonah stood back to allow Coldhardt and Motti to investigate. Their torches showed a high, narrow recessed panel of carved stone, set into the rock. It was topped by a kind of reed matting.

'What's that?' Tye whispered as her torch played over it.

'In some Egyptian houses, closing the doors on rushes helped keep them closed.' Coldhardt examined the door carefully. 'But this is a fake. A false door – like those you find in tombs of the first dynasty. They were set in the west, left so that the deceased could pass from the living world to the dead land.'

'*Catena Mundi* again,' Tye muttered under her breath. 'Could be a real door behind it.'

'Yeah, but this door is set East,' Motti pointed out, taking a closer look for himself. 'And why is there a heap of bones outside it?'

'To put people off entering?' Jonah suggested. 'Works for me.'

'It could be another trap,' said Con.

'Must be.' In the thick silence you could practically hear the workings of Motti's mind. 'Some kind of poison on the handle maybe, absorbed through the skin? Nah, the victims dropped right outside the door. If it was poison they'd have had time to wander. And these rushes . . . at the base, it's like they've been singed or something.' He snapped his fingers. 'It's gotta be the recess in the door. The stone around it's blackened, just like outside when I blew off some of that plaster.'

Coldhardt studied the recess. 'There's evidence of several layers having been built into this panel.'

'That could be it.' Motti gently stroked the door. 'What if the panel's made of layer upon layer of something volatile? A kind of paste mixed in with gunpowder – permanganate maybe, I dunno . . . the elements mixed in an exact quantity and left to harden. Then when enough force is used on the door . . .'

'The panel ignites,' Coldhardt concluded. 'A lethal, carefully measured blast.'

'The rest of the panel burns away and melts a protective lining – leaving another exploding panel exposed for when the next poor son of a bitch comes knocking.'

'You're either a genius, Motti, or totally paranoid,' said Jonah, shaking his head.

'Sounds a bit elaborate,' Con agreed. 'But I suppose it fits the facts.'

'Why not try knocking? Then we'll see how

elaborate it is.'

'That's exactly what it is,' said Coldhardt. 'An elaborate challenge. A false focus to keep us occupied.'

Patch thought he understood. 'You mean, they *want* us to think that this is the way inside? That because it's so tough to get past, it's got to be the entrance?'

Tye's voice sounded quietly from the darkness. 'So where's the real entrance? I've searched every inch of this place.'

'Including the floor?' asked Jonah with sudden inspiration.

'Uh-huh. Only thing in here besides those old bones, us and the dark is this big chunk of rock with copper handles. I can't shift it.'

'Limestone, most probably,' mused Coldhardt. 'Used for polishing the rock floors, to make them smooth.'

Patch scraped his trainers on the floor. 'It's not that smooth in here.'

'Maybe it was the Spartans' job and they sucked at it,' said Motti. 'That's why they got *fired*.'

'Not funny,' muttered Con.

Tye shone her torch on the block of limestone. One by one, every other beam fell upon it too.

'This is an antechamber – it has to lead somewhere.' Coldhardt slipped his fingers into one of the handles, gauging the stone's weight. 'The real entrance must be linked to this block.'

'We'll check it out,' said Motti. 'No saying what's beneath it. Tye, how about a pre-emptive *pouin* to offset any *wangas*.'

tail flexing, pincers raised. Coldhardt stamped down his heel, cracking the creature's carapace. It writhed for a few seconds, then lay still.

Jonah stared in the tense aftermath, cringing, but nothing else stirred from beneath the rock. 'So . . . so were those things magic scorpions or something?'

'Magic scorpions?' In the torchlight he saw Motti look at him like he was nuts. 'Shit, man, they was just living under the rock. You got some weird ideas.'

'*I've* got some weird ideas,' Jonah muttered.

Patch swept his torch around, then stopped. 'Uh . . . Jonah. You've got a scorpion on your leg.'

'That's not funny.'

'He's right,' said Tye quietly. 'Hold still.'

Jonah chanced a glance down. Jesus Christ, there it was. The fat brown scorpion had hooked hold of his jeans just below the knee.

'Get it off,' he whispered. 'Please, get it off, get it off.'

Tye reached out with the muddy toe of her boot. The scorpion crawled a little higher, its hard brown body glinting in the torchlight.

Then she kicked out, knocked it from his shin. Patch followed it with his torch as it slunk off into the shadows.

Jonah swallowed hard. 'Thanks.'

'You're welcome,' said Tye. 'You really hate those things?'

He smiled weakly. 'Them and spiders.'

'And snakes,' Motti added.

'They're the real reason I sleep with the lights on,' Jonah joked, but Tye didn't react.

'Let us proceed,' said Coldhardt, gripping one of the copper handles. Con and Motti took the other and together they dragged the weighted stone millimetre by millimetre across the floor.

'There's a hole underneath,' whispered Patch.

Tye went to see. 'Wow, and it's warm down there.'

'You three, take over,' said Coldhardt. 'We'll move it in shifts.'

'It's OK, Jonah,' said Tye as she gripped the handle. 'No more of your little friends.'

Jonah took the other handle with Patch, and together they put everything they had into budging the stone. Alternating with the others in short, hard shifts, whoever wasn't heaving at the weight was training torches below, checking for traps.

'Whatever treasure's kept down there,' Patch panted, leaning on the stubborn stone, 'it had better not be heavy. I'm knackered.'

'We can get through it now,' said Coldhardt. 'Though it'll be tight. It's a shallow drop, two metres maybe, into what I imagine is a kind of access tunnel.'

'I don't like it,' said Tye. 'We're leaving all the doors open. If Samraj gets here early she can just breeze right in.'

'I take your point. Motti, seal up the entrance.' He was already lowering himself into the hole. 'Only do be certain we can open it again.'

'Yeah, that thought did occur to me.' Motti walked back down the tunnel. Jonah decided to give him a hand, still uncomfortably aware of the scorpion in the shadows somewhere behind him.

Motti came to a sudden stop. 'Well, here's a hell of a thing.'

'What is it?' But even as Jonah spoke he saw for himself.

The stone was already back standing. The maw had closed, sealing them all inside.

'Probably a safety feature thrown in by the architects,' said Motti, studying the ancient mechanism. 'The counterweight drags the slab back up by itself after a time delay, to keep people out.'

'Yeah,' said Jonah. 'Or in.'

Tye swung herself carefully through the hole in the cavern floor and landed safely on warm, dank rock. Then she hurried over to join Coldhardt, Patch and Con in front of the doorway at the tunnel's end. The small effort left her skin beaded with sweat.

'It's like a sauna down here,' she muttered.

'Heat's being generated from deep underground,' said Coldhardt. 'Plate tectonics. The whole region lies on an active crustal plate margin.'

'Say again?'

'Earthquakes and volcanoes,' Con explained.

'The only volcanoes in Macedonia are long since extinct,' Coldhardt went on. 'We should be safe enough.'

Tye nodded gloomily. 'Safe' didn't feel like a word you could use in this dark, cramped, suffocating space.

'Door's not locked,' Patch reported. 'Looks straightforward. Hidden catch here at the side. Ought to just swing open.'

'No sign of booby traps?'

'Can't find any. Doesn't mean they ain't there, though. It's like them swords in Lima –'

'Would you shut up about Lima?' muttered Jonah.

Suddenly, Motti's voice floated along the tunnel. 'Everything OK down there?'

'Wait up there, you two, while Patch opens an inner door,' Coldhardt commanded. 'Con, Tye – stay as flat as you can against the walls.'

Tye pinned herself back against the warm, sweaty rock, angled her knees away – then frowned to find Patch was staring unashamedly at her chest.

'Keep looking and I'll show you a *real* booby trap,' she hissed in warning.

Patch shut his eyes and quickly pressed down on the catch. With a sucking, scraping sound the door opened, the heavy slab bumping against her hip.

'Anything?' Patch asked nervously.

'Nothing,' said Con, starting forward.

Just then a two-headed axe swung down vertically into the entrance. Con was almost impaled on the curved, vicious blades. They stopped short millimetres from her ribs.

'Well, nothing much, yes?' she added shakily.

Coldhardt placed his hand almost tenderly on her shoulder. 'Move when I tell you to move,' he whispered, moving cautiously past the axe and through the doorway. 'Tye, get the others while I scout ahead. Wait here until I say.'

'All right you two, get down here,' she called, shining her light up the shaft. Her voice sounded strangely dead with no echo. 'Careful as you go.'

Soon Motti and Jonah had joined them at the threshold.

'Is it safe to go on?' Con called to Coldhardt, her hand still caressing the shoulder where he'd touched her.

'Enter,' Coldhardt called back, from somewhere far ahead. 'But be careful where you stand.'

'Traps?' Patch asked nervously.

'No. I think it's snake-root.'

Tye exchanged some apprehensive looks with the others and crossed through to the tunnel beyond. The floor sloped down steeply at first, then levelled out. The air was stale and fetid, the heat oppressive. Her lungs seemed to crackle with each breath.

Then she realised the darkness was lifting, it was getting lighter. Coldhardt and his torch up ahead –?

No. The lower halves of the walls weren't just dark, clammy rock any longer. Stuff was growing there – misshapen, fibrous balloons shot through with little luminous veins and patches. They clustered over the dank surface like pustules on skin, their sickly glow lighting the tunnel like weak moonlight.

'So it's real,' breathed Jonah behind her. 'Flesh of the gods.'

'Never thought of gods as having bad skin days,' said Patch nervously.

'Round here,' said Motti, 'I got the feeling the gods might do things different.'

Even as he spoke, a menacing shadow loomed up from around the corner. Tye shrank back.

But it was just Coldhardt. He wasn't even using his torch any more. 'It grows thicker the further in we go,' he said. 'Even the floor's covered with it. It can't have been harvested for a long, long time.'

'Thank God,' said Jonah with feeling.

'How can this stuff grow out of rock,' Patch wondered, 'with no water or sunlight?'

'Fungi don't need sunlight to grow,' Coldhardt explained. 'They don't have chlorophyll like plants do. They feed on dead or dying things.' He dug out some dark grains from a bare patch in the wall with his fingers, and nodded. 'This isn't rock, it's a thick coating of volcanic loam, full of ancient organic compounds pushed up from the depths of the earth's crust. And this stuff seems to thrive on it.'

'Plus there *is* water,' Jonah pointed out. 'This whole place is damp.'

'An underground spring maybe?' Coldhardt looked around him. 'Or rainfall through vent shafts in the rock? Air must be getting in from somewhere.'

'Who cares how come the stuff's here,' said Con. 'It just is.' Her eyes gleamed greedily in the half-light. 'We should think about what else is here, no?'

'Yes,' grinned Coldhardt. 'Follow me.'

The hot, claustrophobic tunnel wound onwards like some alien artery in the rock. The fungus got thicker around them, squashing wetly underfoot with a creaking noise. The air grew rank to breathe as they trekked on, and Tye clamped a hand over her mouth and nose. They passed smaller passages branching off like veins, so thick with snake-root as to be impassable. Pressure built in her ears as they went ever deeper. How far underground were they now?

Then the walls started to widen again. Strange

designs had been daubed on the walls here in pale oils: a man clutching a serpent; a serpent coiled about a man, while strange, misshapen figures watched on. The pictures were like little seams of gold, glinting in the snake-root's slimy light.

Coldhardt stopped.

Ahead of them was a pair of huge doors set in the rock. They seemed beaten from solid bronze.

And they stood open.

'The markings on the walls suggest we are nearing some kind of inner sanctum,' Coldhardt whispered, smoothing back damp hair from his forehead. 'The shrine of Ophiuchus. The dark heart of these catacombs.'

Tye didn't trust this at all. 'And it's just left open? Unguarded?'

'Maybe they didn't expect the average tomb robber to get this far,' said Jonah. 'Or else someone got here before us and cleared the place out before they left.'

Motti shook his head. 'Those traps were set from the inside. Someone stayed behind.'

'Let's take a look,' Con suggested.

'We cannot be complacent,' Coldhardt told them. 'Motti, check those doors for any surprises.'

Motti nodded and started forward cautiously.

Tye watched him in uneasy silence. Her head was starting to pound. 'Anyone else got a headache?'

'Yeah.' Jonah led a general chorus.

'We're probably dehydrating,' said Con.

'It's so hot, even the air's getting smoky,' Patch moaned.

Coldhardt looked around, as if staring into space. 'Does anyone have a sore throat? Itchy skin?'

'No,' said Tye, glancing round to be sure she wasn't alone. 'Why?'

He produced a white handkerchief from his pocket and shook it out. 'That's not smoke in the air, it's spores.'

She felt suddenly sick. 'From the fungus?'

'Yes, released as we've trodden through the stuff. Unavoidable, I'm afraid.'

'Gross!' Patch pulled his top up over his nose and mouth – he looked like a kid hiding under the sheets. 'Can this stuff hurt us?'

Coldhardt placed the handkerchief over his nose and mouth. 'I can't imagine it's toxic – the fungus itself is supposed to be edible. Besides, we shouldn't be here long enough to experience any ill effects.'

'You hope,' said Jonah, speaking through his sleeve.

'Our work isn't without risks, Jonah,' Coldhardt snapped. Then a sly smile played about his lips. 'Nor is it without reward.'

'You hope,' Tye echoed, under her breath.

'It's safe to go in,' Motti called back to them. 'Totally safe.'

Coldhardt's eyes sparkled like diamonds. 'Shall we see what we can find?'

As they approached, Tye saw that the doors led on to a weird circular cavern hollowed painstakingly from the slates and silts of the foothills. It was palatial in size and might once have been in decoration too. The flesh of the gods grew thickly here, encroaching on intricate mosaics, blighting strange, stylised wall paintings.

Tye switched on her torch to probe the chamber's deepest darknesses as she and the others fanned out, still covering their mouths. Crystal tapestries hung from the high vaulted ceiling, catching the light and playing with it in a hypnotic display. Huge stone statues loomed out at them from the thick shadows, their abstract shapes twisted and unearthly. With a chill, she realised they reminded her of the figures on Coldhardt's frieze in the hangout back in Geneva.

Pressing on deeper into the gloom of the room she saw a small wooden writing desk piled high with parchment scrolls, and all sorts of bric-a-brac scattered about the floor: coins and jewels . . . amphorae . . . another lekythos, discarded on its side but intact . . .

She heard Jonah breathe in sharply. 'Oh, Jesus holy Christ.'

'What is it?' hissed Coldhardt.

But the torch beams were already lancing out in the direction of his voice through the mist of dust and spores. He was standing before a great stone altar, ornately carved. Horrible, contorted shapes that might have been faces laughed and screamed out of the sides in bas-relief.

And on the altar was a body. It was emaciated, swamped in a long, decorated tunic and a cloak. The rich red folds hung down over the sides of the stone, as though the body was dripping blood.

'It's a man,' Jonah whispered. 'He looks . . . he looks about a million years old.'

Tye felt the coldest shiver creep through her, pushing up gooseflesh. 'Ophiuchus?'

When Coldhardt finally spoke it was in a sepulchral whisper: 'The body's intact?'

'You could say that,' said Jonah.

'What's that supposed to mean?' Con complained.

'I – I think he's still breathing.'

CHAPTER TWENTY-THREE

Jonah stared down at the ancient figure, both revolted and fascinated. The broad face was more like a mask it was so leathery and lined. The eyelids were almost transparent, shot through with veins like threadworms preserved in the crispy skin. The nose was a haughty hook, the mouth tugged down in a disapproving sneer. There was no peace in the old, old face, as though it had seen such things, such horrors, that it could never rest easy again.

Again, the chest shifted slightly under the rich vermilion robes. Patch must have caught the movement too. 'Trick of the light,' he said uneasily. 'Gotta be.'

'Let me see.' Coldhardt went up to the altar, pushed Jonah aside, studied the body himself, tentatively pressed a finger to its wrist. The figure didn't stir.

Jonah waited expectantly. There was a long, deathly pause.

'A pulse,' Coldhardt said softly. 'Slow . . . barely anything at all. But this man is *alive*.'

'Probably the caretaker,' said Patch nervously. 'There – there must be a safe way in he uses.'

'These robes, the jewellery on his fingers . . .' Coldhardt stared round at his apprentices. 'They're all ancient. All genuine.'

Gingerly, Con stepped forward. 'So let's take them and get out of here.'

'Better make it quick, too.' Jonah looked at her. 'Before he wakes up.'

Tye turned away from the scene at the altar. It was one thing looting from the long-dead, but if this man was somehow *alive* . . .

She felt suddenly afraid.

'After so many traps . . .' Tye walked back over to Motti, who was still waiting beside the huge, bronze doors. 'If that *is* Ophiuchus, why would these have been left standing open?'

'It's safe to go in,' Motti insisted.

'You see what this might mean, don't you?' She turned at the note of awe in Coldhardt's voice and found him staring round at the others. 'It could mean that the legends are true, that the cultists' faith is based on reality. Which means the Amrita is not myth but *biological fact*.'

'So Samraj really could synthesise it?' asked Jonah.

'There's no shortage of the fungus here.'

'Then we should burn it,' said Con. 'Or maybe save just a handful and make her grovel on her knees to buy it from us.'

'It's safe to go in,' Motti said again. 'Totally safe.'

'Motti?' Tye waved her fingers in front of his face. No reaction. 'Jesus, Motti, come on, this isn't funny any more.' She snatched off his glasses, looked into his eyes. His pupils had dilated to pinpricks.

'Totally safe,' he smiled.

'Coldhardt,' Tye turned and shouted, 'something's wrong. I think something very bad is going down here –'

She broke off as something cool and hard pressed into the side of her neck.

The barrel of a gun.

'Oh, my dear child,' said Samraj, her finger tightening on the trigger. 'How right you are.'

Suddenly the sweat ran a lot colder down the back of Tye's neck. Six veiled acolytes stood ranged just behind Samraj, almost as one with the shadows in their dark robes. At the front of the line was her would-be killer from Cairo again, the woman with the hooded eyes – Hela. She pointed and the man behind her held a knife to Motti's neck.

Then Yianna shuffled in, supported by two more acolytes. Her skin looked waxy and pale in the weird light from the snake-root and torches, and her wide eyes burned with spite.

'None of you move. None of you try *anything*,' said Samraj, her tone as cold and clinical as a surgeon's knife, 'or this girl dies.'

Jonah raised his arms. Con glowered, fuming and helpless, while Patch settled for sighing noisily: 'We're screwed.'

Everyone had frozen, save for Motti – who already seemed oblivious to everything – and Coldhardt. Now he slowly stepped down from the altar and smiled in casual greeting. 'You were quick to find your way here.'

'The drink that Hela gave poor little Con contained tiny transmitting filaments,' said Samraj triumphantly, her thick make-up starting to come loose in the stifling heat. 'I have been using them to track her movements ever since.'

Con started forward. 'You poisoned me, you bitch!'

'The filaments will have left your body entirely within a week. But knowing Jonah's reputation, I suspected that would be more than enough time.' She smiled. 'And that once he had cracked the cipher, you would all head straight here – so I might follow.'

Tye closed her eyes. 'You *let* us escape from your villa.'

'Of course.'

'You've allowed your patients out for a field trip, I see,' Coldhardt went on.

Samraj played it humble. 'This moment of glory is theirs as much as it is mine.'

'And since we left the way in so obligingly clear for you, you have arrived with minimum casualties I trust? I don't see your bodyguards.'

'The acolytes afford me ample protection, I assure you. I would not insult Hela and her brethren by seeking to bring non-believers to this holy place.'

'You mean *Hela* refused to allow them inside.' He grinned suddenly. 'Goodness knows there are enough heathens here already. Ah, and here's poor Yianna. You must have found the trek particularly draining, my dear.'

'I would not miss this moment,' she hissed.

Samraj left a blue smear across her temple as she wiped at her eye with the back of her hand. 'Your arrogance was always your Achilles heel, Nathaniel. Now it has led to your final humiliation. Your time is over.'

'Time is a concept that has little meaning in these catacombs,' said Coldhardt airily. 'Just ask Ophiuchus here.'

Now Samraj tore her eyes away from Coldhardt and took in properly the altar behind him. Tye felt the gun barrel waver as she reacted. 'It is him?'

'Who else would lie at the heart of this place, surrounded by such grandeur?'

'Is he dead?' Yianna whispered, afraid.

Tye looked at her. 'Your father said Ophiuchus couldn't die, remember?'

'He also said that Amrita means "deathlessness",' said Coldhardt. 'And I'm beginning to suspect that's no accidental mistranslation.'

'Ophiuchus still lives, Samraj!' Yianna clutched at the arm of the acolyte supporting her. 'I saw breathing! I know I did.'

'Yes, he still breathes,' Coldhardt agreed. 'His old heart bumps feebly in his breast. His thin blood still drips through his veins.'

And something *has gone to work on Motti*, thought Tye grimly.

'Then the snake-root does sustain the body,' Samraj breathed, staring round at the black fungus as though it was the true treasure here. 'How potent it must be . . . to let him keep a hold on life for all these thousands of years . . .'

'You call that living?' Jonah looked revolted. 'Dried out on a slab for all time?'

Samraj licked her lips. 'I must see this.' She spoke to Hela in a strange tongue, and Tye found a stiletto pressed up against her jugular. The dark spark in the woman's hooded eyes left Tye in no doubt – when Samraj's game was over and it was time to kill, Hela would enjoy every slow second of the knife's insertion.

As Samraj slinked slowly towards the altar, savouring the moment, she trained her gun on Coldhardt. 'You are such a fool, my dear Nathaniel. To turn your back on eternal life. To turn your back on *me*.'

'The snake-root doesn't offer eternal life,' he retorted, looking down at the body on the altar. 'Jonah is right – there's no *life* in this bag of scrag and bones. Only an absence of death.'

'Better a slow decline over five thousand years than this handful of heartbeats the rest of us are given,' she said. 'And now the truth of Ophiuchus's discoveries is within my grasp, I shall go on to taste true power – and wealth beyond imagining.'

'We'll share it for ever,' Yianna called, 'won't we?'

'You thought I wanted eternal life for its own sake, didn't you, Nathaniel?' Samraj shook her head. 'You underestimated me. As the years stretch to decades, as the decades stretch to centuries . . . I shall probe every last secret of the human genome, unlock every last cell of the human mind.'

'She'll learn how to make me well again!' Yianna bragged to Tye and the zombie-like Motti, as though she was desperate to be a part of the moment.

But Samraj was on a roll. 'No longer shall death be the price we pay for progress. All secrets shall be mine – and I shall use them for the betterment of humankind.'

'Totally safe,' Motti said happily.

'When I can cure cancer with a routine operation,'

said Samraj, 'when I can banish disability from the human race . . . When I can extend the lifespan indefinitely of anyone I choose . . . What will people not give me in return?'

She paused, surveying her audience. They all were standing still and silent as statues in the stinking, smothering gloom. Tye realised that even Yianna was waiting to hear.

And finally, Samraj answered her own question.

'They will regard me as their saviour.'

Jonah would have shaken his head in bewildered disgust if he hadn't been afraid Samraj would blow it off at the slightest provocation. Standing there, sweaty and dishevelled, her make-up smeared over half her face, she was at once both frightening and pathetic. And she had clearly lost the plot big time.

'So there you'll be, saviour of a world full of perfect people, all living for ever.' Coldhardt didn't bother to hide the sneer in his voice. 'Driving out the impure. Driving out the different.'

She stared at him like he just didn't get it. 'Improvements must be made.'

'And when you have grasped every last genetic root of humanity's design, what then? What will sustain you, stop you from decaying like . . .' He gestured down at the body on the slab. '. . . *this*.'

'There is much I must learn from this man,' said Samraj. 'If the snake-root reveals doors to higher realities then I shall kick them down, map out every perception of which the mind is capable – every higher sense.' She smiled, looking at him almost hopefully. A thick dribble of mascara stained her cheek like a black tear. 'Don't you see, Nathaniel? In time, anything can be mine. *Everything*.'

She'd still share it all with him, Jonah realised, *no matter what he's done.*

'It would never have worked between us, Samraj,' said Coldhardt bluntly, taking a step towards her. 'You see, we're both takers in life. I take precious treasures, chances, risks – pleasures, where I can.' He looked down the barrel of her gun, perfectly calm. 'You simply take things too far.'

'*I* take things too far?' She shook her head, gritted her teeth. 'I know what you did. The bargain you made when you were young. The way you sold your soul.' Jonah stared, terrified, as her hands squeezed over the gun as though she were trying to wring sweat from the handle. 'I offered you a way out. A way to cheat what's coming to you. To cheat death.'

He took a step closer to her, looked tenderly into her eyes.

'And end my days with you . . . looking like that relic on the slab?' He smiled and shook his head. 'Shoot me now. It's hot as all hell in here. I won't have far to travel.'

Her face twisted as she fought to contain her anger. A crazed smile forced its way through her lips and she spoke in a low, trembling voice. 'I wonder . . . if in all the years before me . . . there will ever come a sweeter moment than when I kill you. But first, I think we should watch your children suffer.' She glanced back at her acolytes, shouted at them in their own language, then smiled back at Coldhardt. 'Slowly.'

Jonah heard Tye gasp as the blade pressed into her throat, saw Con and Patch assume uneasy fighting stances as the acolytes started towards them.

'No!' Coldhardt made to grab Samraj's gun, but her finger was already flexing on the trigger. All but forgotten, Jonah lunged forward over the wizened, shrivelled old body, grabbed her wrist and twisted it as she fired. The shot went wild. The report was like a bark of thunder and a glass tapestry shattered above them, showering them with shards.

Then there was a quieter sound, like eggshells crushing, and Jonah found himself violently thrown aside. He fell to the slimy floor and rolled over.

When he looked back up, the shadowy scene before him made little sense at first.

The acolytes had suddenly abandoned their tasks, even Hela. They had fallen to their knees as if in worship, muttering and wailing, singing strange prayers in ragged unison. Yianna was lying on her back on the floor at Motti's feet, shouting for help; she had been abandoned. And why wasn't Tye moving? Why was she just staring at the altar like Con and Patch, like they were all rooted to the spot? Even Coldhardt was . . .

Then suddenly he saw the force that had sent him sprawling.

The old, bony body of Ophiuchus was sitting up in the crimson puddle of his fine cloak.

His skin was like thin grey chewing gum stretched too far over the sticks of his old bones. The eyes were dead yellow jellies, pricked with specks of blackness, unblinking as they stared, affronted, at Coldhardt and

Samraj. The cadaver's jaw sagged open – and for a moment Jonah thought it would snap straight off.

But then a word formed in the creases of his leathery lips, rode out on a heavy breath.

Jonah didn't understand the word, but he guessed it would sound bad in any language.

'Ophiuchus,' Samraj breathed, lowering the gun. She started speaking to the apparition in what might have been its own language, but which sounded like a frightened babble to Jonah's ears.

Then his sight began to blur. The smoke of spores was thickening, distorting his vision. Lights were sparkling in the broken tapestry, and sinister shapes resolved themselves from the shadows they cast. The misshapen statues seemed to shift on their plinths. A low boom was building in his ears. The wall paintings were folding into the blackened, scabrous walls – strange windows opening on some wrong, forbidden world. Letting in *things*.

Jonah clutched his hands to his head as the funereal chamber seemed to warp all around him. The prayers of the cultists were growing wilder, higher in pitch. They started to sound like screams.

'Samraj!' That was Yianna. She was shrieking. 'You hear the acolytes? These are the visions of Ophiuchus. He's showing us what he's seen. *This* is the evil the old mages linked him to.'

'No!' He could hear Samraj but no longer see her. She was lost to the darkness like Tye, like Coldhardt, like all of them. 'Superstitious rubbish! This . . . this is some kind of mass hallucination . . . brought on by the snake-root –'

'Flesh of the gods!' Yianna screeched. 'He ate of their bodies to feed his soul. Now the gods have come for *our* skins!'

'Don't believe it!' That was Tye's voice. 'This is our reality, here in the chamber *here*.'

'*Catena Mundi*, the link between worlds, yes?' Con shouted. 'Yianna is right, they *have* come for us.'

Jonah joined in with the acolytes' screams as weird, willowy phantoms drifted from the shadows towards him.

CHAPTER TWENTY-FOUR

Tye stared around the chamber in horror. Hela was down on her knees, clutching at her throat, tearing at her veil. Jonah was lying on his back near the altar, arms flailing as if a cloud of invisible wasps had descended on him. Con was curled in a ball beside a pillar, rocking herself for comfort, while Patch all but drowned out the babbling prayers of the acolytes with his screams of 'Get away!' repeated over and over again. Yianna was silent now; her face a grimace of sheer terror, trapped in some private hell.

Of Coldhardt there was no sign at all.

'Totally safe,' murmured Motti. Something had happened to him when he'd first checked the doors to this place. Had he tripped something – some ancient last line of defence – or had the snake-root spores somehow altered his perceptions ahead of the rest of them?

Tye kept catching intense colours at the fringes of her vision, blindingly bright patterns at the backs of her eyes. Either the spirits she had invoked earlier in the antechamber were helping to keep her sane or this *had* to be an illusion brought on by the snake-root spores. Tye had sat through enough voodoo rituals as a child to know how certain substances could mess up your mind, cheat your senses – and to know how faith and fervour could feed into that hysteria, keep it going, lift you higher.

If you were prepared to surrender yourself to that ride, it could be a euphoric experience. But if you didn't want to let go, if you were afraid . . .

The old figure was sitting up like his back was locked in place, like it might splinter if he ever moved again. His face was just as rigid, fixed and imperious. Samraj was weeping, wailing, her reason lost, beating her legs in frustration.

Where the hell was Coldhardt? Had he run out on them for real this time?

The room was starting to bend around her. Tye knew she didn't have long before she was as helpless as everyone else. She guessed that whether hallucination or some kind of psychic attack, these visions could drive them all mad.

She needed a distraction. Phosphor cap? She had one stuck beneath her collarbone, though she was so sweaty now it had almost come free. She threw it down between Patch and Con, shielded her eyes from the explosion of light . . .

When the smoke cleared, Tye saw that Patch had stopped shouting. Had she brought him round? No – he was just standing there, looking up into the shadows, gibbering. She had thought that with just the one eye, perhaps he wouldn't be so easily affected by –

The eye.

Tye stumbled over to him. The pressure was building

in her ears, she couldn't swallow it away. It was so damned hot, and every step she took broke more of the fleshy mould and spilled more spores. *You idiot! You could be making things worse,* she thought, but she had to reach Patch, and this stuff was everywhere.

She lifted up the leather patch over his eye.

Ick. Ick. Ick.

And she hooked her nails around the ceramic eyeball and plucked it out.

Patch didn't even flinch as the leather slapped back down over his face, hiding the little pit beneath.

'Gelignite,' she muttered aloud, her fingers trembling as she tried to undo it. 'He said he kept gelignite in this one . . .' She gasped as she walked into something.

It was one of the creepy statues, like a wraith captured in marble.

Suddenly it was leaning down, shoving its huge shadowy face into hers.

She closed her eyes, bit hard on her lip, scissored her teeth on the flesh till the pain and the shock of the blood on her tongue made her gasp.

When she opened her eyes, the statue was just a statue. But the patterns behind her eyes were starting to circle and spin, the same sickly yellow as the glow of the snake-root.

'Motti!' she shouted, pushing a wailing acolyte aside to get to him. 'How do I use this stuff?'

'Totally safe,' he said.

Tye shouted in pain and surprise as her left ankle was grabbed tight.

It was Hela, unveiled. Her old face was thick with

blue veins, twisting in despair as she clutched hold of anything for comfort. Tye tried to yank herself free but she was held fast.

And she felt the colours edge round from behind her eyes for a full-on assault. This time she might be dragged under.

'Motti, it's *not* safe!' she shouted, reaching out to him. 'How do I set this stuff off?' She could almost touch his hand . . . 'You went under before any of this started happening. Now I need you here with us. It is *not* safe, you stupid bastard, d'you get me?'

She grabbed hold of his hand, staggered in Hela's grip, opened out his fingers, slapped Patch's eyeball into his palm.

'Look what Patch did to you!' she yelled. 'He's totally got one up on you now. He's laughing his ass off at you, Motti! He'll dine out on this for months!'

Slowly, Motti looked down at the thing in his palm. At the grey eye staring cheekily back at him. And suddenly he cringed, roared with disgust and –

'No!' Tye yelled. 'Don't!'

He threw the eyeball away.

It sailed into the wall, cracked against one of the mosaics.

And exploded in a white inferno that drove every shadow from the place.

Tye felt a wave of heat break over her. It felt hot enough to strip skin. Motti was thrown forward by the blast, smashed into Tye, breaking Hela's grip.

So that's *how you set it off*, thought Tye as the cavern started falling in around her.

* * *

In the aftermath, Jonah's ears screamed with the noise of the explosion. The heat of the blast had barely warmed him, but its light had seared through the engulfing darkness, driving away the phantoms – for now at least.

With a frisson of fear, Jonah saw that the twisted, ancient body was lying on its back on the stone once more, as though it had never moved at all. How much of the last few minutes had been delusion and how much real, he didn't know – but he could still see the nightmare shapes of the wraiths every time he closed his eyes, as if the brightness of the blast had burned the images on to his eyelids.

A severed stone head stared across at him from the floor – one of the statues, brought down in the blast. He stared at it dumbly for a few seconds. Another few metres and it would have crushed him flat.

Focus, he willed himself. *This is still a nightmare and you're trapped in it*. He choked as he brushed dust and debris from his body. The cavern was brighter now – the fungus on the wall around the mosaic had caught light and was starting to blaze with a thick, orange flame. And blearily, Jonah saw someone stagger in front of him.

It was Samraj, swaying from side to side as if she were trying to charm some vast, invisible serpent.

The gun swung up to cover him. He stumbled away, backing up behind the altar for cover.

A sound caught in her throat, then another – more of a cry. A choking cry for help. The gun wavered.

Then Jonah saw the blood and shrapnel peppering Samraj's shoulders. His stomach turned as he saw the blackened gash in her head. She was holding a sharp flint in her other hand, a big, bloody stone splinter she must just have plucked out.

He watched her hard, beautiful eyes roll in her ruined face as she pitched forward and collapsed on top of the ancient body, pinning it to the slab in a final embrace.

Disgusted, Jonah looked away. Then a sudden shower of rock dust came down beside him. It built in a heap at his feet, like sand in the bottom of an hourglass. *None-too-subtle metaphors of our time*, he thought, getting weakly to his feet.

Time was running out for this place.

A weird wailing noise started up – one of the acolytes was rushing about between his fallen buddies. Jonah knew he must do the same for his own band of brothers. He had to find them fast, check they were OK, because if these flames kept spreading . . .

'Jonah!' It was Tye's voice, some way off. 'Where are you?'

'I'm here!' He choked through a billow of smoke, glanced up nervously at a fresh creak and crumble from the ceiling. The shadows were thick about him. 'Where are you?'

Then someone rushed up behind him. Jonah whirled round, raised a fist, ready to lash out.

'Fine way to say thanks,' said Tye, half-smiling.

'Thanks for what? What the hell happened?'

'What the hell happened *here*?' she said, pointing to where Samraj lay sprawled on top of the body.

'You'd think they'd get a room or something, wouldn't you?' said Jonah. 'She caught some flying rubble from the blast. I think she's dead.'

'I thought *I* was a goner for sure.' Motti appeared from out of the gloom, looming over Tye's shoulder like some scrawny Goth familiar. 'I remember going over to the doors, then . . . nothing. Nothing till I found Patch's goddamn eye in my hand.'

'I was trying to shock you awake to give me some help. Didn't expect you to be *that* squeamish about it.'

'Who's squeamish?' he challenged hotly.

She half-smiled. 'Who's back to normal?'

Then the ground bucked suddenly beneath them. 'Whoa,' said Jonah. 'What the hell was that?'

'This whole place sits on a fault line in the earth's crust, remember?' Motti stared at Tye almost accusingly. 'And we just let off some high explosives. It's seismic fun-time.'

'Let's get the others and get out of here,' said Tye.

'We're already here. We're OK.' Con emerged from the shadows, dragging a bewildered Patch behind her. 'The explosion gave us something in our own reality to focus on, yes? Reset our senses, if you like. A shock of that force can break through the strongest mesmerism.'

'That's really all you think it was – mesmerism?' asked Jonah. 'Those visions, those . . . well, they *weren't* real?'

Con looked away, troubled.

'Where's Coldhardt, anyhow?' Patch started staring about nervously. 'We've got company.'

Hela and some of her brethren were heading in their direction, looking for Samraj, or to their master for guidance – or perhaps making ready to kill their enemies.

'Time we left,' said Jonah, as grit and pebbles hailed down from the rocky sky.

'We can't go without Coldhardt,' Con insisted.

Tye grabbed her by the hand. 'Coldhardt might not even be here. He may have gone without us!'

'Then the old bastard had the right idea,' said Motti, 'because we ain't going nowhere.'

More cultists were closing in, encircling them.

'We'd better buy some time,' said Con grimly. 'Jonah, help me.' She started wrestling Samraj's body up from the altar. 'We'll threaten to kill her if they don't let us go!'

Jonah stared at her, appalled. 'Bit late for that isn't it?'

'Bit late for losing your bottle, too,' Motti hissed, pushing Jonah aside and giving Con a hand. '*They* don't know she's a stiff, remember?'

'I don't know if you can understand me,' Con called to Hela, gripping Samraj by her bloodied throat. 'But if you move a step closer I'll . . . Oh, God!'

'What is it?' hissed Tye.

'The bitch has got a pulse.'

Jonah swore. 'She's got a gun too –'

Suddenly Samraj jerked into life. She screeched with rage, elbowed Motti in the guts, doubling him over, and kicked Con aside into Patch so that the pair of them fell sprawling at the feet of the approaching acolytes.

Then she brought the gun up against Tye's head.

'No!' Jonah yelled, and threw himself at Samraj. He'd stopped her once this way, he could do it again. But this time he was too slow. Her dark eyes burned darkly with spite as she twisted her wrist away, brought the gun up hard under his chin.

Jonah tried to roll with the blow, tumbled backwards over the body on the altar. He felt its old, brittle bones crunch beneath his weight. Caught a wheeling glimpse of acolytes surging forward to grab hold of Tye, of Samraj, her bloodstained leer as she aimed the gun straight at him.

Heard the thunder of the weapon as it fired.

Tye yanked herself away from her attackers as the gun sounded. 'Jonah!' she yelled.

But Samraj, injured at least, was a lousy shot. The first bullet bit into the stone altar. The next two slammed into the ancient body that crowned it.

The thing that might have been Ophiuchus twitched once – twice. Then the wizened head lolled to one side.

Samraj stared in horror and dropped the gun.

Tye ran behind the altar and helped Jonah up. 'You OK?'

Rubbing his bloody jaw, he gestured to the ruined body on the slab. 'Better than him.'

There was a moment's horrible calm. Hela and the acolytes stared at the grisly scene in shocked silence. Samraj staggered forward, pawing over the old man's body with a careful composure spoiled only by the way she had to keep wiping blood from her eyes. Con and Patch pulled away from their attackers and joined Tye and Jonah behind the altar, as did Motti, clutching his bruised stomach.

Then Tye became aware of a fierce heat on her

back. The fire had spread behind them – they were hemmed in, nowhere to run. The ground rumbled again, as if some giant far below was laughing at them.

Slowly, the acolytes were closing in.

Samraj pinched the figure's nose, pressing her lips against the leathery flaps of the sagging mouth as she tried to give mouth-to-mouth. But the nose pulled away in her fingers like a crust of soggy bread. She tutted crossly and dropped it to the floor. The old man's emaciated jaw sank into the wrinkled neck and did not rise again.

Tye saw the outrage, the anger in Hela's eyes mirrored in those of the other acolytes. And she knew that they were no longer interested in the heathen.

Samraj was now their target.

Uncertainly, the once beautiful woman turned to face Hela, spoke a few words in the strange language, then paused to spit out some blood. 'Your god is not dead,' she began again in English. 'He . . . he lives on through you. And – and I can heal you now.'

Hela drew her knife, took a further step towards Samraj. Her brethren did the same. The ground trembled again, as if in anticipation.

'We should get the hell out of here,' hissed Motti, edging away from the altar. 'Now, while they're distracted.'

'I can take genetic material from him and give it to you,' she told them desperately. 'You will be flesh of his flesh – truly! You will *all* be gods!'

'Not everyone wants the same things you do,' muttered Tye as she and the others crept warily after Motti.

'Stay back,' Samraj said as the acolytes formed a tight circle around her. 'Kill me and your cult will die out too!'

But with their god dead at last, Tye wondered what could be left for these people.

Samraj's voice rose to a bloodcurdling scream. '*Help me!*'

As the cry choked off, Tye didn't look back.

Then there came a terrific splitting sound from above. Fresh dirt and pebbles rained down like the chamber itself was weeping. Tye was soon choking on dust and smoke and spores and God knew what.

'We've got to find Coldhardt,' Patch almost whimpered. 'We can't deal with this by ourselves.'

'Looks like we're going to have to,' said Jonah. 'Face it, Patch – if he's not dead, he's run out on us.'

'On the contrary.' Coldhardt stepped out from behind a nearby pillar, weighed down with scrolls and coins and jewellery and vases. 'Help me with these.'

Patch grinned. 'I knew you wouldn't leave us!'

'You've been busy,' Con observed, stuffing the brightest of the jewels in her pockets.

'Yeah, hiding out the way while we were nearly killed,' muttered Jonah.

'Simply doing what we came here to do.' He smiled thinly at Tye as she grabbed an undamaged lekythos and some scrolls from his bundle. 'In the end, wealth is the only reality that matters. And after all that's happened, I'm damned if we're coming away empty-handed!'

Jonah took an urn from him, almost dropping it as one of the crystal tapestries crashed down from the blazing ceiling and shattered into a million pieces close behind them. 'Did you honestly come back for us? Or did you just realise you couldn't carry all this crap by yourself?'

Coldhardt's wintry smile was his only answer.

'What about Hela and her barmy army?' said Patch. 'You think they'll let us just walk out of here?'

'I don't think they're a problem any more,' said Tye.

She could see them through the gusting smoke; the followers of Ophiuchus had gathered round the corpse on the altar in a close circle, their heads bowed in mourning. The ground shook as if it might split apart, but they did not shift in their vigil, didn't react as a heavy statue toppled over with a crash close by. It was as though their own lives had ended with their god's.

Of Samraj's body there was no sign.

'Move!' Coldhardt barked.

Con led them out, struggling under the weight of their treasure, through the ruins of the cavern.

'Please! Don't let me die!' came a weak cry from the smoky shadows near the great bronze doors. 'I was going to live for ever . . .'

'Yianna,' Tye realised. Through the dust and smoke she saw the girl had been half buried by falling rock.

'I'm trapped. My leg . . .'

'Someone help me get her out.' Con stuffed a thick handful of jewellery down the waistband of her jeans and started scrabbling at the chunks of rubble. 'We can't just leave her.'

'She's right.' Coldhardt directed Jonah and Tye to help her at the rock pile.

Motti scowled. 'Why the hell should we take her with us, after all she's done?'

Con smiled up at him. 'Because like you said – it is a gift, yes? Demnos offered us a fortune to bring her back alive.'

'That's gonna be the tricky bit,' said Patch, wincing as another chunk of ceiling came crashing down around them.

With Yianna dug out and slung over Motti's shoulder like a sack of potatoes, Jonah followed the others out of the great hall. He paused for a second in the doorway, glimpsing the dark figures motionless in the flames as the altar became a funeral pyre. Then he turned and stumbled away feeling sweaty and sick.

The rest of the catacombs were no more secure. Huge cracks had opened up in the walls and parts of the roof were caving in. The tunnels were ankle deep with scalding water bubbling out of the ground. The glowing veins in the snake-root seemed to seethe and pulse with angry life as the tremors grew stronger and longer with every passing minute.

Dazed and disturbed, the rest of Jonah's journey back passed in a succession of nightmare moments. The pounding vibration of falling stone knocking him off his feet. Priceless relics slipping from his grip, vanishing beneath the steaming water. His ashen reflection staring back up at him. Crossing a cave-in, trying to squeeze through a tiny gap, a moment with the weight of a mountain on his ribs while Tye and Con dragged him through. Yianna dangling upside down ahead of him, tears rolling over her high forehead, her long hair trailing through slimy puddles.

And through it all, the fear of being entombed here for ever. The awful feeling that the wraiths he'd seen before were following close behind, ready to pluck him back into the fetid darkness.

But somehow they made it back to the dark, cramped access tunnel that led up to the antechamber.

'We're on the final stretch,' Coldhardt shouted, stuffing precious relics and ornaments inside his shirt to free up his hands. His torch beam flicked into life now the fungus was too patchy to light their way, but its glow was faint. 'Has everyone still got their torch?'

'No,' Jonah realised.

'Must've dropped mine in the big freak-out,' was Patch's answer. Jonah's heart sank to hear everyone but Motti give the same story.

'Someone else take Yianna,' Motti shouted from somewhere up ahead. 'I'll go on and light the way, open the outer door.'

'Take as many of the others' treasures as you can carry,' Coldhardt instructed. 'Patch, Con, go with him. Jonah, you take over with Yianna – pass her up through the gap when Con and Patch are in position. Tye, take my torch and lead the way.'

'He would have made a good schoolteacher,' Jonah muttered, offloading the few treasures he'd kept hold of on to Motti, who took them without a word.

'Schoolteacher, huh?' Tye forced a half-smile. 'And what have you learned today, Jonah Wish?'

'That nothing lasts for ever?'

Yianna lay where she'd been dumped on the hot, dank ground, passive and tear-stained, all the fight wrung from her. Jonah could almost feel sorry for her. He tensed his already aching muscles to lift her, but she actually weighed very little. With Tye lighting the way ahead and Coldhardt following behind, he shifted her along the narrow tunnel in a fireman's lift, as fast as he could.

But then a fresh tremor, the largest yet, shook down more dirt and rock from the roof. Jonah and Yianna fell back against the tunnel wall as a huge crack opened up in the ground beside them.

A searing heat welled up from the split, together with a red, dangerous glow like molten metal.

'Magma!' Coldhardt shouted. 'Jonah, get up! If it spills into here it'll burn the flesh from our bones.'

Jonah was already struggling to his feet when he felt Yianna twisting free of his grip as she tried to fling herself into the chasm.

'I'd sooner die than go back to my father!' she screamed.

Coldhardt grabbed her by the back of the neck and hauled her away from the smoking split in the rock. 'After what you did to my children,' he hissed, 'a death like that would be far, far too quick.'

He squeezed a little harder, and Yianna collapsed to the floor, unconscious.

Jonah dragged her body along to where Tye was waiting beneath the exit hole. Together they handed Yianna up to Con and Patch. 'Good riddance,' Jonah murmured as the girl was yanked away from them, her long, bloodied legs vanishing upwards into the darkness. Jonah made a stirrup with his fingers and gestured to Tye he could bunk her up. She used him as a springboard, Con and Patch helping her through.

Then a further tremor and a fierce wave of heat almost knocked him over. It was like being trapped inside a volcano about to blow. He knew he should jump up for safety, quickly, before . . .

But he found himself turning. Coldhardt was watching him. The old man's features seemed almost satanic in the ruddy glare of the underground fire.

Jonah kept his hands in the stirrup shape. 'Come on, then!'

Coldhardt advanced on him and gripped Jonah by the waist.

And Jonah found himself lifted up to where six reaching hands were grabbing for him. They snatched him up through the hole to safety. The ground was hot and hard beneath his back, and in the fading torchlight he looked up at their grimy, grinning faces. Saw the relief there.

Then Jonah rolled back over and offered his own hands to Coldhardt. He pulled up with all his strength, the others helping him, until suddenly Coldhardt lay panting on the ground beside them, clutching his treasures tightly to his chest.

But still they weren't safe.

'Goddamn torch!' Motti shouted. 'The door's jammed, mechanism's fouled up. I can't see to fix it.'

The ground shook again, the noise of the rending rock almost too low to hear.

'We have to get out of here!' Tye shouted.

'Duh!' said Motti. 'Anyone got a match? I can't see a damn –'

Con had reached into Coldhardt's pocket and

pulled out the old arrowhead. 'Get ready, Motti,' she shouted, drawing back her arm. 'I don't know how long you'll have – but make it count, yes?'

And she hurled the arrow at the false door in the shallow alcove. The impact detonated the incendiary panel, which burst into white fire like a miniature sun, so bright and hot that Jonah thought his eyes might boil away. At the other end of the short tunnel, Motti whooped for joy.

'That's good!' he shouted. 'I can see. All right, people, get ready. I'm gonna lick this sucker!'

A roaring, rumbling noise began to build over the sound of the incendiary. 'And make it fast, Motti!' bellowed Coldhardt, back on his feet again.

The trembling ground was littered with treasures and relics, and Jonah grabbed at them just as greedily as the others. No longer scared. Determined.

This had to count.

'Open sesame!' Motti shouted as the stone slid slowly open.

'All right, everyone out!' Coldhardt ordered, leading the charge for the exit. Jonah picked up Yianna and half-dragged, half-carried her out of the smoky cave and into the cold, damp Macedonian night.

The light rain felt intoxicating and cool against his skin. Jonah dropped Yianna and collapsed in a pile of wet grass, pressing his burning cheeks into it, revelling in it.

'We must seal the entrance,' Coldhardt insisted. 'Use the rest of that plastic explosive, Motti. Whatever's down there now, stays down there.'

'But we could set off an even bigger earthquake –'

'*Do it!*'

'Understood.' Motti spoke it like a salute and grabbed hold of Patch to give him a hand.

'Don't get comfy,' Tye told Jonah, dragging him back to his feet. 'This won't be a very healthy place to be in a few minutes.'

'Tell that to them,' said Jonah, pointing behind her to where two men in ranger-style uniforms were shouting and yelling in some foreign language, scrambling down the side of the gully to get to them.

Coldhardt crossed to help Motti and Patch at the cave entrance. 'Con, deal with them, would you?'

Jonah watched, bemused, as Con walked up to the men, all smiles, then floored one with an uppercut to the jaw and knocked down the other with a chop to the neck. He knew it was bad of him, but he couldn't help laughing.

'What?' Con glowered at him. 'You think I'm talking to park rangers in Macedonian after a night like this? Go to hell!'

'Hell?' Jonah looked at Tye, marvelling that they were all still standing. 'Been there, done that.'

'Next time,' she said, 'we'll have to get T-shirts done.'

CHAPTER TWENTY-FIVE

With everyone safely out the way at the top of the gully, Motti let off the charges. The rainy night was lit up firework-bright with a fat explosion. It seemed as though half the foothills were thrown up in the air. In the back of the Jeep, Jonah watched as ton after ton of rock and silt came crashing down over the entrance to the ruined catacombs, burying it for ever. The ground juddered and shook, and soon the car roof rang and rattled with the rain of debris sweeping down from the sky.

The tremors kept on as the echoes of the explosion rolled out to the dark shades of the horizon. Had they triggered a full-scale earthquake?

Then, at long last, the ground was still beneath Jonah's feet. He waited tensely but as the minutes stretched by it stayed still.

And he thanked God for it.

The rangers dozed through the whole thing, lying side by side in the back seat of their 4x4. One of them had the keys to Samraj's Range Rover stuffed in his pockets with a note reading KEEP ME, I'M YOURS in Albanian, which was the closest Con could get to their native tongue. After all, she'd argued, no one else would be coming to claim it.

Both men were sweetly oblivious as Coldhardt, his children and their captive drove away into the night's treacherous terrain.

On board the plane, Patch and Con had fallen asleep and Coldhardt was in a private reverie, gloating over the jewels and chains and coins he had taken from Ophiuchus's fiery tomb. Yianna was bundled up in the hold, out of sight if not earshot. She'd finally tired of the angry tirades and had fallen quiet, at least for now.

Tye was flying them over an ocean of dark cloud, through the long purple bruise of the night sky.

Jonah wanted to relax, but his mind was still choked with all he had seen. He turned to Motti, who was sitting next to him, idly polishing his glasses on his dusty T-shirt, leaning his head against the window.

'What're you thinking?' Jonah asked quietly.

He shrugged. 'Just about what happened to me down there. And what happened to the rest of you . . .'

'And here I was trying to forget about all that.'

'You gotta peg it in your head, man, or it just eats you alive,' Motti told him. 'I mean, I'm sitting here wondering why I didn't go head-crazy like the rest of you. I just went *out*, you know? There was something there I tripped, man, some trigger – gas, a blow dart, I dunno. Made me all, "Yeah, come on in, water's great", so I didn't notice the sharks circling.'

Jonah nodded. 'So you think maybe that whatever hit you stopped you tripping out on the snake-root spores?'

'If it *was* spores,' said Motti quietly. 'I ain't never heard of shock bringing anyone round from a bad trip before. And why didn't we just fall straight back under when the blast faded?'

Jonah wasn't sure he liked where this conversation was heading. 'What, so you think what happened down there was for real? That Ophiuchus really *did* open those doors to the – the higher realities or whatever? And that those demon wraith things were waiting on the other side?'

'For you to *join* them on the other side,' said Motti in a spooky voice. He laughed unexpectedly. 'Well, it's one explanation. But then, try this for size. What if the old guy on the altar was just another cultist – one who had the real long lifespan thing going down? Say he'd found a back way in at some point, probably known only to the real-deal cultists – the ones who'd sooner die than go to someone like Samraj for help. And 'cause they know they got some serious secrets to keep down there, and 'cause they know they got, like, this rogue group splinter cell thing going on, they rigged up this state-of-the-art intruder alarm. Some projection-system set up. A big VR rig – virtual reality, right? Anyone comes in uninvited, they see bad, freaky, weird stuff. Drives them out of their skulls, turns them crazy.'

'But like you said, you never even saw the trip-out stuff,' said Jonah slowly. 'Something got to you before that all kicked off.'

'Right.' Motti nodded. 'So perhaps the first person through those big bronze doors – the first intruder – gets hypnotised somehow. Gets *programmed*. While his buddies stand around helpless being driven crazy by the VR projections, this post-hypnotic suggestion thing kicks in – and it makes him kill every one of them. And the last person he kills is himself. Total wipeout.'

Jonah frowned. 'You really think that's possible? That it was all computers and special effects and not . . . not demons and stuff?'

'Man, I gotta believe it.' Motti turned and looked back out at the dark, brooding landscape through the plane window. ''Cause if I *was* under some devil-charm shit . . . if I wasn't meant to see all that scare-you-out-of-your-mind stuff . . .' He swallowed. '. . . then just what did those creatures down there have waiting in store for me?'

Jonah felt a shiver run through him. It stayed in his spine till the first pink rays of sunlight came to rouse and warm the uncertain sky, and they were close to home.

Home, he thought.

He closed his eyes and lingered on the word. It stayed solid and real, while the horrors slowly ebbed away.

The next day Tye found herself back in the driving seat – although this time, the ride was far smoother. Besides the sale of the treasures looted from the Macedonian tomb, there was just one other piece of business to take care of: Yianna.

So with Coldhardt for company, Tye had driven the girl back to Demnos's mansion outside Florence. Now, while Demnos and Coldhardt talked business in private, she kept watch over their charge in a luxurious sitting room. And as she watched Yianna, miserable and distracted in the home that had become her prison, Tye felt just a trace of kinship. She knew what it was like trying to measure up to a memory – though thank God her own father had been too poor to reach Demnos's levels of obsession. That was the privilege and curse of the truly loaded, Tye decided. You could come so close to making your dreams reality, but then you had to live with the consequences.

She looked up as Demnos and Coldhardt re-entered the room. Yianna gazed coldly ahead; Tye had the distinct impression that if the girl's good leg hadn't been half-pulverised in the rockfall she'd have been kicking the place in. As it was, she was a captive audience in every sense.

Demnos looked at his daughter, his eyes brimming with tears and compassion. 'Coldhardt has told me how Samraj abducted you. Brainwashed you. Turned you against me.'

'She did no such thing,' Yianna hissed. 'I have *always* hated you, Father.'

'You see?' said Coldhardt sadly. 'Samraj did her job well.'

'He's lying, you idiot! Can't you see that?' Yianna cried. 'He was working for her, against you! His people broke into here when you were away, photographed your pieces of the Ophiuchus parchment –'

Coldhardt sighed. 'Such a shame to see a young mind so poisoned.'

Tye wasn't sure whether to feel happy that they were getting away with it, or sorry for Demnos. It was obvious that he didn't believe Yianna's accusations for a moment – or, more likely, didn't want to believe that his daughter could despise him so deeply without an enemy's help. 'Oh, my poor child,' he said, 'I have neglected you so badly. You shall see the finest psychiatrists, specialists –'

'There's nothing wrong with my mind, you useless old fool!' Yianna shouted. But Tye could see that with every mean word she dug her grave a little deeper.

'These people will help you . . . no matter how long it takes. I will have you back again, my own sweet Yianna.'

Coldhardt cleared his throat. 'Of course, now it's clear that Amrita is a dead end, perhaps conventional medicine can help Yianna's body while you care for her mind.'

'We shall explore every possible route,' said Demnos, putting a bearlike arm around his skinny daughter, who held herself stock-still in his grip. 'From now on I shall tend you more closely than ever. Whenever you turn around I shall be here. Ready to cherish you.'

Yianna let out a deep, mournful wail.

Demnos smiled and nodded fondly. 'From now until our dying days.'

Coldhardt and Tye saw themselves out.

'Yianna may not live for ever,' said Tye, 'but I've a feeling it's going to seem like it.'

Tye was glad to learn that Con had put the champagne on ice for their arrival back in Geneva. The job was pretty much a wrap, and it was time to celebrate

– a good result, and no casualties.

This time.

Demnos had paid Coldhardt well for his services, not only for laying bare the truth of Samraj's entire operation, but for bringing back his daughter. Now he had information on Serpens Biotech's horrible researches on the cultists' genomes, he intended to use it to his own advantage. Revelations of illegal human experimentation could knock millions off Serpens' stock value, allowing him to steam in and buy up the whole enterprise – always assuming he had any money left once he'd attended the forthcoming auction of Ophiuchus's treasures and relics. A select handful of private collectors had been invited to Berne to bid. Coldhardt was expecting record levels of profit – and his Talent would each receive ten per cent for their labours.

'*Enough to keep the wolf from the door for a while*,' he'd said thoughtfully. '*The wolf and her many familiars.*' A familiar, haunted look had crept into his eyes as he spoke. Even the memory of it sent a little chill down Tye's spine.

But she'd decided there would be no dwelling on things. Not tonight. Tonight they would go out and party. The *Fête de Genève* was in full swing just twenty miles away, with food and fireworks and music from all over the world. For a few hours they would give themselves over to normal life, blend in with the faceless crowds, forget the darkness and the shadows. Act their ages for once.

'Someone go get the geek outta his room,' Motti grumbled, wrestling the cork from a magnum of Krug in the hangout. 'Coldhardt's gonna show in a minute and I wanna get swilling.'

'I'll go,' said Tye casually.

Con gave her a knowing look but Patch and Motti didn't seem to notice.

She ran upstairs and knocked on his door. 'You decent?'

'No, I'm doing unnatural things to a computer,' he called.

'Again?' Tye opened the door. Jonah was looking good in blue Diesel, getting up from his office chair, turning his back on a screen full of sums and squiggles.

'Sorry,' he began, 'I was working on another decryption. Lost track of time.'

But Tye wasn't listening. She'd seen the two fat suitcases by the foot of the bed.

'So you're leaving again,' she said quietly. 'Thought maybe . . .'

'Yes?'

'That you were maybe sticking around.' She stiffened, turning to go. 'Doesn't matter. You're still coming out with us tonight, yeah?'

'Yeah, but –'

'So get your ass in gear.'

'Tye,' he said, catching hold of her arm. She looked down at his fingers, then up into his blue eyes. 'I'm staying. That's luggage I'm moving *in*, not out.' He smiled bashfully. 'It was good of Con to pick me out a wardrobe, but her tastes and mine . . .' He shook his head. 'We're not a match. Not in a million years.'

'Oh,' she said.

'So Coldhardt let me kit myself out. My way. But I haven't unpacked yet, got waylaid . . .' Jonah smiled a little awkwardly. 'So. Pleased I'm staying?'

She turned quickly to go. 'Motti says you're to hurry. He wants to get mega-wasted, and you're holding him up.'

'Yeah, of course. Sorry. It was the computer that distracted me.'

Tye glanced at the computer again, caught a dark sparkle there. Pressed into a blob of Blu-Tack in the top left corner of the monitor screen was Jonah's smokestone.

'Motti's right. I really am just a geek.' Jonah paused. 'Except . . .'

'Except?'

'Well, I'm meant to be bright, right? So how come I can crack secret codes and forbidden ciphers and all that stuff, no problem . . .' He looked at her, his eyes bright and brilliant. 'But when I try to work out how the people I care about are feeling, I get nowhere?'

She held his gaze for a few moments. Then she smiled.

'I guess that will come in time,' she said.

Jonah came downstairs with Tye to a round of ironic applause.

''Bout time!' Motti shouted, offering an overflowing glass to each of them. 'We have some serious partying to do, my friends, and I want no wimping out till the last of us has spewed in a stranger's lap, 'K?'

'Me, I love him for his sophistication,' said Patch, knocking back the last of his glass.

'Funny, Cyclops,' said Motti. 'But not as funny as you being on Appletise for the rest of the night.'

'Come off it!'

'Poor little Patch,' said Con, pulling him to her in a theatrical hug. 'Maybe I'll slip you something later.'

Patch grinned. 'That was gonna be *my* line.'

She shoved him away in disgust and Jonah joined in the laughter. But then Coldhardt walked in and a more respectful atmosphere prevailed. He looked fully his old urbane self – the dark, impeccable suit, the black rose in his lapel, the icy smile about his craggy features.

He surveyed each of them in turn. 'Our car is waiting outside.'

'But we ain't finished the Krug!' Motti complained.

'Good. I trust there's enough remaining for our traditional toast?'

Jonah noticed the others smile between themselves. 'Toast?'

Coldhardt took a brimming champagne saucer from Motti and raised it aloft. 'To talent,' he said, 'and to our continued success. While it lasts.'

'While it lasts,' the others chorused. Jonah swigged back his drink and chanced a glance at Tye. Just in time to catch her looking away.

Nothing lasts for ever, he'd told her, back in the crumbling catacombs. Not helplessness. Not fear. Maybe not even love.

But while he was here, Jonah was going to make the most of every second.

Draining the last of his drink, he followed Coldhardt and his children out into the balmy night, towards the distant sound of fireworks and the cheering of happy crowds.

STEPHEN COLE

Stephen Cole was born in autumn 1971 on the darkest night of the year. He grew up loving books, went to the University of East Anglia to read more, and now writes them for a living. In other walks of life he has been a magazine editor, a BBC radio interviewer and a singer in a band.

www.bloomsbury.com/stephencole